D0511690

Bone Dancing

Bone Dancing

JONATHAN GASH

MORAY COUNCIL LIBRARIES & INFO.SERVICES	
2O 14 68 42	
Askews	
MF	

This edition published in Great Britain in 2003 by
Allison & Busby Limited
Bon Marche Centre
241-251 Ferndale Road
London SW9 8BJ
http://www.allisonandbusby.com

Copyright © 2002 by Jonathan Gash

The moral right of the author has been asserted.

This book is sold subject to the conditions that it shall not,
by way of trade or otherwise, be lent, resold, hired out or
otherwise circulated without the publisher's prior
written consent in any form of binding or cover other than
that in which it is published and without a similar condition
being imposed upon the subsequent
purchaser.

A catalogue record for this book is available from
the British Library.

ISBN 0 7490 0637 4

Typeset by Old Tin Dog Design,
Brighton, England

Printed and bound by Liberduplex, sl.
Barcelona, Spain.

A story for memories of Joan, Mary, Comets and
scribblers everywhere

Thanks: Susan, for the graft

When a doctor does go wrong, he is the first of criminals.
He has nerve and he has knowledge.

Dr Arthur Conan Doyle

The girl knocked on the side door, irritated by the weather, always rain at this stupid hour.

"Who is it?" A man's voice.

"Deirdre."

The door opened. A taller priest tonight. He scared her, in his black cassock down to the flagstones.

"You have it?"

"Yeh." She never knew what to call them. "Sir."

She handed him the package. Its weight killed her. Tablets didn't weigh so heavy. What on earth was with them? Third night in a row and everybody in bed.

"Step inside. Don't move. I'll be a minute."

"Yes, sir."

She stood in the vestibule. Etched glass, colours showing on the walls when car headlights came down the street toward Canal Road. She smelled incense. Why'd they need more smelly stuff, then, Christ's sake? She caught herself guiltily, thinking that name in this place.

Footsteps, returning. A motor bumped down the street. The priest opened the vestibule door.

"That is all. You may go."

So he'd checked her parcel, suspicious swine. She was turning when the passing motor's headlights caught on glass. A glim reflected into the dark passage.

Onto the face of a frightened little boy. He was white from terror, standing rigid behind the priest man. He tried to flatten himself against the wall. If the man groped behind himself, he'd have grabbed the lad.

Deirdre knew about doing a runner. She made herself pause and smiled up.

"Isn't it terrible weather? Good night, sir."

The priest seemed startled by her sudden warmth. "Yes. Good night."

She left. For almost ten minutes she waited, across the cobbled street under the big drooping trees where the street lamp's light didn't reach. What if the lad got out? She knew that she'd help him if she could. She'd escaped three times from places like the Home Orphanage, and knew terror when she saw it.

He didn't come. No racket, so he'd not been caught either. Disappointed, she went up the street towards Liverpool Road and the Deansgate corner where she was to meet Set. Like prisons, children's homes were, and orphanages these days were nothing but evil, if you believed half of what was in the papers.

The figure standing in the alley watched Deirdre go. Why her hesitation? What did she say to the priest? She had strict orders. Hand over. Good night. Out.

Set sighed. A promising girl, Deirdre. But women always did something wrong just when you thought everything was okay. No wonder they got themselves killed.

2 | Glove Man – the chief one who executes violence to order

The meeting of the City Medical Foundation started Clare's ruinous day. She missed being elected the new doctoral chairman by one vote, thanks to Dr Emil Kotscha. A good enough physician, but a self-serving guerrilla fighter in committee.

"The question is," he interrupted smoothly when the matter came up, "whether Dr Clare Burtonall would be an effective voice in hospital – I do mean *hospital* – services."

His famed sneer, one lip slightly curled, the glance a provocation, made Clare rise unwillingly to the bait.

"We've already had this out." She tried for cool. "GCU, Graded Comparison Ultrasonography, is an accurate early – I do mean *early*," she added sarcastically, " – diagnostic determinant in appendicitis. The Farnworth General should have that twenty-four hour facility. *All* hospitals should!"

"It's not essential." Dr Kotscha kept far cooler. "Research papers all show that. There's Alvarado's Point Score, for a start."

Since the 1980s, the ten-point Alvarado System had been regularly used in the diagnosis of appendicitis, house doctors relying on peripheral blood leucocyte counts and combinations of symptoms and clinical signs.

Clare was smarting because the real issue was that Emil Kotscha wanted less hospital money channelled into Accident and Emergency, prime competitors against his new Orthopedics wing. She and many other doctors favoured improving A & E services.

"It *is* essential," she blazed, foolishly letting her anger show, "if you're a junior houseman at two in the morning with the consultant tied up in theatre, the registrar at some carnage on the M6 and the technicians have all knocked off the previous afternoon as bloody usual!"

Clare's friend, haematologist Dr Laura Howden, had been the first to propose Clare for the doctoral slot on the Medical Services Resource Committee at the Farnworth. Now she joined in to help, but her manner was guarded.

"Dr Burtonall does a valuable job among the inner city vagrants," she said to the orthopaedic surgeon. "Since she took up her Charlestown post, charity donations to the Farnworth have almost doubled." She grimaced in sympathy at her friend, but Clare knew she was in there batting for herself more than A & E. "Perhaps in the circumstances..."

Emil sighed theatrically, looking round the table at the other six doctors.

"Seeing Dr Burtonall's loyalties are so divided – for excellent medical reasons, of course – I believe we should select a doctor fully within the hospital, rather than one who has a foot in other camps."

The vote went against Clare. Everyone was unfailingly polite, Dr Emil gave his celebrated beam now he was their representative on the important Resources panel. Clare left in a restrained temper, relieved she would have time to cool off while having her hair done.

Her day would go downhill.

*   *   *

"You're a doctor, aren't you?" Sylvia asked.

The young hairdresser was fussy, her every action seeming pure guesswork.

"Yes," Clare reluctantly admitted.

Warily she eyed the girl's reflection. A doctor's time was never her own. It was always the same. She'd been shown abdominal scars at parties, even asked to palpate mammary

12

lumps during the intervals at theatres. What now, she wondered. A hairdressing saloon should be a refuge, not an extension of Out Patients.

"Listen to this," Sylvia said, leaning close.

Clare sighed, prepared for boredom. It would be somebody's hernia operation, a girlfriend's mysterious pelvic infection after getting blotto at an office party.

"You're a doctor of medicine, yeah? Not science, things like that?"

"Medicine, yes."

There were three answers. First was the full confession: yes, I am Dr Clare Burtonall but please remember that I am only here for a wash and set, so please let me doze untroubled under the drier. Second came the dismissive laugh, that might prevent Sylvia's inanities about some pregnant "friend". Third came her usual cop-out, the tired plea to simply be left alone, hopeless because of her reluctance to turn people away.

The one manoeuvre she could have used would have been a cold description of the previous day's suicide case – it hadn't reached the papers or telly yet. It would be a sensation in the Talk Bark Hairdressing Emporium. Or maybe recount the possible results of the post-mortem examination on the dead girl scheduled for this afternoon.

Except that might set Sylvia off asking gruesome questions, which meant Clare would have to change hairdressers for good.

Sylvia stifled a giggle.

"Well, did you know that lady? The one who's just left?"

Clare thought with relief, mere gossip after all. "No, I'm afraid not."

"You know what she does?" Hidden laughter, then quietly the shocked whisper. "Bone dancing!"

Sylvia had been bursting to tell her this nugget the instant the receptionist had returned the departing customer's card to settle her bill. The desk girl had since gone through to the staff area. It was Sylvia's moment.

13

Clare smiled in the mirror at Sylvia.

"Some new craze?"

"Old one, more like!" Sylvia tittered, leaning back to judge Clare's ends. "Straight up! Can you imagine the cost?"

"An ethnic thing?" Clare asked, blank.

Sylvia glanced at the staff-room door. Clare watched and listened with amusement. Sylvia's news would already be common talk in there.

"She hires *men*."

"Hires…?" Clare's heart constricted.

"True! Has them out to her home, and they *do it*!"

"When you say 'do it'…?"

Sylvia nodded, hands busy on Clare's hair.

"Sex!" She mouthed the word, face aglow at the scandal of it.

Clare couldn't speak. An image of Bonn's face rose in her mind.

"Is that…?"

Is that what? Clare wondered. Is that sort of thing possible, when she knew only too well that hiring Bonn was her own great release? Or had she been about to ask something even more banal, like was it common among the city women?

"Definitely!" Sylvia assured her, satisfied now she'd treated herself to a scandalmonger's thrill. "All sorts of women do it, evidently. Costs a fortune. And people say there's no money about!"

"Bone dancing?" Clare had never heard the expression. It suggested a macabre tribal ritual. "What sort of name is that?"

Sylvia dissolved, trying to suppress her laughter.

"You've heard of lap dancing? Well," she said, eyes shining, "bone dancing. Y'know? Like men's thingy? Bone?"

Clare felt herself redden. She pretended to laugh along, making a show of innocence.

"I've never heard of it." A lie, cheap at the price.

"See? I told my friend Bianca, works in Martin's. She bet

14

me even doctors didn't know about it. Well," she went on, "you wouldn't want folk knowing, would you? And she's married." Sylvia's eyes watched for the desk girl's return. "Her husband's a builder near Atherton, son at university!"

Clare felt a mixture of emotions. A fragment of compassion for the departed customer, and her all unsuspecting. But mostly Clare tasted venom. The woman could possibly be some bitch who hired Bonn. The thought almost made her cry out. She tensed with sudden anger.

Even so, the woman must be a legitimate customer of the Pleases Agency Inc., paying for the usual expensive arrangements. Clare tried to remember the woman: clothes, age, which way she'd gone on leaving. She caught herself. For God's sake, what had the woman to do with anything? Yet her mind chipped away: had Sylvia spoken her name? Had the receptionist? Clare drew herself in, ordering herself to stop thinking of the woman as a rival. She composed herself.

Sylvia mercifully misunderstood. "Sorry. Did that pleck?"

"No, it's fine. How do you know, Sylvia?

"My friend's a newspaperman. He sells stuff – you know, stuff?" Sylvia rolled her eyes.

"Drugs?"

"Maybe." The girl drew back from more revelations. Clare realised she had gone too far.

"How sad," she said with feeling. "How very sad."

"I think," Sylvia said, teasingly, as the outer door opened, "that she's a naughty lady. It makes you wonder, though, dunnit?"

Two customers entered and the receptionist had to be shouted for. That gave Clare a respite. She was able to read a magazine under the hood while Sylvia shot her conspiratorial half-smiles.

Half past the hour, Clare left the Talk Bark, crossed Victoria Square against the stream of mad traffic, and sat in her old maroon Humber SuperSnipe in the car park. She found her carry phone.

"Pleases Agency, Inc.," the voice intoned. "How may we help?"

"I wish to make a booking, please."

"Do you have a reference, madam?"

"Yes. Clare Three-Nine-Five."

"One moment, please." Then, "Confirmed, Clare Three-Nine-Five. Have you a specific request, or may we advise – ?"

Stupid woman, Clare fumed silently. I've been booking Bonn all year and still the ignorant old cat goes through the same stupid litany.

"Bonn, please. Today, if possible."

"One moment, please. This evening, eight-thirty?"

"Yes, please. Two hours."

"Would the Time and Scythe, Bolgate Street, be acceptable? It is handily situated north of Victoria Square – "

"I know it," Clare almost shouted. The robotic woman sounded some ageless crone.

"Suite Four-One, eight-thirty. Is there anything?"

"Thank you, no."

"Your booking is confirmed. The Pleases Agency thanks you for your custom and wishes to assure you that we are committed to…"

Clare rang off, leaving the old hag to her closing patter. She put her phone in her handbag and sat thinking.

Sylvia's gossip disturbed her deeply. It was almost terrifying. It could undermine her very existence. Bonn had to know that the Pleases Agency's activities were a topic for popular chat, with known women clients readily identifiable. It was alarmingly unexpected.

Bonn was the leading goer in the city, hired out by the Agency to offer sex to whatever women clients could afford that luxury. Yet all booking calls were meticulously screened, and security was iron hard.

Until now, though?

"Maybe I'm only pretending," she told her vanity mirror, inspecting her new hairdo in the old saloon's interior light. "Perhaps I really mean that Sylvia's gossip threatens me."

In any case Bonn would have to be told. She had no means of reaching him. His whereabouts were unknown except to the Pleases Agency.

It would have to keep until eight-thirty tonight, then, Four-One at the Time and Scythe Hotel. He would be waiting, never late.

She felt her breathing tighten at the thought of seeing him, but pulled herself together. If she ran late at the hospital in Farnworth, she might be late back and miss Bonn altogether. It didn't bear thinking about. She drove sedately down the ramp into Victoria Square's traffic mayhem, heading for the clinic.

3

Goer – a male hired by a
female, implicitly for sexual
purposes

Rack leant on the pedestrian railing at the corner of Victoria Square, watching Hassall, idlest police bumbler in the city. The plod was standing near a busker who was doing his cymbals and chains act watched by a few shoppers.

Hassall had been there half an hour. Soon he'd drift across to Market Street for a cuppa then amble back to the nick and report that he'd slogged all day gaping at sod all. Rack saw the woman doctor's cumbersome maroon SuperSnipe trundle round the square, just making the Warrington exit on amber.

"Silly cow'll do it once too often," he told Louse. "Know why women jump lights? They can't see proper. Different shape heads. Know why?"

Louse was today's messenger. A Wigan idler, he affected tatty sports gear and fancy trainers even on wet days. He stood reading a newspaper, except he couldn't read but it was what Rack said he had to do.

"No?" he prompted. Rack got well narked if you didn't listen to his barmy theories.

"Women are born faster than us, see?"

"Never knew that, Rack."

"Listen ter me and yer'll learn summert."

Nobody believed Rack's ballocks but pretended otherwise because Rack was Martina's glove man and well violent. Martina ruled the city centre.

Rack turned his attention back to the girls across in the Central Gardens. He'd been here for over an hour, waiting for contacts to show. So far not a frigging sniff. It was enough to

19

make even Bonn swear. No, Rack thought quickly. Bonn never cursed, swore, smoked; it was a fucking wonder Bonn even ate or blew his nose. Bonn was the Pleases syndicate's paramount goer, and he was true class. Pity the poor sod didn't know how to live proper. Bonn proved Rack's theory that education damaged you.

He saw Grellie emerge from the bus station loos across in Victoria Square gardens. She gave him a look. Rack had once wanted Grellie, but Grellie only wanted Bonn.

Grellie, pretty and dark, twenty-three give or take, was street boss of the Pleases Agency's stringers, the girls who did street business. Evidently she'd just done a motor job – white-collar worker nicking time off for a quick gobber. Rack often told her it was high time she stopped that malarky and shacked up with Bonn, though that was against the Pleases Agency rules, meaning that Martina said no. It would snap Bonn out of all that silence. Thinking and reading was dangerous for a bloke who was hardly twenty. Your mind sent you mental. Everybody knew that. Except Bonn.

Having Bonn would be superb for Grellie, who was crazy for him, though nobody had better tell Martina because females were hatred waiting to focus and that was a right fucking fact.

"Know what, Louse?" Rack told the world for nothing. "I believe in professional."

"Right, Rack." Louse stared at his paper like he was told, wondering what the printed words meant. There were actually people who looked at words day after day. Bonn was one. Unbelievable.

Rack watched Bernice, Grellie's newest stringer, taunting football fans arriving off the Burnley bus. Grellie glared at the stupid girl, to no effect. There'd be trouble. Sixteen and full of herself, the Swansea lass had done two gobbers in her first afternoon, thought she was Cleopatra.

An example of Rack's professional approach to life: He'd fixed a couple of loose girls to get done for shoplifting, get rid of them off Grellie's patch. It took ten minutes. That's what being a pro meant, you always got clear but left others in the clag. Both girls had been junkies, trading a shag for money, and the money for scag. Addicts, serve them right, shot themselves with their own arrow. Not his fault if they went mad. Crackheads shouldn't go ape in the first place, getting their powders by crazy burglaries or knee tremblers just to get their hands on some fucking dust. Un fucking believable. He'd told this to Bonn, but Bonn just said, "Oh, Rack," in that sad way. Never argued. Yet you felt so frigging bad it was like you was weeping inside for nothing. Oh Rack. What sort of naff talk was that?

It was no way for a bloke to behave, going *Oh, Rack* when you got the Pleases Agency syndicate off the hook. Maybe Bonn, clean as a flute and who thought that being silent all day was frigging normal, maybe Bonn couldn't see how clever Rack had worked it. He brightened. That was it. Bonn was too educated to see the obvious.

Bonn sometimes got upset. It was new in Rack's experience, for a bloke. Hurting inside, for nothing? It wasn't healthy. Bonn was well weird, come from nowhere with his phenomenal success with women clients. Rack guessed that maybe Bonn fed his clients tablets or summert. Martina said no, it was just Bonn. She put Rack on as Bonn's special stander.

Truth was, Bonn was the Agency's main key goer and the women clients knew it. He could be hired out to a dozen women a day, only Martina had ruled that one was plenty. Rack was the syndicate's head stander. He'd taught Bonn all he knew. Well, nearly almost. Maybe.

"Louse? How many different birds could a bloke shag in a week, if it was a race, like?"

"Dunno."

Rack saw Grellie speak sharply to Bernice the Swansea girl, who flounced off towards the Butty Bar where the city queers congregated after five o'clock. That's birds for you, he thought. Top cheeky, then sulk all frigging afternoon.

"Louse. Go and ask Grellie what."

"Ask what?"

Rack looked at him. Louse went instantly, almost getting himself run over by a taxi in his fright to obey.

See? Rack fumed inwardly. That's why a scurf like Louse wasn't pro. Tell him straight and the gripe just gapes. He'd work out a theory why some people were born pro and others duckeggs. He saw Bonn among the shoppers.

"Wotcher, Bonn."

"Good afternoon, Rack."

"Why are some blokes pros and some fucking pillocks?"

"Language, please, in public."

Rack almost exploded. Like, the drivers of the heavy goods vehicles chugging past northbound would be shocked to hear somebody say pillock? He leant on the barrier, sacrificing a view of Grellie's response to Louse's message. He swallowed. You didn't explode at Bonn.

He looked at his charge.

Bonn was average everything. Bump into him, you'd think here's a young bloke day dreaming and hardly worth noticing. Painfully polite, his clothes hardly fashion, he'd not under-stand if you told him the best joke on earth. Silent, no style, not a laugh in him. Pity that Bonn didn't tog himself out in Weird Wear across the shopping mall or – better – Beggars Choosers beyond the Textile Museum. God knows, Rack thought, irritated at Bonn's silence, Martina the boss would be over the moon if Bonn asked her to pick him some new gear. Probably choose it herself, if Rack sussed Martina right. And Grellie's girls'd scrap all the way down George Street to kit him out, buy him something with real style. Rack thought Bonn would look dead smart in yellow-and-pink seersucker shirts, maybe with an orange kerchief. Great.

Bonn was well odd, and that was that.

And now Bonn was clearing his throat. Rack thought, oh, fuck, what now?

"Rack," Bonn said quietly, among the noisy pedestrians pouring from London Road railway station. "That poor lass."

"Who?" Rack demanded instantly.

"One of the street girls."

"I ain't heard that, Bonn," Rack lied. "Who?"

Bonn stared at the pavement. He held out a hand to prevent a child wandering off the kerb, looking round for its mother. The harassed woman thanked him. Bonn gathered the child back into its pushchair, carefully strapped the toddler in, finally stood to resume the conversation.

"She is one of Grellie's, ah, stringers."

Rack craned to peer into the Central Gardens, wondering why Louse and Grellie were taking so long. "Can't be. You heard wrong, Bonn. I'd know about it."

Bonn hesitated while Rack signalled an okay to something Grellie did. Louse started back. "I am relieved. Thank you, Rack."

"It's okay, mate." Rack felt horrible, which was a right pest, just because he'd told Bonn what was necessary instead of what was true. "You've a booking, Bonn. Clare Three-Nine-Five. Time and Scythe, Suite Four-One, half eight, okay?"

"Very well."

"You want anyfink, Bonn?"

"No, thank you. I ordered a book at Smith's."

That narked Rack almost to fury. Belligerent, he stood in Bonn's way.

"For fuck's sake, Bonn. You buying your own effing books now? Look about." Rack was almost hopping on the spot in rage. "Martina owns the whole fucking city. You've only to say you want summink and somebody'd bring it. What the fuck you playing at?"

"Please, Rack. I must ask you again to abate your language. There are ladies and children about."

Rack subsided, seething. "Okay, mate. Get your book."

He glared after his key.

Bonn had shagged a City Mass Transit Corporation magnate's missus stupid the previous day, and the day before that done the same to an assistant headmistress, all for money. And done a dommy, a home visit, to a woman's house in Altrincham, who wanted to take Bonn cruising to the Seychelles or somewhere oceans away. So he does God-knows-what to women, then it's mind your bleeding manners? When the pavements were crammed with rogues and ponces as far as you could see? It wasn't normal. And Bonn'd just accepted a booking to shag that woman doctor mindless at eight-thirty.

Rack despaired at the state of Bonn's brain. He wondered if Bonn was secretly mental, hadn't developed proper when he'd been a kid. Watching Bonn move off in the crowd, Rack marvelled. His behaviour was a right blagging outrage. He decided to talk to Martina, boss of all, tell her straight that Bonn was letting the fucking side down. He wasn't using the syndicate's people like a key goer should. Christ, the other goers milked the Pleases Agency's credit dry. They were expected to.

Martina, going over the Pleases Agency's books every third day, took satisfaction in her goers' expenditure. Bonn was the exception, paying for his own tea, queuing with ordinary people at the Vallance Carvery while the counter girls squabbled to serve him. It was a frigging sore, that's what it was. What would folk think? Respect was down to Rack. Bonn's frigging politeness weakened the system.

He felt really terrible, sort of an ache, having had to tell Bonn that Tamina, drug sick, best friend of young Deirdre, who shared her personal pimp Set, wasn't anything to do with the syndicate. But Martina was right; Bonn couldn't take news. He was like a kid; you'd to pretend there was a Father Christmas.

"Rack?" Louse stood there. "Grellie says – "

"You say summert?" Rack looked hard at the messenger.

Louse only managed to speak third go from fright. "No."

24

Rack held the glare until Louse was almost white. "Follow Bonn till he's had his tea. Be at Fat George's newspaper stand at nine."

"Right, Rack."

Louse fled. Rack stayed there fuming. Grellie came over.

"How's Bonn, Rack?" she asked.

That was standard greeting. How's Bonn? The stringers said it instead of wotcher. Ought to get a frigging paper printed, Bonn's okay today so don't anybody go worrying.

"He asked after Tamina." He gave it like an accusation.

"You said nothing?"

"Leave orf, Grellie," he said sourly. "Grell, it's time you and Bonn shacked up. He wants his corners knocking off. Shagging these hiring bints is okay, his job and all. But a bloke oughter have his own bint, come home to and knock about a bit."

"Martina'd go spare."

"Want me to have another word with Bonn?"

Grellie stared, scarlet. "You've not said anything to him?"

Rack could see he'd have to be even more tactful. "I told him he needs you to shag."

She groaned, struck him ineffectually. Then, "What did he say?"

"Couldn't say anyfink, could he? Knowed it's true."

"One day, Rack," she said through clenched teeth. "One day."

She stalked off among the people crossing towards Mealhouse Lane. Rack looked after her, mystified. Birds didn't understand. You needed tact, like he had. Bonn was too cackhanded and silent when he ought to be having a few pints of an evening with the lads in the Shot Pot snooker hall in Settle Street.

People didn't know what was best for their own good. That was a fact. Rack knew he should have been a headshrinker. He was a natural, telling folk what they didn't know. Helping people was a gift.

"Rack?" A girl stood by, Blossom from Raglan Street,

worked off the barrows. "Martina."

"Right."

He jaunted off along the pavement, thinking Oh Christ. That's all I need today, Martina giving me her hard blues. Life was one war after another.

*   *   *

"Just look at that silly sod down there." Gary the movie cameraman watched from the third floor window of the porn studio on Quaker Street. "Thinks he's a superstar."

Ray was the electrics man and just as bored. He watched Rack's progress with Gary, waiting for the two tarts on the bed to get going. The girls, Steela and Ironia, were naked, talking in desultory tones about their moves.

"I seed him yesterday. Going paw-paw-paw, thinks he's a cowboy shooting Indians. Crazy."

"Couple of minutes, Gary. Ready to go."

Bondice, half Yank who sometimes acted but now less and less, stood arranging the two girls. Always cold, she wore her usual overcoat, no makeup, drab hair, hands in her pockets. Once had a famous name for billing on porn movies, but now she directed, getting script money, distributor's deals, and director's gelt. And she had the power. Nothing surprised Bondice.

"Right."

Gary left the window and positioned his camera over the two girls. The rooms were virtually decomposing, paint fraying on the walls, showing damp patches, radiators on the blink and Bondice's cold blood kept going by trivial fan heaters about the place. The bed's exotic pink coverlets lay on a concealed electric blanket Ray had rigged up.

"Here, Bondice. Any more about that loony message we got?"

"No," the director told Gary. "From some jerk called Rack, fancying his chances." She almost showed a smile. "He picked the wrong mark. I've paid protection money to real extortioners."

Gary looked at her as the girls worked out the first embrace, legs in a simulated writhe. "Want me to ask around? Only, we're new here. Don't want to cause ripples."

"I'm not shelling money out for fuck all," Bondice said.

"No, no!" The girls looked up, one mopping her mouth. "Didn't I tell you stupid cows? Steela's the one who lays down. Ironia does the slaps. Got it? Same as in the Lurk Turk, yeah?"

She sighed as the girls rearranged their positions and straightened the bed. "Right. Go again."

It seemed risky to Gary, who raised his eyebrows to Ray's shrug, but Bondice paid the piper and had got everything right so far.

He said nothing more as the action began.

4   **Dommy** – (domicilary) older
    term for the hiring of a goer
    for sex, by a woman in her
    own place or home

Tired, Bonn walked towards the Deansgate shopping mall.
The irony was almost humorous, for tiredness did not count
in considerations of the soul.

He had learned this during the seminary's unbelievably
hard years. The Order's justly famed religious ingenuity taught
such essentials, every step a compelling orthodoxy.

His problem, he thought candidly as he passed the Asda
centre, was misjudgement of small actions and unguarded
words. Here in the living streets of girl stringers, goers – of
which he was the least likely success – the slightest injudicious
glance could lead to open war and end up with blood on the
tavern pavements. Since becoming a Pleases Agency goer, he'd
realised that there were only two options. One was withdrawal
into seclusion, the other total acceptance.

He went through the mall and out by the opposite exit. Some
of Grellie's girls said hello as they emerged from the multiple
chemist. He was conscious of being unable to manage a smile at
such short notice, then they were gone, looking back after him.
He saw their reflections in the shop windows near the hugely
spacious budgerigar cage that towered by the waterclock, which
proved that he was guilty of cynicism – why else would he have
glanced so, if not to catch them at their whispering and staring?
Pride was never far from the surface; a great sin, but by no
means the most condemnatory.

He held to the pavement in Liverpool Road, past the
Rowlocks Casino, one of the few independent leisure sites;
independent meaning not under Martina's sway. He turned

into a narrow ginnel before the canal. An old pendulum bell clonked overhead as he entered the shop. The whole place was desperately old-fashioned, nothing more than a single room with a counter, just space enough for maybe two customers. *Tootal Herbalist* was the sign. Mr Tootal was weighing out dry pods on antique imperial scales.

"Good day to you."

Mr Tootal, no first name for a Dickensian caricature, seemed as desiccated as his herbs. Jars, amophoras, winchesters, demijohns, every known type of glass container occupied shelves to the ceiling. The herbalist himself affected a leather brat apron, slim wire spectacles and wispy silvery hair. Bonn was not taken in. The very aromas were probably chemicals from industrial synthesizers at St Helens. The women of the city believed however in Tootal's performance, their custom maintaining the sham. This was what Bonn had gleaned from listening to stringers in the Butty Bar. He had never visited the shop before.

"Mr Tootal."

"What may I get you? Aniseed? Some nice liquorice, spanish, coltsfoot rock?"

Bonn hesitated, not knowing whether to join the patter or ask his one question outright. He remembered the herbalist bringing incense and candles to the seminary chapel and the bursar. Maybe the other didn't remember Bonn, the young cassocked brother, seen only at a distance. They had never spoken.

"No, thank you."

"All I sell is legitimate herbs and slimming foods."

Mr Tootal had assumed that his customer was police.

"A girl died," Bonn said, courage in both hands. "I trust that you heard."

Mr Tootal sighed, emptying the pods into a paper bag. Bonn observed these preparations gravely. Tootal carefully returned the brass weights into a mahogany box, snapped it shut. He leant on the counter in his shirt sleeves, cuff links gleaming, a picture of Victorian propriety.

"Poor lass," he echoed.

"I need to know if she was your customer, and what she purchased, please."

"I only know what I read in the papers. She got taken by drugs. She was a stringer, not with some working house. You police?"

Bonn was still learning the street lingo. The word prostitute was eschewed. A working house was a brothel, a stringer a street girl openly plying for hire. Grellie's four strings were named for colours, Grellie's own idea to clarify her girls for Martina and Rack, one colour for each corner of the central square. Green, blue, yellow, red. There was talk of adding orange, for the growing numbers of Grellie's trollers who worked the streets south of Market Street and Moor Lane, but not even Grellie could cope with such a mad increase.

Stringers shared the Pleases Agency's fierce concern to protect territory, and demanded terrible sanctions if they suspected some amateur working girl poaching in their area. Ammie intruders always vanished without trace. Martina alone had the power and the veto.

"See, son, I never hear anything. Dead-and-alive ginnel, this. I hardly break even. Commercial rates are up another tenth this year."

"Please tell me what has come to your notice."

The herbalist leant away, regarding him through his spectacles. He said finally, "Friend of hers?"

Bonn felt a taste of iron. Had he accidentally bitten his lip? It had happened once when in the throes with a client, a Breightmet lady who owned two retail shoe shops, stout and anxious to show she was a capable lover for reasons he never fathomed. He tried to recall how Rack established himself as a person of menace. Ludicrous to emulate, though. Bonn would simply look a fool, his growl a pathetic bleat. He was sorry to threaten, but if Tootal really had been dealing in drugs with Tamina, *requiescat in pace*, then sanction was unavoidable. He cleared his throat.

"No. I mean yes. I do not know."

"Who told you to come asking, lad?"

"I came of my own volition."

Mr Tootal observed him. "Boxed, are you? Wired?" And explained to Bonn's uncomprehending silence, "Are you taping this conversation?"

"Of course not."

Mr Tootal took his time, wiped the counter with a wash-leather before speaking.

"You remind me of somebody I seed once, at a place I used to deliver to. It's closed these long months. To hear mass now, I've to go all the way out to St George's on School Hill. Can't stand St Michael's, young priests with guitars and bare feet like a sword-and-sandal film."

"Please."

"I heard some youngster made key goer." The herbalist looked at him. "Not that it's any of my business. What folk were and what they become is their own affair."

Bonn's attempted threat had clearly failed. He said with sorrow, "Be frank, or your shop will close for good tonight."

"Right, son." Strangely, the old shopkeeper brightened as if the bluntness had resolved some inner conflict. Words poured out.

"That lass Tamina come in a week back. She were on her own. Her bloke's some goldie but I never saw him. She want-ed me to buy a skip of miraa, cash coin. I said how on earth. She left. A goldie watched across the ginnel while she was in."

"Please clarify what you mean." Bonn was out of his depth.

"Miraa is like grass, hash, ganja, marijuana. You'll have heard of that. Except it grows in Kenya, the miraa tree, see?"

"It is a drug, I presume."

Tootal smiled ruefully at Bonn's difficulty. "Isn't everything these days, son?" He paused and said shyly, "I'll have to stop calling you son, you nearly being a seminary father and all, eh?"

"You rejected her offer to sell this material."

"How could I afford that much money?" He named a sum that would have bought the freehold of at least three Deansgate shops, almost making Bonn exclaim aloud. "I decided long since to stay clear of drugs. Herbals or nothing, me."

"She left."

Tootal smiled, nodding. "You're Bonn, aren't you? I've heard lasses talk, how you never ask a question outright like you don't want to give offence. Don't worry. I keep myself to myself." He pointed. "She went out. The bloke clouted her. They went towards the bus station."

"This, ah, miraa drug is some kind of…" Bonn indicated the dried bunches of herbs hanging from the ceiling.

"We used to call it khat. I was in the army over there." Tootal smiled, all nostalgia. "Tribesmen chewed it all day long. Mostly old duffers having a chat. *Catha edulis* is its proper name. There's no clear law yet for it over here, though you'll sometimes see some blokes chomping wedges of it. Legal, see? Chewed like coca leaves, gives you the same sort of amphetamine rush but slower. They say it's easier on the system."

"You qualified in pharmacy, I might suppose."

The herbalist gave a mild grimace, finally nodding. "No harm me and you knowing that betwixt ourselves, eh? I'm not registered any more. Makes it easier all round."

"Please inform me if any more information comes your way."

"I shall, son. How do I reach you?"

"Please be circumspect when you try. Good evening."

Bonn left, thinking hard. He had about two hours left before his next client, Clare Three-Nine-Five. He had enough information to have some person killed on Rack's say-so, so he must constantly pretend ignorance. He failed to notice Louse at the canal bus stop further along.

A thickness lay in Clare's throat as she left the SuperSnipe. No fancy electronic alarm systems in a vehicle this old, no flashing ambers to say it had got the message and was intruder alert. You locked the old thing and hoped for the best.

The Time and Scythe was an ancient hostelry, with bars downstairs and thick black posts setting off the white dash walling. Bright flowers, of which Clare approved, brass furnishings, leaded windows, a grandfather clock chiming in the lounge bar, quiet and discreet. It was a wise choice, this reserved place so close to the city centre. She walked straight through, ignoring the girl at the reception desk. A mere two lifts, each capable of holding only four people. That sort of hotel.

The lift started with a judder. She inspected herself in the mirror. Not bad, perhaps a suggestion of too much lipstick. No time for repairs. She heard two men and a woman laughing, closer as the lift rose. She didn't want other guests to be there when she alighted. They would dart those who's-she glances, want to exchange greetings. She heard the other lift's doors gently clash to, just as she reached her level, a mercy. Nobody there as she stepped out. Four-One was to the left, signed on a brass panel.

Absurd to feel her heart beating faster as she stepped to the door. It was tempting to knock, just as she had when first meeting Bonn – God, was it no more than a few months ago? She resisted, turned the handle and entered coolly as if it was her own place, looking about with a smile. It took courage, this act, call it a woman's assertiveness, announcing her absolute right to be here.

Bonn looked up from doing, what, nothing. He came forward with the start of his usual smile that never quite made it, and took her coat. She stood and let him minister. This was the awkward moment, that newness that each arranged encounter never quite lost.

"Good evening, Clare."

Fleetingly she wondered if there were grades of warmth in customary greetings. "Hello, Bonn. I'm not late?"

"You always look so smart."

"Thank you." She crossed to the couch, laid her handbag on the sofa table. Perhaps her reserve was created by the recognition of some trace of other women, some mental residue in him of having served previous clients? Medically speaking, some fragmentary molecules of pheromones signalling the presence of past physiologies, perhaps, or merely her awareness of how he was employed? He had a grim street life among prostitutes and hoodlums, that she knew, yet he remained sacrosanct, somehow above the mayhem and killings.

The couch was floral, the curtains new and the lighting different from a fortnight before. They had met in Four-One before. The entire suite had been re-upholstered. New furnishings, too, she observed. A different Wilton carpet, Persian design, with marginally too much intense red. At least it showed they were trying to please. Would the bedroom too be different?

Bonn seemed frozen, holding her coat. She beckoned. Gravely he hung the garment in the wardrobe, slid the closet louvres to and came to sit with her.

"There's a problem, Clare," he said. "The tea."

"Tea?" she asked blankly.

He took his time. "I'm afraid it may be the wrong sort," he said at last. "You like Lipton. I think they omitted to supply – "

She laughed. "It can wait until afterwards, darling."

There again, she thought, taking his hand. Saying darling, and reaching for his hand. Her fingers ruffled his hair, arranged it about his forehead, no thought of getting his agreement. She was in charge. It was a new feeling, no negotiations before she imposed her demand. That rush to union was now a natural conclusion, and it was all at her pace.

"Do you remember how we talked of the biochemistry of sexual congress?" She smiled to see him redden. "The chemical pathways, the brain's actions? I was so anxious to explain!"

"I remember."

"I took an hour, yacking about the duration of male-female attraction, and how it was limited by the hormonal factors. I talked of orgasmic molecules."

"Yes." He showed anxiety. "However, I do not recall details."

"I shan't ask questions!" She concealed her amusement so as not to give offence. Who else but Bonn would speak phrases like *I do not* or *however*? Or, for that matter, express concern over tea leaves when hired for sex. "There's something new now." She was being mischievous, and saw his face change. "About what we do."

Eventually he managed to say, "I have done every sexual thing to you that a man possibly can, Clare."

Her cheeks coloured, even after all their times together.

"Not that, darling." She almost giggled. "They implant a subcutaneous microchip in you. It emits signals, and your computer tells you if you have had an orgasm. It's quite a simple device, and functions by signalling on threshold trips."

He went silent to contemplate this. "But one knows when one has."

"It shows on the screen, degree of response, blood pressure and everything. Cybernetics at Reading University, I think. It prints it out afterwards."

"A souvenir of a romance, to prove that it happened," Bonn said gravely. Slowly he began to smile now he saw her purpose, to ridicule all comparisons.

She clapped her hands at his amusement, getting there.

"Progress!" she said, rising and taking him with her into the bedroom. "Like this. No computers, no planning, no measured steps."

The bedroom too had been refurnished, she observed with pleasure. A Regency flock wallpaper, muted silvers embossed on fawn, with matching curtains and bedspreads on the twin doubles. Different lights now, she saw with interest. She couldn't recall if she'd expressed reservations about the lampshades. Maybe she had, and these were the result?

Yet as she perched on the edge of the bed to remove her shoes and tights she wondered how many of the alterations to the décor of the various hotel rooms she'd shared with Bonn were made in response to remarks of his other clients. It disturbed her. Not quite so much progress as all that, then.

In silence she undressed and slipped between the cool sheets. She lay on her side to watch him. He was usually slower, sometimes even pausing as if at a sudden thought, at other times casting off his shirt, trousers, uncaring for tidiness. She liked that.

"Confidence," she said.

He turned to face her along the pillow.

"You do not lack confidence," he said quietly, making no move. "You couldn't."

Because I am a doctor? she almost blurted out in sudden anger but held her peace.

"Grace," he said eventually. "You possess grace."

There it was again, his vocabulary a reliquary from the seminary where he'd studied all his teenage years. She moved her hand and felt his flanks, his back, his chest. He was twenty years old, she knew, and she in her thirtieth year. That meant, working it out, she was half as old again. Putting it another way, he was two-thirds her age. Was this the attraction? It would be, for some women. Youth always was, and had a compelling attraction. She could see that. Her questions about his other clients had always failed. Infuriatingly, he never seemed to actually know any answers. Yet if he didn't, who on earth did?

Youth was everything these days. Young, you were monarch of all. Middle-aged, or simply getting on, you were made for derision. Bonn served older women, though she was still mercifully young. Youngish.

"Can you refuse?" she blurted out, just like that.

"Refuse in the sense of decline, I take it."

Never a question, merely stepping from statement to statement. The hallmark of theological debate was assertion to counter assertion. Psychiatrists too pretended their every utterance was a question. Lawyers insisted that the witness answered the question, often when no question was put. Before Bonn, she would have seen psychiatry and law as prime movers. Now, she knew them for mere beginners. The oldest thought system was laughably more expert. It was Bonn's, yet in him was so innocent.

"Yes." He said nothing to that and she went on, "Like, if you're booked for some woman who's too old, can you say no? Maybe wait for some woman more attractive?"

He looked past her. She watched his face, inches away, feeling his breath. She decided she disliked the wallpaper design and resolved to tell him. That would test the Pleases Agency's system. She would then learn for sure whether he was reporting back, change that décor in Four-One at the Bolgate Time and Scythe, please, because Clare Three-Nine-Five hated it so get a move on.

"Women do not understand the compulsion," he said finally.

"Whose?"

"The male needs women. I believe that I never question a client's desire, or her compulsion. I cannot claim the right."

She drew back to see him better. The curtains had closed, maybe something automatic as he'd slipped in beside her. The room was in gloaming. His eyes gleamed.

"Why ever not?" But she was sulky, wanting him to say he selected, and that she was one he would always eventually choose, given the choice. "That's stupid."

"I simply respond."

"Like with me?" She was furious but strove to conceal her anger. "So I could be anyone?"

"You are unique to me."

She considered this. Was it a negative? His hands were on her breasts now. She wondered what it was about breasts that fascinated him so. Something from childhood, a lack he revealed as an adult? That was the glibbest, hence the phoniest, of psychologists' usual claptrap. No. He was actually in awe of the love process, overcome at the merest glimpse of her in a way that was nothing to do with upbringing. To him, her very body seemed to be mystical in ways she'd never even thought possible. Certainly she had never felt that magical response in Clifford, her husband.

And in the final throes, flailing and spilling into her – the very thought made her breathing deepen – Bonn seemed lifted to some level that made her wonder.

Experiencing it for the first time, it had stunned her, as if she'd encountered something almost holy. Foolish word, when she'd tried to think it through afterwards.

"With everyone?"

"I never broach a lady's confidence."

"Other clients in general, then."

He was silent, but spoke quietly without hesitation. "I do not betray a confidence."

"Bone dancing," she said harshly. "A girl said it in the hairdresser's."

He looked away.

"Well?" Clare demanded. "That's what it's called, isn't it? This? When a women hires a man?"

"It has many names." His calm maddened her. "Women are addicted to words. At first, when I encountered women, it was one of my disappointments. Now, I sympathize. It is as if they suffer phrases as an affliction. Some collect them, not to use but to convince themselves that they know. They feel empowered."

Sexist! The accusation would come easy, but he would not fight back with the obvious retort, that she was prostituting him by the hiring process, not the other way round. In that way he was defenceless.

And sexist was one word. It was unfair to press him. She quietened, tracing his features with her fingers, eyes, mouth, hair line, chest. She felt him. He was already stiffening. Her hand moved. She saw his eyes close.

"Some goers do marry, don't they?" They had been over this, when she had moved into the new surgery out at Charlestown to take up working for the charity.

"I am not at liberty to say."

"Can a key do it, like you?"

A key was, Clare knew, the ultimate goer, highest paid of all. From her intense association with Bonn, and the criminal cases they had accidentally, maybe not so accidentally, happened on together, she knew a little about the street hierarchies. There were very few keys, special youths who, each leading a trio of goers, were regarded as vastly superior. They were the elite. Their booking fee was quadruple that of the ordinary goer. A long waiting list for a key was practically routine. She knew she was specially privileged and that she received priority. That could only be at Bonn's instigation.

"That would not be contrary to rule."

She felt her spirits lift. She propped herself on her elbow, fed her breast into his mouth, touching his moving lips, feeling his cheeks narrow as he took the nipple.

"Come on, darling," she said huskily. "Enough talk. Over me this time." She tapped her hands along his flank by way of instruction, and slid quickly onto her back.

He complied, his weight driving the air from her. She accepted the pressure, wanting discomfort as he entered her. Evidence of a sort, she thought, but for what purpose she did not know. Reason did not come with the process. Then she was away, as if feeding voraciously at a last chance of a meal.

*　*　*

Clare felt unused, which was a new experience for her after Bonn.

She entered her small flat in Charlestown, near the city centre but sufficiently far not to irritate Martina and her Pleases Agency. She now saw the tactic so clearly. She ran a bath, thoughtful. Usually she allowed Bonn's sweat to linger, savouring the faint musk of him through the evening until bed. Unless she had to do a spell at the hospital, that is, for her two worlds were never to merge. She stuck to that. She clicked the radio on, local news, leaving the door ajar.

Soaking, she reviewed her position.

A well qualified consultant less than a year ago, she was then offered permanent posts in Farnworth General Hospital, including a special medical fellowship in cardiology. Instead, she had opted for a highly paid independent private practice in Charlestown, funded by a discreet charitable foundation with seemingly unlimited resources. It had promised more time, time that would let her see more of Bonn. The career change had coincided with her divorce. Poor Clifford, though now he was wassailing it round the city, deep into his beloved party politics, golfing, running his lucrative investment office. He still lived in his original house in the Wirral, with the same elderly housekeeper who knew his every foible. Clare had been more relieved than sad. The separation had been what sociologists termed amicable.

Which left her in solitude. Not solitude, perhaps more independence, and it had reclaimed her freedom. Of course marriage had immense benefits. The solidity, financial ease, the sex of course, married woman's status, companionship. Erosion set in, as she realised that Clifford was involved in city crime. She had been able to provide him with alibis only so long.

Then came Bonn, literally at a road accident in Victoria Square, and she was drawn in. Soaping herself, she wondered if it was the anonymity of sex that first dared her. Now, it was a compulsion born of partial understanding and was becoming more compelling than ever.

The radio was going on about a young woman found dead. Her next of kin were being informed. Clare thought a moment. That was one angle. Prostitutes never seemed to have relatives or permanent addresses. Hassall might know, but what would he think of a doctor's sudden request for information about a chance suicide?

Clare had no doubt about her own position. She was the doctor employed to care for the girl stringers and goers employed by the Pleases Agency, plus a miscellany of odd vagrants and street mumpers. Painted into a corner, in fact. She tried to recapture the image of Martina who owned Pleases: lovely, quiet, bright and alert. They had only ever met in some grand office, where Martina was attended by sober professional lawyers and fawning ingrates, whole clones of decorative secretaries and silent besuited youths straight from the Stock Exchange.

Bonn was the key to everything, though. To her own personal desire, to her destiny if you liked.

She reached for a towel and rose, nudging the plug chain to set the water draining. Time for a warm drink, then bed. One day Bonn would be here too. She smiled into her living room almost seeing him there. Perhaps reading, looking up, saying, "Shall we turn in?" or some such.

That was one aim in her life. If opposition stood in her way, she would meet it head on. She was determined enough. Her failure at the City Medical Foundation vote still stung. She would get even, repay somehow.

6 | Rig – necessary apparatus for the intake of drugs (syringe, foil, matches, needles etc)

Dark was no friend, though Jecko waited for it. Night was pally to some of the kids in the Home but never to him. Dark was filthy in the black, in threats it brought. He always heard the faint shuffles the Home made after lights-out. Soon as Brother Monitor's shouts dowsed the lecky and the shadows turned traitor, then came the whisperings and that deep guttural chuckle.

Jecko hated that word as much as he hated darkness. Chuckle. It sounded made up, somebody evil's invention. It sounded like the start of punishment. No questioning what it was, not in the Christian Brothers' Home Orphanage.

Chink on the other hand was a lovely word. Chink meant escape. He wanted a chink through the railings onto the road. Out there the city's glow shone like rescue.

Chink truly was brilliant. Chink. He'd heard Bentie, big of size for all his twelve years and able to kick a ball further than any boy in the Home, talk of some Hollywood picture. It had been about a mouse or something. This mouse hated a prison gaoler who'd been right bad. It had found a chink in some walls. Where there was no chink it had gnawed one.

It got away.

Then it had thought. It had gone back, to help some prisoner who'd given it crumbs and that. Bentie told Jecko the story. In his version, the gaoler had a crucifix on his black cassock.

The mouse killed the gaoler. Bentie couldn't say how, but it had. The mouse. It done it, then got away.

Fottso, who came from Walkden and said he could swim

45

but he was a liar, Fottso said electrocution didn't hurt because it was better than hanging. The rest of the lads said no. Fottso was a liar. He said he had a brother called William who would come and buy him out, but he hadn't so it wouldn't happen.

It was dark. Time.

Jecko knew he could escape. He could get away tonight. If it rained, he'd give it a go tomorrow night.

He'd still got his clothes on. Some children in the dorm kept their Home pullover on for warmth because one lecky switch did heating and everything. He'd kept his pants underneath his blanket. As soon as the lights went out he pulled his socks on. Underpants, trousers, vest, shirt, no tie because that was a give-away. Three kids had been caught like that, caught easy. Jecko wasn't going to risk anything that daft. Shoes were always kept downstairs. Brother Ernest counted them. Shoeless with a tie was a clear sign that you were from the Home Orphanage of the holy Christian Brothers who were responsible for you to Almighty God in thought, word and deed.

Jecko wondered whether to pray for help to the Virgin Mary. Something like, please get me escaped and I'll light a candle for ever and ever. She was on their side, though, not on Jecko's, and she'd see Jecko clear as day and tell on him.

So no shoes and no tie and no prayers. Take your chance. Boys who talked of escape always kept on about whether prayers would help, and who you said them to. Like, one group of three lads were cousins and always fought together as a pack. Take one on, you took on the lot. Well, them three reckoned the safest was Saint Anthony because he was Lost Causes.

But people you told secrets to told on you. That was how you got caught. That was Jecko's experience. Even if he only got half way across the roof, it would be worth it. The other night had been a near thing, but the girl in the vestibule hadn't told on him, when he'd been trapped there. She'd been on his side, seen him in that passing car's lights but not grassed. A miracle.

He slipped from under the rough blanket. It pricked his chin in farewell. He remembered a story in English about a tree that nodded in the wind at some escaping child. "It nodded in the wind as if in farewell," the story said.

His heart thumped, surely so loud everybody in the Home could hear. He was deafened by his heart. He could hear Grock snoring and coughing. Grock was going to try to learn how to cough blood because he'd heard of some lad in the Christian Brothers' places in Ireland, which was across the sea, who'd coughed blood. Ever after, the bastards left him alone. He got no exams and they kept him separate. That was why Grock kept trying to cough up blood so the bastards'd leave him alone. Sess said coughing blood meant you were going to die, which was okay because you could go to heaven and tell God the Brothers were shagnasties and God would be like an avenging angel. Jecko said that was all ballocks.

Then Brother Jason had come across the playground calling out what are you boys arguing about and remain in mute holy contemplation for the rest of playtime. It showed what a cruel bastard Brother Jason was, though he'd never had been a shagnasty like some of the others, especially the Bursar and the Brother Ritualist who'd already been moved twice from one Home to another to hide his evil.

To creep, you kept your socks on or your feet squeaked on polished lino. If your noise wakened the lads, they'd keep quiet, even Ray who was the smallest and lived in terror of everything. The lads made him jump by shouting or bursting a paper bag. Jecko alone guessed why Ray cried when they made him jump. It wasn't the bang. It was relief, when he saw it was only his pals and not the Christian Brothers coming to get him and leave him hurting so everybody would know what had happened.

If anybody woke up they'd think Jecko was going to pee. Except one might whisper, "Heigh! Jecko! You got thih clothes on!" Peddle got caught climbing the gates in a sudden electric glare, now gone to the Christian Brothers in Ireland, his mate said in a cattle truck. Peddle's exclamation had fetched Brother Dietrich running in his cassock. He'd smothered Peddle in a horrible grappling match that had all the watching boys silent and pale. Peddle got tied up and marched off and was gone next morning. His desk was empty, his crayons and pencil case that he'd brought with him also vanished.

None of the lads dared ask. The sermon at Holy Mass next day had been about Punishment for Sins Condoned. None of them understood it, except they knew from Brother Francesco's tone that it meant keep your mouth shut.

Bentie said God would forgive anybody who told on the Brothers. Nobody risked that. They weren't daft.

Jecko crept down the staircase. Always a light on the narrow landing where the Brothers kept their black overcoats and outdoor shoes.

There was one playground, with a footer field that did for cricket. They played against other religious schools, but only the teams got to play. The rest of the Home lads watched. When the visiting teams wanted to talk they were blocked by the Brothers. It was supposed to be because they were Proddy Dogs, not Cat Licks – Protestant, Catholic – but the Home lads said it was so they couldn't tell how rotten it was with the Brothers. It was a sin to tell and you'd go to hell. Brother Jason's sermons were about lads who didn't Stand By The Faith going straight to hell. God saw to that.

He reached the bottom stair. He heard voices, too distant for separate words. Jecko wondered what it would be like to have a voice like that. His would break one day. Except when your voice broke you were sent away to a different Home in Gwent in Wales or Ireland that was just as bad as this. His heart was almost clanging. The stone flags were cold. His toes went numb.

He took hold of the door handle, astonished his hand was slippery with sweat. Fear did that. Noiselessly he turned it and pushed.

The door was shut.

Panic took hold. He almost tried to run back, but remembered Peddle.

Somebody chuckled at something said in a bass voice. No prayers in there, just talk among the Brothers waiting for heavier, more poisonous dark to fall. For a moment it came to Jecko that some Brothers – maybe Brother Jason? – didn't really know, but that couldn't be true.

His hand hit something, and he stared. There was a key sticking from the lock. He gaped, almost exclaimed aloud. Could anyone be that lucky? He grasped the knob and the key. For quiet, you pulled a door close to you, until there was no more give. Only then did you try to turn a key. That's what Bentie and Grock said. They actually had burgled houses before they came to the Home.

He did it. The key turned in utter silence and the door opened. He stared at the darkness of the quadrangle and stepped out.

He closed the door, careful, careful. No noise. The ground was wet, some rain earlier. He walked – never ever run when burgling, so escaping must be the same. Running made you obvious, and obvious got you caught.

One of the glass doors was suddenly lit with lecky that shed yellow light across the quadrangle. He froze. It was one of the lay brothers in his three-piece suit and black boots, locking up, coming round the square. Brother Arthur. Jecko waited until he reached the far corner, then slid low along the wall, ducking under the windows. He reached the near corner, opposite Brother Arthur, and caught the drainpipe. He climbed slowly. Clinging, he thought, like ivy on the old garden wall. Some song he vaguely remembered, maybe from in that small house he sometimes imaged, an old woman rocking on a chair and singing in a wail. She'd taught him to sing "Down With the Demon Drink". He could still sing the words except the lads

49

laughed at him.

He reached the roof, scrambled up and lay flat. No sound from below, but that didn't mean somebody like Brother Arthur wasn't already peering upwards through his bottle specs and taking out his whistle. Jecko still didn't move. Then he heard Brother Arthur's measured tread – that phrase from some poem, *measured tread*.

And the door closed, the key turning, the handle being shaken to test it stood firm. Jecko couldn't believe it. Free?

Almost. Meaning stuck up on a roof. No way he could say he'd walked in his sleep like that little pale lad who was always found wailing asleep standing in some corner, hands in front of his face.

Jecko spread himself out like a frog, moving his limbs slowly, one at a time. Never hurry, another edict by Bentie.

His hands were so cold now they didn't do what he wanted. He rested his chin on the ridge tiles.

He was amazed at the view. Down there, under a tree almost as tall as the roof, there was a lamp post. A man had a woman up against the lamp and was ramming himself at her. Her legs were apart, heels off the ground, her hands on his back. It wasn't like how the Brothers did it to some of the lads. It was the other way round.

She was laughing sort of, like she was making it up.

And another woman was there, casually smoking a cigarette, looking back towards the main road. Jecko could see motors and people walking against the coloured lights from cinemas and pubs. People! They were safety, so many and different. They were escape.

For an instant he imagined himself on a moorland farm, that you could see from the upper Home classroom on clear days. Himself driving sheep to the river, maybe on a wild mustang. Then he was back to clinging on a roof, looking down on some bloke shagnastying some woman while she pretended laughing.

The man cried out then slumped and stood away. Jecko heard the zip, saw the woman straighten her skirt, chewing gum. She asked the man something. Jecko couldn't hear.

She took tissues from her handbag, wiped herself between her legs like it didn't matter and lobbed the tissues into the gutter. The other woman approached, not caring. The man walked along the pavement to a motor. He drove off.

Jecko crawled along the roof crest to the end slope and slowly slid down until his stockinged feet lodged on the guttering. He grabbed the groove with both hands and looked down.

Down it went. He tried working it out in measures like they taught in class, maths with Brother Pius. Four times his own length? More, much more.

He saw the sheen of a drainpipe some three body lengths along and crawled towards it, to freedom down there on the street.

The girls were standing talking, having a smoke. Jecko longed for a smoke. In the Home the teaching was that you died from fags. God in His infinite wisdom had given you a temple for a body, and there you went making it sick. That was spitting in the face of the Almighty and landed you in hellfire, serve you right.

The women didn't look like they gave a toss. One was saying something about the man in the motor.

"…didn't give a prick like that, I'll tell you, Rita."

"What's he want for a couple of notes, Chrissakes?"

"I'll tell Rack if he starts that again."

"That's Grellie's rule, Joy. Do any different, she'll knife you. Remember that Manchester girl."

"I wouldn't, would I?"

By the time they'd had their fags and looked like moving on Jecko was almost above them.

Then the terror began. Somebody called in that deep voice from inside the quadrangle. Jecko almost voided in fright.

The two women walked off. He saw the black sky above lighten as lecky switched on in the Home. No whistle yet.

He scrambled over the guttering and found the drainpipe. He started to shin down, scraping his feet, the pavement suddenly jarring his heels and almost stunning him. Shakily he tried to run but slammed against the younger of the women, the one who hadn't shagged the man.

"Here, you," the Rita one said, cuffing him.

"What the fuck?" Joy said.

"Please missus, let me go."

Jecko was in the shagging woman's grasp. He saw in the feeble glim of the street lamp that she was barely an adult.

The inner door opened flooding the pavement with light. Somebody called, another responded. Lights came on.

"It's only some kid," Rita said.

"Right, you little bastard. Let's have it!"

"What? What?"

Jecko had never been so scared. Shadows were moving against the porch screens now, large dark figures silhouetted against the Home lights. The place was coming alive.

"I didn't pinch anything, missus, honest!"

"Search him, Rita. Little bleeders get younger every week."

"Look, titch," Rita said, shaking Jecko. She was stronger than he thought. "Give back what you nicked and we'll let you go."

"Please don't send me back. Please."

"Thieving little bugger."

He stood there, palms pressed together in supplication. "Please. You don't know."

Both now had hold of him. The outer door opened. Out came Brother Paulo and Brother Pius, swooping forward, cassocks flapping, shadows cast across the street from the porchlight.

The two Brothers stood facing the girls. They reached out to Jecko. For one instant he shrank back then he sagged in the girls' grip. It was hopeless.

"What's he done?" Rita asked.

Brother Pius sighed. "What a child!" he intoned.

"So poorly last week, and now this!" Brother Paulo said, smiling.

"Thank you ladies, for returning him to our care." Brother Pius kept a hand on Jecko's shoulder. "He hasn't been well, poor boy. Quite deranged."

"Soon better, though, eh?" Brother Paulo smiled. "We really are very grateful to you two young ladies. But for your presence here, we should have had the police searching the city centre."

"Providential, you might say." Brother Pius beamed. He paused, smiling, and spoke with meaning. "We always deplore having to call the police."

Jecko looked up at Rita, then at Joy. All of them were in it together.

"We thought he'd stolen something," Rita said.

"It's what some kids do," Joy explained. "Bump into you, nick your handbag and off."

"He's a good boy," Brother Pius said fondly. "Just been slightly unwell lately. Soon have him back on his feet, good as new."

"Here," Rita said, checking her handbag. "Just let me see. You can never tell."

"Yih." Joy pulled Jecko to her and turned her back on the two clerics, patting Jecko's pockets. She leant down.

Both girls were suddenly stooping over Jecko, fingers prodding his pockets.

"I haven't anything, honest, missus!"

And Rita whispered, "Run. Run."

And when Jecko stared, she shoved him forcibly away towards the lights at the end of the street. For an instant he stood wondering what the trick was, then took off in his stockinged feet, going like the wind as the two Brothers shouted and started after him. The girls got in the way, screaming in exasperation and calling out for the two men to be careful, mind out, that's my foot. Jecko heard the thud of somebody falling, heard the girls screech, one shouting filthy abuse at the Brothers.

The sound behind dwindled. He ran into the main street, slowed, winded, and walked on. Nobody took a bit of notice, and he thought, I'm free, I did it, I'm out. They can't put me back in there ever again. He saw the lights of the bus station and went towards it.

7

Mumper – one who sleeps
without shelter.

Inside the Shot Pot, in its usual turmoil before the big
Thursday betting night began, Rack held court. Various
standers, the goers' minders, wanted to see him. He hated
these niggles. They were nothing to do with gelt – and everything on earth was money. He suspected something was
always going on.

Frol he saw off sharpish, the whining git.

"Look, Frol," he told the casual stander in his smart single-
breasted and custom shoes. "You either do the job proper or
you get your fucking head knocked in, see?"

"It's how do I get time for a pee, Rack."

"A pee?"

"Three stands on the trot, all on different floors."

"How old are you?" Rack asked, doing his hooded eyes and
leaning as if about to leap. "Twenny-free?" His Cockney
showed at such times. "Default, and I'll tank you myself. Out."

The whinger left through the curtain, shrugging to the next
stander. Rack caught that but didn't call him back. He'd find
some reason to tank Frol anyway.

"What, Set?"

The back room was actually a small bar, but Rack sometimes wanted it cleared for crap like these moans. The waitress Josie insisted she was a mulatto, whatever that was.
Question her, she'd draw diagrams on her order pad to show
how some grampa was from Sierra Leone, that she said was
next to Argentina. Rack told her she was stupid, because
everybody was coloured something, like he was coloured

55

white, but telling birds anything was like talking to the wall. She just kept on.

Josie was looking out of the hatch, entertained by the snooker lads in the hall, laughing at the players' antics. She'd been done for starting a fire once in some school. Martina had barred her from becoming a stringer. Martina and Grellie had had a right ding-dong over her, but Martina still said no. Rack didn't know whether he wanted to use her himself or not. He kept imagining waking up to find her going on about some ancestors. Drive him mental.

He decided he'd stick to Georgina who ran a taxi stand. She was married but was a definite plus. He'd used her for over a month, a good find.

Set glanced at Josie so Rack told her to clear off. She left, grumbling. Set drew breath. He knew that the next few minutes would decide his fate. Play it well, Deirdre would be up for it and he'd be in the clear. Forget the opposite.

"It's Deirdre," Set said.

He was a sharp dresser, but had the sense to look just that bit shoddy when on his stands. You could go anywhere then, but not if you're tarted up like a fucking flag day. Set had a gold lighter, a snappy trilby, flashy gold teeth, reckoned he deserved a place in them TV soaps. He'd done seventy auditions. Twice he'd asked to be made a goer, or somehow helped into acting. Rack had doubts, but Set was a safe stander, done as he was told.

"What about her?"

"She's a stringer, does the – "

"Get on wiv it."

"She's on chalkies. I found her stoned out of her skull."

Rack shook his head. One stringer turning a junkie last month, now another. That woman doctor over in Charlestown should earn her frigging keep, stop the silly cunts doing it.

"Where's she getting it?"

Set looked round, carefully brought out a small satch of

white powder and another glassy holding small yellowish tablets. He laid another bag beside them. It held three rigs, syringes, needles still in their sterile plastic hoods. Standard orange, green, blue, different sizes.

"No idea. I left her sleeping it off."

"Leave them here."

Chalk, meaning cocaine or morphine, and Ecstasy. Rack put his hands behind his head, looked up at the ceiling.

"The money, Set."

"It was in her handbag. This is it all."

The stander had it ready taped in a lavatory roll. Set had taken trouble with it, even scenting it with a dab of her perfume. Rack counted. More than any working girl should be carrying.

"She's dealing?"

"Looks like it."

Set seemed really sad, standing there pale and evidently worried sick. Deirdre's transgressions were down to him, he being her bloke. Crossing, the discreet pairing off of a stander and one of the Pleases Agency's working girls, was forbidden, but an exception had been allowed in this case. The reason: Deirdre was a charity worker in her spare time, collected money and stuff for good causes. Martina said it might be good cover, if Deirdre ever got picked up by the Squad. Rack had been against it and Grellie hadn't been so keen, but Martina ruled otherwise so there you go.

"How long?" He only asked because Martina would want to know where Deirdre stashed her money. Greed undid them.

"Recently." Set winced. "I think she's seeing some other bloke who was milking her."

"And her milking him, eh?" Rack fell about, laughing at his wit. "You know the rules, Set."

"Only," the stander said, nervy, "I come to tell you straight off, Rack."

"Okay." Rack floored his chair with a crash, shooting his non-existent cuffs like a saloon gambler. "You're clear. Bring

57

Deirdre in to see Grellie. As soon as she can walk. Where is she now?"

"Waterloo Street. You know that four-storey? There."

Set didn't move, stood waiting for his punishment.

"You're on stand tonight."

"Yes. Vikram, the goer from Hulton. At the Vivante."

"Eight o'clock, innit. Do it. Grellie'll send word. And Set?"

"Yes, Rack?"

"If it's like you say, you're okay." Rack did his hooded eyes threat for a count of ten. "If it's not…"

"Thanks, Rack. You're a gent."

Rack saw him go, feeling a glow of pleasure. See? Even scurf knew a gent when they saw one.

He still had three groaners to see. He shouted for Josie to bring him a pint of Newcastle but the lazy cow wasn't where she should have been. He'd pass the news to Grellie. Let her sort it out, give him a bit of peace to work out his new card gambling system. Cards depended on the weather, his best theory yet.

Some women astonish by their presence. Bonn felt taken aback by Annabel One-Seven-Three-Six, who entered the room flinging off her coat and simply dropping her handbag, laughingly exclaiming that she'd gone to the wrong floor. He felt unprepared, almost like his first sexual encounter, so decisive was she.

"What a fool! Missing the third level!" She bussed him, ruffled his hair playfully, flung herself on the couch.

He could not manage a word.

"Lovely to see a real fire! Got a drink? Whisky and virtually no soda."

"Whisky and soda, Annabel."

Another worry was drinks. Posser had given him a brief lesson, mix brandy with this, gin with tonic but only when … and so on. He still was unsure, because a lady could make assumptions. They held social power, having given (he was sure) politics and theology over as male playthings while they held the terrain that mattered. Which, he noted for future thought, was possibly the only apt definition of social intercourse.

He stared at the array of bottles. How many kinds of whisky existed? Were whiskey and whisky identical? If yes, why then all these different spellings and bottle shapes? One seemed so dark. Single malt, was there a double malt? He searched, failed to find such a label. Were some ladies inclined to single, as perhaps sweeter or less potent, leaving men the other stuff? Or vice versa?

"So you're the one who costs five times as much?"

He looked round from the drinks cabinet, anxious.

"If you have any queries..." The Pleases Agency had accountants for money. All the front people were shrewd girls, eager to explain these arcane details even though he never wanted to know. And Martina had Money Evenings with her dad Posser, usually a Tuesday, while Bonn usually read Gibbon's *Decline and Fall* in the living-room, unless he was hired out.

"I'm just wondering what I'll get extra, that's all."

He heard the smile in her voice but was nonetheless concerned.

"Annabel. I am afraid I'm at a loss."

She laughed, eyeing him over the couch backrest. "Pouring the drinks? I thought you looked new. A good three fingers, dear. Half that of soda. No ice."

"Thank you."

She smiled at him as he returned.

"You're not having one?"

"Thank you, no. Unless..."

"No. Fine." She took it and sipped, eyes large, smiling, knee raised onto the couch, taking him in. "How new, exactly?"

"Rather recent, I'm afraid." He felt his cheeks warm. It seemed to add to her amusement.

"*Rather* recent?" She laid her head back to laugh and patted his face in a way he hoped was intended as reassurance. "You'd not last a minute on the stage, Bonn. It is Bonn, right?"

"Yes." The stage? He recalled Rack's words: That singer. Was she famous? Television had not been allowed in the seminary.

"You are on the stage, Annabel."

"My posters are all round the city for tomorrow night's gig, and here I am with an assumed name. Is that stupid or what?"

"You took the name before you became famous."

"That's right." She took a drink, almost a gulp, and sighed with relish. "You don't know what a benefit you lot are. You save my life, I can tell you. The public are beasts. You can't trust them."

He listened in bafflement. We lot? Who saved her life? "I do not understand, Annabel."

"What don't you?"

"You must love the public," he said gravely.

"*Love* the *public?*" She sat up, no relaxation now. Not angry, just astonished at innocence. "You're joking!"

She slumped, groped for a cushion. He reached, plumped one and placed it behind her shoulders. She subsided with a purr. After a moment she started speaking.

"Showbiz is grimsville. Don't let appearances fool you." She sighed, licked the rim of her glass absently, eyes distant as she remembered past nights. "The times I've longed for company, a man to talk to. Sometimes nothing to do with sex, maybe nothing more than just a drink. Or maybe a quiet session with somebody who'd be restful after supper. You know? Women are right bitches on tour or pitched, I'll tell you."

"I fail to see, Annabel. Showbiz. I take it you mean members of the audience."

"Doesn't matter whether they are or not, Bonn." She finished the drink, held it out for him to take and nodded that she wanted another. "Don't drown it this time."

Her voice raised to follow him, calming as she began to relax.

"Know what I used to do, Bonn? I'd pick the best looker after the show. Even a musician from the band. They were always a laugh, but usually drunk. A horrid mistake, every single time. It was ghastly."

"Ghastly," Bonn repeated. Ghastly, yet it had been her usual practice.

He concentrated on pouring. She had not complained about the whisky, so presumably he had chosen a correct brand. Drown the drink? Was that the soda? He had heard the expression somewhere, possibly in some old film. He trickled the soda water in. He ought to have made the same drink twice, kept one in reserve to check colour for comparison.

"How difficult," he murmured as he took the drink across.

"Bloody evil, darling." She sipped while he watched anxiously, then rolled her eyes in pleasure. "You're learning! Nearly eight out of ten. Sit close."

He obeyed, his hip against her knee.

"I find it hard to imagine the process."

She smiled at his choice of words.

"Picking a man up from a stage door queue? It's sordid. They stand there – there'll be ten, fifteen, tomorrow – for autographs. Maybe a dyke or two, always a couple of queers. Ominous that, because it tips you off you're becoming a fag hag." And explained, amused at his ignorance, "When you're of a certain ... vintage, a female performer can become a special focus of interest to the fag clan. Y'know? Like Judy Garland."

"You cannot mean old."

She looked at him with less amusement but greater interest.

"You meant that!" She inspected him quizzically, his clothes, his hair, his hands. "I'm beginning to develop a certain feeling that you might actually be real. Are you?"

"I do not follow." He felt real.

"I've had more roadies than you've had dinners, Bonn, dear. Dicks for a night, y'know?" She looked into the fireplace, unseeing, flames reflected in her eyes. "Just for company. You can't know the loneliness. Even Grade One tours can be hell. And you're the star." She gave a mirthless bark of a laugh. "Or what passes for one when the lower billing start playing up."

"Company." He could carry the concept no further. He tried to read her expression but she quickly looked away.

"On stage, you are the show, Bonn, see? You have your dresser, yack with the stage manager about lights, timing, bully the musicians to get the notes right for once. Then you perform well enough so the idle bastards get paid. They're leeches."

"It seems so hostile."

She looked at him in astonishment.

"I thought you were going to say glamorous!" She smiled.

"You're simple, innocent, or a hell of a sight too clever for your own good. Which?"

He wished he could drink, talk about her loneliness as alcohol took over. Except, would he like the taste of whisky? And would she be pleased if he shared the same? Wine he quite liked, but at this early evening hour it would stifle him.

"I find life outside almost incomprehensible."

"Outside where?" she asked shrewdly. Then, "You're not an ex-con, are you?"

Presumably meaning a released prisoner? Not in the sense Annabel One-Seven-Three-Six meant.

"I have never been in gaol."

Now she was alert, scrutinising him in silence a moment before her eyes drifted to the fire and she sank into reverie. She had booked him for two hours. Why, if she was in such a rush? Had she no show tonight?

"What's incomprehensible, Bonn?" She made a rueful face, eyes averted. "That I maybe hope to find someone to confide in? What's wrong with that?"

He himself had no one, so had no basis for an answer and stayed silent.

"They began to use me, taking pay from magazines to 'Reveal All'." She made a bitter quotation of the words. "And the photographs, when some bastard lets the paparazzi know where you'll be, which hotel's back exit you'll be slinking out of. I've done all that."

She shook herself, offered him her empty glass. "Get me another." He remained beside her. "Then I heard about Pleases Agency. It was a miracle, sudden reassurance. I didn't believe you existed. I tried it seven months ago. And been a regular ever since when I've been here."

"I am pleased, Annabel."

"The relief! Knowing that I'd not be followed, never have to explain some chance dickster away to some pushy magazine tart hooked on getting promotion to a by-liner."

Bonn, listening attentively but could not quite follow her meaning.

"No comebacks, Bonn. No stories going round, nothing except doing the shows. I suddenly felt I was getting away with it all. Everything perfectly clean!" She hugged herself. "Nobody pointing the finger, no talk-show host making double remarks about how you got laid by some casual nobody. No taxi driver's knowing grin. Ugh! Thanks to your agency."

She laughed at Bonn's face.

"Isn't this where you do your plug, advertise your services? Tell me that The Pleases Agency, Inc., aims to give every satisfaction?"

He began to suspect her frequent laughter, but not her amusement, even if she was a performer.

"That would be impertinent."

"You talk funny, like you just learned the language, picking your way through. Worried I'll think you're saying the wrong thing?"

He thought a long while, then said, "Yes."

"Where's my drink?"

"Please do not ask for another just yet."

She gaped. "*What?*"

"Please allow me to bring one later." He laid her glass aside and took her hand. "You deserve better, Annabel. Better than you want."

"I what?" She glanced about, a star angry at an obstruction.

"And better than you think you have a right to expect."

"Here, mister. You just fucking listen to me – "

"I enjoy your presence. We shall enjoy your time so much better if you delay." Bonn studied her hand so intently that she started to draw it away in sudden apprehension. "Please."

"What are you looking for? Are you a palmist?"

He did not answer, laid her hand palm upwards on his. Still looking, he began tracing the lines.

"Hands are so beautiful. I love them. They express a lady."

64

"I've always been ashamed of my hands." She peered with him. "My sister had such lovely long fingers. Dad praised her for picking blackberries from our hedge without popping a single one. She always went home without a single purple stain. I was covered."

"No comparisons, Annabel." He decided how to say it, and got out, "I remark that your hands are beautiful, and you immediately tell me about those of a different lady. That is the strangeness."

"You're telling me off, Bonn." She didn't withdraw her hand from his. "You tell me what I can drink, where I go wrong. Yet I pay the piper."

"And so call the tune, Annabel." He tilted her palm to catch the light. "You cannot go wrong. Not with me."

She examined her palm with him. "What *is* it?"

"I like the terrain, Annabel, its contours. Like looking at an entire body."

Her other hand fell on his thigh. She moved it, observing its passage.

"Time for the melody, Bonn?"

He turned gravely from her hand to look into her eyes.

"Whatever you wish, Annabel. If I fail to comprehend, please say."

"Oh, I'll do that, honey. I'll do exactly that."

She pushed him aside, somehow retaining hold of his hand, and waited for him to raise her to her feet. She smiled honestly now, shaking out her hair. She kicked off her shoes.

"Leave them there. Get the door."

"It will have been fastened after you entered."

She stared, frowning. "Who by? Some watcher down the hallways?"

"There is no watcher in the hallway. But you are secure. I suggested that it be so," he said. They walked slowly into the bedroom.

"And it was? Just like that?"

She stood while he buzzed the curtains to.

"When do I learn what I get extra?" It was her attempt to reassert her control.

Slowly he started to undo her blouse, pulling its hem slowly from her skirt and parting it to slip her arms from the sleeves, frowning with concentration.

"There is only me, Annabel. I am obligated, not you, for this occasion. Perhaps you don't understand. I am the beneficiary of the loveliest living thing. It is you. I am at a loss," he continued while she looked at him as he undid the skirt waist and dropped the garment to the carpet, "as to why you fail to see that yours is the stupendous gift to me."

"And my question?" she asked, her voice thickening. "More money for what?"

"I can only rejoice," he said softly, his breathing shallower, "that you give me your gift of life. There is nothing beyond."

He pressed his mouth on her breast. She leant in to make his kneeling position easier, wanting to hear more.

"Okay," she said finally, "Tell me after."

9

Fluffer – a female employed to arouse actors prior to the commencement of filming porn

Brother Jason smoked a cigarette that morning, though he insisted that he "no longer had the smoking habit," in his carefully designed phrase. He kept a twenty pack in reserve. The occasions on which a cigarette was called into use were never mapped in detail, in the sense should this or that happen then secretly light one up for comfort. Yet why had he kept them in his desk drawer?

He leant against the wall, in the vegetable garden. There was a paving flag set in the grass verge just there, exactly right for an illegitimate smoker. Out of sight of the vestry, the classrooms and the bursar's office. Brother Stephen ran the gardens. He stacked implements here, and talked endlessly of erecting a rack of pegs to prevent tools falling. Brother Frederick, a clever grinning man, said that enterprise would be enough to keep Brother Stephen occupied for years. No teacher, Stephen. A gardener, and that was all. Safe.

Brother Jason finished the cigarette, folded the stub on itself and spat on it in his fingers, carefully wrapping it in a piece of tissue. There should be no trace. Two minutes later he flushed it down the lavatory, went to do his teeth and gargle, and visited the refectory kitchens. There loomed Mrs Charnock.

*   *   *

"We have a missing child, Mrs Charnock." Eight other women were busy working in the kitchens. It was getting on for seven o'clock, the boys all at Holy Mass. Brother Jason felt careworn, no acting needed. He sighed, used his hands to show deeply felt distress. "I'm afraid I must notify the authorities."

The overweight lady wiped her hands on her pinafore. "Are you sure, Brother Jason?"

He gave his enduring smile. It suggested piety, saintly work reviled by ingratitude.

"Absolutely certain. The boy they call Jecko. Rupert Scowcroft."

He knew instantly he was making headway. The other women glanced over, lifting containers, the aroma of frying and the clashing of pots a constant here.

"Little, talks nineteen to the dozen? I know him!" Mrs Charnock was shocked.

Does he now, Brother Jason registered, and what would all those spoken words be about? He caught Mrs Charnock's glance darted across to the oldest of the kitchen helpers, the one the other women, and some of the boys, called Marj. She did not look up, using two boards to shovel peelings into large bags suspended below her work surface. Extraordinary how so small a woman could heft such weights. She would later carry them out, quite unaided, to Brother Stephen's compost corner during the women's elevenses. Brother Jason had seen her do it on countless mornings.

But why that glance?

"Some valuables seem to be missing, Mrs Charnock," he intoned, heavy with sorrow. "It would be wrong to guess that Rupert took them. I shall check. The poor boy must be so frightened out there."

"The poor mite! During the night, Brother Jason?"

"Presumably. We shall inform the boys, of course, and ask for their assistance in trying to identify some cause." He truly did feel doleful at all this. "I sometimes wonder how much good we really do, Mrs Charnock."

"Don't fret yourself, Brother Jason."

She held up some massive shining container and a helper

hurried over to take it. Remarkable the strength these women displayed.

"Possibly it is some trivial cause," he said with sadness. "A childhood argument, perhaps. I sometimes think we don't deserve children. So much is Providence."

"He'll be back, you see. Please God unharmed, just hungry." She smiled hopefully, wanting her work to bring in the lost prodigal, a success to brag about.

"Please God." He sighed. "But I fear for him in the world out there, Mrs Charnock."

"Let's pray he'll be back."

Brother Jason left then, hands behind his back, head down, moving with long raking steps, cassock kicking ahead. He was conscious of the growing quiet behind him. The women would be talking of the missing boy. In itself that was harmless.

That glance, though. The boys called that old woman Marj. He knew that and, he thought with a stirring of unease, that was all he knew. He must find out more.

Safely back in his study, he concealed a silver inkstand, an amber penholder and a miniature gold and garnet crucifix, then rang the police to report a missing child who had stolen certain objects, and asked if he could please have the help of the authorities.

*   *   *

Steela was in a sulk, after the ballocking she'd had from Bondice the previous day. She'd complained about the director's story lines. "Same old same old," she'd said straight out. She'd been threatened with the sack, which shut her up, but it had been close.

On the way to the Bondice studios, Quaker Street – a right laugh, "Studios" like it was Warner or MGM instead of two shoddy upstairs rooms with everything on the blink – Steela defiantly took her time, ten minutes for a nosh in the Butty

Bar across the Square.

It wasn't as if she was a beginner. She was an actress, got star billing. Find another girl half as attractive with her talent who'd put up with Bondice's crap. And that Ironia was a pest, shoving her drooping tits into the camera. She gave Gary the cameraman some on the side for it. Steela didn't blame her, because what actress wouldn't? It was career or no career, life's only choice.

While risking two slices of toast and honey, couldn't resist, she noticed a young girl giving some old bloke the come-on. Quickly Steela pretended to borrow the salt from his table. As she did, she casually touched her forehead as if brushing her hair back, making sure the silly tart saw. The universal street gesture for police, Steela's mind shrieking, *He's the filth, stupid little cow!* The girl instantly left the caff.

Steela sighed and finished her tea. The girl would get herself in trouble. Shouldn't be working this early anyway, save caffs and bus shelters till later, early evening always best for punters on the move when they wanted a quick shag. Quick dick, dash cash. Everybody knew that. But maybe the girl was desperate, money for a rig, drugs, her pimp knocking her about for faster takes, you could never tell. Steela had been there, done that, until she'd got into showbiz – movies, no less. She'd made three films so far, the last two for Bondice.

Today, she thought, leaving the caff, Bondice was going for a routine story, boy-girl-girl, the most saleable prial of the threesomes that were porn movie standards. One-sexers were flatly out, except for the porn market's corner shelf. Even Bondice agreed on that. The boy-boy-girl was least favoured, girl-boy-girl second. Bondice rang the changes – teacher, nurse, mechanic, doctor, dentist, except Ironia had almost killed herself in that fucking dentist's chair that Ray couldn't work properly. Thinking, Steela almost bumped into the girl she'd tipped off. She'd been waiting by the traffic lights.

"Wanted to say ta for the warning. I'm Anj."

The girl could only have been seventeen, Steela saw with envy. What she'd give! Now twenty-six, youth threatened her.

"I wanted to be one ahead of my mate," the girl Anj explained. "Early start, see?"

"Take care." Steela was moving on with the other pedestrians when somebody almost knocked her over. She drew breath, raised her arm to give the bloke a clout, but Anj caught her arm, hissing like a warning snake.

They stood, Steela watching the rude bloke cross into Central Gardens. He went like a maniac, joshing people, dancing, shouting to friends – mostly street lasses – and cracking jokes to anybody who'd listen.

"Who is he?" Steela caught Anj's sudden fear.

"Rack," Anj said. "He's the boss stander, does everything round here. You do as he says or else."

"Everybody?" Steela was fascinated.

"He's an animal. No telling what he'll do if he goes into one." She shivered.

The lad called Rack – what, twenty-two perhaps – was dressed like a crazy western gambler with eyeshade, sleeve bands, cufflinks the size of wheels, brilliant yellow cravat studded with diamonte, and striped waistcoat over threadbare jeans. He looked stupid.

"Ta, then." Steela gave her a smile as they parted. She'd heard Bondice say that name.

In the shooting room Ray had rigged up a kitchen set. Bondice was already there, grumbling, How d'you think I can get Hump in there when he's the size of a bus, etc, etc. Gary was fiddling with his lenses. Rows of them on a cotton sheet he carried everywhere. Ironia was ready, smarmy cow. Man Beast Hump was working himself erect before mirrors, always took his time, really needed Bondice to hire a good fluffer, but the bitch was too mean. Steela hated the amount of skin oil he used, bloody stuff getting everywhere.

She chose her moment.

"Bondice," she said donning her tatty dressing gown. "Did you mention somebody called Rack?"

"Rack?" Bondice's brow cleared. "Tried to screw us just for being here? Yeah. Why?"

"I heard he's somebody to steer clear of."

"You been talking about my business?"

Her business. "No, honest. I heard a girl talking. She seemed scared."

"Fuck him." Bondice gave a laugh, more concerned with Ray's set. "I mean *don't* fuck him! Make him buy the movie!"

Steela shrugged. She'd passed word on, in the clear.

"Who's first?"

"You and Ironia are talking in pretty pinnies at coffee time. You start doing it – Ironia's the butch, you're the feather – when the doorbell goes and you're both whoops for Christ's sake you're caughty naughty and it's Hump, sack of tools come to mend something…"

10 | Suss (suspicion) – wariness, on lookout

Set sometimes pretended he was Jewish, sometimes Muslim. Other times he claimed French ancestry, Danish, Russian or Australian descent, depending on the conversation. His colouring helped. Thin, he adopted a chameleon garb, bright yellow trainers. White socks would change several times a day to checks, tartan, then discreet fawn. His suits swapped with blazers and flannels or even plus fours. He paid fortunes for trilby hats that could emerge crumpled from a pocket and look Jermyn Street. Movie heroes assumed disguises, but his worked better.

Finding Deirdre had seemed like perpetual Christmas, just blew in one day when Tamina came in for the night bringing his cut. After Tamina passed on Deirdre slotted in like a natural. She had youth, willingness, an aching desire to be wanted. She was protected by Grellie's outfit, about which he knew little but had the sense never to ask. He made it right with the swaggering loudmouth Rack, by slipping him notes now and then.

Set knew to keep out of the way. Too much always going on in the city centre. He stayed away from the Central Gardens. Others weren't so clever. One bloke was so fascinated by the different activities that he haunted the tram stops, the railway station, even the Butty Bar and the Rum Romeo where gossip was everywhere. He'd gone, got off lightly.

Instinctively Set knew that gossip was for the mighty, not for the likes of him. Prattle was good, to those on the payroll. Deirdre soon came to live in his pad down Raglan Road where he rented a whole house, genuine landlady's rent book kept up to date. He went shopping twice a week, once for main food-stuffs, once for forgetfulness. Deirdre he looked after.

One trouble was she was too sorry for everybody. Why else had she taken up with him? He was nothing to look at. But he was kind, gave her things, made her shop for herself, once took her out to the Pier and gave her a supper she was proud of and told her girl friends all about. He bought a sapphire from Emden the jeweller, paid honest money and warned her against losing it.

He let her go to church, Methodist. He never pretended he was one of them, gave her windage that way. He was her sav-iour, he told himself. What would she have been without him? He saved her from becoming just a whore, a loose street cow who'd get herself tanked or topped inside a twelvemonth.

The biochemist he came across touting Ecstasy at a street corner. He was another Christmas, something from outer space. This specky geezer in a college tie for Christ's sake, standing there trying to look like part of the brickwork outside a Saturday night social. Shoes shining, crease in his trousers, hands in overcoat pockets saying as kids went in, "Want some E?" The youngsters just looking. It was a fucking miracle he'd not been robbed or blanked. Silly cunt had even parked his motor at the street corner, like everything he did was invisible.

Set went up to him and said, quiet, "Come round the corner. I've something to tell you, okay? It's okay."

And drifted.

Unbelievably the thicko had followed, glancing about like a movie villain. It had crossed Set's mind that he might be a plant, some plod, except even they weren't so dim that they'd stake out like a tailor's dummy from Wessex's in the Arcade.

The biochemist had come, obviously mystified but hoping for the international drugs deal of all time. Set told him that he was being watched, sending him white with fear, and said to meet him in the bookie's in Sebastopol Terrace. From there, he'd sent him on to the ice-skating rink near Trafford Park.

Safely there, Set asked where he got the supplies, but only after he'd slipped him a fortune, all the money he'd had on him at the time. It dazzled the poor bleeder.

"I make them," Dennis told him.

"Make?" Set's turn to be mystified.

"Yes. It's quite simple," Dennis answered. "I find the solvents are hard to get rid of on account of – "

"Look." Set couldn't believe what was happening. "Make? Like, start from fuck all, and *make?*"

"I'm a biochemist," Dennis said with pride.

He started on about getting a two-one, whatever that was, from Manchester University or somewhere, that he'd not had the funds for a higher degree.

"A real scientist?"

"I like experimentation," the buffoon explained, eyes shining in his specs. "The cutbacks stopped the research programme. I had hopes for one of the new universities, but it went belly-up. I deplore…"

Set heard him out, nodding sympathetically while the skaters went round and round. He could hardly believe his fantastic luck. A real scientist who could make – as in starting out with powders, and create drugs – E, maybe hash, speed, that LSD that Set was truly scared of, Christ only knows what else. It was like a dream.

"Listen, Dennis." By then they'd exchanged names, Set giving Set, though that was invented since coming out after a five-and-two for robbery with violence. "Listen. You're going about this all wrong. You should be in partnership."

"Partnership?"

Dennis was worried by that. He'd had a friend who'd gone into partnership with a bicycle maker and got rooked, lost his savings, no bikes ever manufactured and the tool shop unfinished.

"A regular partnership, I mean." And Set had gone for it, lying to this gullible nerk's face. "I mean me, Dennis. You make,

I'll bring in the gelt. I'll see you don't miss out on the money."

"How? What?"

The idiot was dazzled, hope and alarm chasing tails across his features.

"I sell. You shouldn't be involved in the street side. You make. I'm the bloke for you, Dennis. I'll pay you up front."

No sooner had he said it than Set almost groaned aloud, because he hadn't a fucking bean, not a carrot, and here he was promising this goldmine a fortune.

Giddy, he mentioned enough to buy a small car.

"How do you know I'll bring you the drugs?" Dennis said, like nobody might be listening in a crowded ice-rink caff, the prick.

"Because I trust you, Dennis."

It was like a melodrama, the burke unable to see anything but wealth up ahead.

That was it. Set had borrowed from a thirty-nighter down the Rowlocks Casino, paying thirty per cent on the loan at a rate of one per cent every evening, eight o'clock. He'd run it up twice, and paid them off in full on the last night of the sixty.

It had been astonishingly simple. Dennis manufactured tablets flat as a pie, each stamped with the familiar apple logo except two bites out of it and an extra leaf. He coloured the e tablets yellow because that was popular. Set told him to keep doing that. Then there was LSD – Dennis called that some lengthy German name. And there was the imported miraa that Dennis swore had no laws against. Bulky, but safer on account of law being stupid again.

And life soared. Set was in clover.

After the first terrible couple of months, in the loan period before Set repaid, Set found a derelict mill. Lot of them about. This still had its immense engines that, sooner or later, some idiot enthusiasts intended to restore as a working model of the city's manufacturing past.

Set took a lease. He had a prefabricated room set up in one

of the immense floors. No assistants, because Set wasn't daft. No helpers, no vans. Everywhere by public transport. Dennis grumbled at that, seeing he had money to burn now.

In the first week of proper production, they made seventeen times the national average working wage.

Millionaires by the year's end, Set promised Dennis with a straight face. Life couldn't be better. Kids going on rave-ups, schoolies wet behind the ears yet somehow able to pay more than their parents earned in a week for a tablet a day. Life was crazy.

Dennis turned out the stuff like there was no tomorrow.

Lately he'd begun to brag, which Set knew he'd have to keep an eye on, but so far that was a small price to pay. MDMA was the winner because every kid over the age of eight knew more about it than the average professor. And fast money was down there among the little bastards, Christ alone knew where from, but it was there a-plenty.

Set was in clover. And Deirdre was a good girl, did as she was told. It was then that, allowing Deirdre to take a whip-round to the Christian Brothers' Home Orphanage, Set happened on the distribution system of a lifetime. An elderly priest who'd been in Africa or somewhere, accepted Deirdre's donation and asked her to bring him a small bag of some imported herb next time she called. Gave her the importer's address, and the money too.

Set took over from there. Within a week he'd met Brother Paulo, and learned that the Home Orphanage distributed religious objects all over the country. The only risk was secrecy, and what was more secret than religion? You had to recognise clover when you found it.

11 | Dib (dibble) – the male appendage

The teacher was sleeping, her hair awry. She breathed gently. Bonn watched her. There was enough light. He retrieved an earring from near her face, leant across and put it on the bed-side table.

She woke, her eyes startled until she remembered and smiled, stretching.

"Thank you."

Had he been given to questioning, he would have asked why she thanked him when it should be the other way round. He did the next best thing. She still had thirty minutes. It barely gave him time enough. She had booked him for two hours at the start of the previous term holiday, and now again. Saved up? It was disconcerting. He worried about how much he cost. He didn't actually know, so would have to ask Posser.

"Gratitude is mine, Jean."

Jean Four-Seven-Nought-Two looked puzzled, then her brow cleared. She burrowed down to his belly, moved aside the bedclothes with an impatient flap of her arm for air, and laid her head on him.

"No, darling. Mine. You don't know."

How could he argue?

"Days go by with no hope of change," Jean told him, her breath on his skin. "These two hours are like a lovely promise up ahead. It helps me to manage."

She looked up at him, held his eyes a moment.

"You think I'm selfish?"

"Certainly not. Women are all gift."

"You're simple." She shook her head as if in normal conversation. "I'm thirty-five. Did you guess I was that old?"

"There is no such thing as age."

"Do you remember me from last time?"

"Yes."

"What?" she asked, mischievously. He felt her mouth move on his skin. Did women know the effects they had? He supposed not.

"Your hair was more pale. Your lipstick is deeper. Your dress was pastel blue with bishop sleeves – if that is the term. As if you were going to a party, or had come from one. Your breath was scented with drink, perhaps gin and tonic, though I'm never quite sure. You had mislaid your spectacles. Your handbag was tan leather. You told me you decided to wear stockings to boost your confidence. I trust that will suffice."

She was silent. "Do they train you?"

"You asked me that previously, Jean."

"Please don't be mad. It sounded a catalogue."

"My image, your appearance. That is all. External characteristics mean little."

"No! They *matter*!" She said it with such conviction that he knew it was her dogma, a cross to be borne.

"Forgive my rebuttal. They do not."

He let his hand fall on her hair and smoothed the strands. Some were dewy from his sweat, but that could not be helped. He always sweated during intercourse. How astonishing that women did not seem to mind.

She wouldn't agree. "I'm ordinary, Bonn. I'm going to start going out in another three months. A woman has less time. There's someone in my school. He's divorced. We might make a go of it, maybe try for a child."

"A woman can't be ordinary. Each has her own beauty."

"Men can't see."

"A woman can have any man, Jean."

"Then why do women have to keep trying like we do?"

80

He looked at her. "You don't."

"I could have you without paying for you to come?"

"If I were not employed this way, yes."

She wanted to dress him. He accepted. She did the chore with frowning concentration, painstakingly straightening his shirt and trousers, aligning his socks, finding his jacket and smoothing it on his shoulders. She dressed quickly.

"You know what I worry about, when I ring the Agency?"

"No."

"If you've become more expensive, gone out of my reach."

He was about to say never mind, it would not be long before she would no longer need to hire him. She would have her fellow teacher from her own school, to marry and live happily ever after. He avoided saying anything. Speech was a fearsome risk. He never knew if he did the right thing.

* * *

That evening, Posser was in the conservatory having his miniature tot of whisky. Bonn found him and sat. Posser had dozed, waiting for the nightly television news. He roused with a slow smile. Bonn worried about the old man, who now wheezed at rest, instead of only when coming back from his walk round Bradshawgate Green outside the house.

"All right, son?"

"Yes, thank you, Posser."

"Martina in, is she?"

"She's doing the accounts in the living room."

Posser sighed, a squeaking tyre. "Time somebody took her in hand, Bonn. I mean you."

"Yes."

"So does she, Bonn. I'd be happy if you two got together. It's time. You know that."

"Yes."

"There's nothing that could stop you, is there? You know

what I mean, son."

"I should have told you if there was."

"Sorry. Come back all I said." Posser smiled. "You lodging in that spare room up here, like a mystery tenant in some Victorian drama. Having your meals separate except once or twice a week, to show us you're still here."

"It avoids giving scandal."

"It gives hell of a sight too much, Bonn. You wanted to ask what?"

Bonn nearly smiled. The astute old man could always tell, but then he had been the first and only goer on the circuit when he had started the Pleases syndicate alone.

"I had Jean Four-Seven-Nought-Two. She books me between school terms. She saves up, can scarcely afford it."

"And you want a special rate for the woman?" Posser was amused. "Can't be done, Bonn. You are their special thing. Don't you see? They crave something outrageous. They know that perfume costs guinea a drop because it does, see?"

"No, I do not."

"Then you never will. It's the way they are. Good job you asked me and not Martina."

"Asked me what?" Martina said from the conservatory doorway.

"If a special rate could be allowed for some uppers."

"Goers on the cheap?" Martina came and sat on the stool by her father, looking out to the back garden where the evening lamps had already come on. "Never. It's principle. The goers wouldn't wear it, for a start. The girl stringers would go mental. The standers would wonder what I was playing at."

"And the clients," Posser prompted gently.

"The clients would shun us in droves."

"I do not understand," Bonn said directly to Martina in a plea for more guidance and less understanding.

Her eyes for once were not filled with ice. They were warm with amusement, almost a new brand of pity. No mistake, either; her pity was pity for him, with another ingredient he saw but failed to comprehend.

She looked away, smiling. He thought her beautiful.

"Of course you don't," she said. "I'd be astonished if you did."

★ ★ ★

The frightened girl in the alcove stayed quiet, her childhood survival tactic when a man's voice changed like his had just done. She prayed Deirdre wouldn't tell him about her being here for a quiet lie down.

"You took one hell of a time. What did you tell that priest git the other night?"

"Me? Nothing."

Weird, but Deirdre's voice didn't even sound scared.

Eileen lay still. Set didn't know she was here. Should she try to creep out? But stairs creaked. People were rowing on the floor below, might come out and see her, and then she was done for. Maybe nothing would happen. The man's voice grew harder.

"You talked with that priest bloke. You said something."

The blow, Deirdre saying she hadn't, she hadn't. Eileen hardly breathed, didn't dare look.

"There was a little lad." Deirdre, coming clean. The sound of a chair being dragged.

"He had a kid with him? The priest bloke?"

"No." Deirdre snuffled. "You made my mouth bleed. I'll catch it, going on the street, my mouth's all swolled. Grellie'll kill me."

"Did the kid see you?"

"Yes." The sound of Deirdre walking. To a mirror, to check her face for damage? "I think he was trying to hide, like escaping. He looked really scared. I felt sorry for him. I saw him when that car went past. The priest didn't see him."

"You kept the priest bloke chatting, distract him from

the kid?"

"Yes. He just took the ull and said ta and I went."

"Is that it?"

"Honest, Set, honey. Nothing else."

Unbelievably there was no more hitting, no thumps, no whimpers from Deirdre, her new friend. But Eileen knew something bad would happen. It was that hard edge in the voice, and she knew. He spoke next.

"You did right."

A lighter clicked. Eileen knew the sounds of somebody toking, the grin-shaped mouth, teeth bared, when the puff was in and they needed enough air to go with it, take the smoke down everywhere inside.

"Here, love. Have this on me." The man laughing, something funny.

And Deirdre said ta like nothing was happening, casual and not guessing right. Eileen felt tears start. She stayed huddled under the blanket in the truckle bed, praying the man with the murderer's blade in his voice wouldn't check round the miserable flat whatever else he did.

Ever since she was four, Eileen had wept soundlessly and with utter stillness. She did it again, and saved her life.

Unbelievably Deirdre giggled, saying, "Come here, you," working her man up to shag the anger out of him, maybe even showing off because her friend was in the alcove hearing what Deirdre got up to.

Except that killer calm in the man's voice proved Deirdre stupid, and wrong, on her way to suffering and maybe worse.

She was going to die.

Eileen prayed and wept, letting the sex noises wash over her, wanting only not to be trapped and somehow to leave unseen.

12 Ull (ullage) – the amount that can be stolen unnoticed

"Faye Ray." The clerk ushered the new girl.

Clare bit back the rebuke. "Thank you, Mrs Hast."

The new clerk showed that irritating sense of aggrandise-ment that all GP office people sooner or later developed. They wanted to be a cut above patients. Their voices became aloof. They gave the impression that they alone decided who was to be seen and when.

Mrs Hast had been with her three weeks and was already showing classical arrogance. Clare had taken a perverse delight in registering the rotund Sheffield lady as "clerk" on her employment form. Mrs Hast had insisted on "receptionist". Clare had coldly faced her down and, in equal silliness, had had *Clerk* put on the woman's door.

Mrs Hast, hair sculpted into bronzed inflexibility, invariably got her own back by entering without knocking and announcing the next patient's name with no preamble or courtesy. It galled Clare. She maintained a smiling affability that she hoped was at least as maddening as Mrs Hast's rudeness.

"Do sit down," she said, deliberately waiting for the clerk to leave.

She noticed that the hatch between her surgery office and the clerk's alcove was ajar and called, "Mrs Hast? You've forgotten your hatch, please."

"Oh, sorry, doctor."

The hatch slowly closed. Clare crossed to it and made certain it was pulled to.

"We've never met before, have we, Faye?"

"No. They made me come because I'm late."

A slight girl, far too slight in fact. Dark hair, perhaps a sallow tinge to her complexion, with nervous hands and a taut neck. Clare smiled gently. There was too much silliness about today. Leave aside Mrs Hast's war, these girls – was she wrong to assume the girl was in fact a vagrant? – adopted some old actress's name as a pseudonym. Another pointless irritation. Imagine how annoyed the real Faye Ray must be!

And all the goers that she saw for routine three-monthly medical examinations did the same. Bonn, she remembered, gave the name James Whitmore.

"They?" Clare was at a loss. "Your employers, your family?"

"My boss, Grellie. She's outside."

"Would you rather she sat with you?"

The girl looked round at the cabinets of instruments in the white alcove, the examination corner with the electrocardiograph and sphygmomanometer already set up.

"She'll have to come in anyhow," she said with resignation. "If you're sure."

Clare buzzed and asked Mrs Hast to invite Faye's friend in. The clerk obeyed with ill grace, pointedly asking the new-comer's name but getting no response. She closed the door with unnecessary firmness. Clare looked and was startled at what she saw.

The new girl facing her was twenty-two, or perhaps a year older. Dark of hair, startlingly blue eyed, instantly seating herself with a disconcerting air of authority. She wore a mauve sheath dress, priced well above the usual range. Her jacket was a fawn Chaumval, enviously expensive. No jewellery except for a single-diamond brooch on her hair band and a gold slave anklet.

The effect was unusual and assertive. Boss, this young Faye girl had said. But boss of what? Clare's patient looked round, showed no reaction. Docility, Clare thought, passive acceptance at the arrival of authority.

"How do you do? I'm Dr Burtonall. Miss Ray is in your employ?"

"Sort of." The voice was low, modulated, level and used to being obeyed.

"Would you mind if Miss, ah, Grellie stayed while I take your history and examine you?" Clare asked the younger girl. "My nurse will be here too." She smiled. "Quite a crowd, but – "

"Just get on with it." Faye seemed bored yet wary.

"Then can I have your full name and address?" Clare pressed the intercom for Nurse Scanlon to come through. "I need to know something about your history…"

Painstakingly she took the details. No significant past ailments, no surgery. No diseases ran in her family. The girl casually said that she had lost touch with her relatives. She hesitated only when asked about her normal weight. Her work was asking people questions about shopping, she said.

"You know, like in the malls."

It sounded fabricated. Clare nevertheless took it all down. Faye's employers, Grellie answered for the girl, were a public polling service researching household items.

Clare asked Nurse Scanlon to measure and weigh the girl and smiled at Grellie as Faye stepped onto the scales.

"What made you bring Faye in, exactly?"

"She doesn't eat right. She's a skeleton."

"And when you say she's late…?"

"She's stopped coming on. She starves herself."

"I don't!" defiantly from Faye behind the screen.

"You spew it up, don't tell me different." Grellie eyed Clare candidly. "If she gets anorexia it's down to me. I'll get blamed."

"How long since you first thought that?"

"Two months. The other girls – her friends – noticed. Twice I sent her here. She wouldn't come. So I brought her myself."

"I'll give her a general examination and do some simple tests, then decide what other investigations I'll want."

Clare left Grellie by the desk and went to perform the

standard physical examination. Nurse Scanlon marked the Body Mass Index chart. Faye's point fell significantly below the norm. Clare was painstaking. The girl seemed almost skeletal, though there was no sign of a systemic disease. Nurse Scanlon handed Clare the result of the simple pregnancy spot test on Faye's urine. Negative.

"You want Grellie to hear what I have to say?" Clare washed her hands, discarding her disposable sterile gloves, and let the nurse remove the tray of instruments.

"It's okay."

Clare made notes as the girl dressed. She laid her pen aside and questioned the girl about her eating, appetite, what she regarded as a standard meal. Grellie interrupted so often that Clare had to ask her to remain silent.

"You seem to have some kind of eating disorder, Faye. You've heard of anorexia nervosa? I've put that down as one possibility. There are other causes of weight loss, but this provisional diagnosis is high on my list."

"Lots of girls lose weight!" Faye shot back.

"Yes, but not quite to this degree. As I say, I shall need to do several tests to eliminate other diseases."

"I eat like a horse!"

"Then make yourself sick, Faye?"

"I don't! That's when you're bingeing and…"

"Look at your hands." Clare lifted Faye's right hand. "You see those calluses on your knuckles? They become noticeable in patients – usually girls – who eat, then make themselves vomit by using their fingers. Doctors sometimes call them Russell calluses, from a doctor's name. And there's your weight."

She looked candidly at Faye's clothes. They hung on her.

"Scales give us only a rough guide. We sometimes work out what people call the BMI, body mass index. We weigh you, and divide that by your height squared in metric measure. It gives us the BMI." She paused, waited for a question. None came.

"Yours is just on 17.5. Most doctors use 20 to 25 or 26 as normal."

"They're just numbers." The girl's mulishness was expected, but Clare was seriously worried. She doubted the girl's given age of nineteen. Seventeen was more likely.

"Is it serious?" Grellie put in.

"Yes, I'm afraid so. Faye, please listen."

"Why should I?" the girl said sulkily, glaring balefully as the nurse entered with a phlebotomy tray. "I'm not letting you do any of that, for a fucking start. I'm fat enough, for Christ's sake. I have real big meals. I don't want to be a fucking balloon."

"Please allow me – "

The girl stood, taking her clutch bag. "I don't have to listen to this crap."

"Sit," Grellie said. The girl hesitated. Grellie looked up. The girl sank back onto the chair, slammed her bag down.

"Faye," Clare said slowly. "Your boss Grellie here has made an accurate diagnosis. That doesn't mean you're guilty, just that you're poorly."

"Why're you telling me this?"

"Shut it, Maeve," Grellie said quietly. The girl subsided. "It's her nickname," she explained to Clare. "What has she to do?"

"Besides the loss of body mass index, there's her recurrent depressions that some young girls call the glums. Faye's circulation is poor. Her pulse is too slow, her blood pressure low. You'll have noticed, Faye," she said directly to the girl, "the soft hair coming on your skin? We doctors use the old word lanugo. Like the furry surface of a peach?"

"She can't work, then?" Grellie demanded.

"It depends what work she normally does," Clare replied evenly, letting her disbelief show. "It is serious and needs treatment."

She was suddenly weary of the deception. The girl was a prostitute, this Grellie her overseer.

"I want to exclude other diagnoses," she went on. "This

eating disorder is usually pretty clear-cut. But there's a whole lot of other possible illnesses."

"What are they?" Grellie demanded.

Clare was beginning to dislike the other's peremptory manner.

"They're my job," she said bluntly. "Yours is to give Faye support. I shall probably refer her to – "

"No, doctor," Grellie said, her voice becoming more incisive, the eyes even more alert. "Just say how likely you are to be right or not."

"With the history, the findings, the BMI and other clinical signs, there's over a ninety-five per cent chance of my provisional diagnosis being correct."

"What tests?"

"Infections sometimes cause this degree of weight loss, some glandular conditions or intestinal illnesses."

"How quick?"

"A fortnight. Following that, I will want to refer her."

Grellie was painstakingly patient. "How soon can she be back to work?"

"Look. I don't want to minimise the severity of this. Yes, Nurse Scanlon. Could you perform a routine urinalysis? Stick tests are fine." She waited until Faye had gone with the nurse.

"The truth is that bulima nervosa and anorexia nervosa sometimes overlap. Some American doctors give them one collective name, bulimarexia, but the two conditions have been recognised for centuries, since the 1590s in fact. Doctors knew about bulimia – hound's appetite, they thought of it as – over five hundred years ago. Nowadays, the popular glossies assume they're new diseases. They're not."

"Get on with it."

Clare held her temper. "A fifth of classical anorexia nervosa patients can die from it. That's the highest mortality of any – repeat *any* – psychiatric condition. And bulimics are almost three times commoner than anorexics. Males are ten times less likely to get either."

Grellie leant forward, not at all put out.

"I'm not getting through to you, doctor." Clare suddenly knew how infuriating all this medical pedantry must seem.

"Yes, you are, Grellie." She felt her anger rise but contained it while she spoke her piece. "Every employer wants productivity. Every boss wants a workforce. But this girl is seriously at risk. She may well not recover. What I want is – "

Grellie rose. "Superfluous."

Clare stared in astonishment as Grellie moved to the door.

"Will you not wait? Nurse Scanlon will be finished in a minute, then we can discuss…"

Grellie was smiling with exasperation.

"No, Dr Burtonall. No discussion. If Maeve can't work, then I don't want her. If she's not up for it, she's out. It's the rule."

"Whose rule?" Clare knew her voice was rising, her anger exposed.

"Mine."

"Where are you going?" Clare felt the stupidity of her question.

"To work, doctor. Tell her I said tara."

The door closed. Mrs Hast poked her head round almost immediately.

"Doctor? There's a query about immunisation for holiday cruises on the line. I said you'd speak to her."

"Mrs Hast," Clare said in a voice of sleet. "*Out!*"

Clare almost rose from her chair and the clerk fled. Clare subsided, looking with surprise at the closed door.

A moment later, Nurse Scanlon brought Faye back. The girl looked about.

"Where's Grellie?" she asked.

"Gone, I'm afraid."

"Did she say where I've got to be?"

Clare drew breath. "Please sit down, Faye. We must talk some more. I should like Nurse Scanlon to sit in with us. Will that be all right?"

"I'm not too sure, Rack."

"It's a pig's arse, Bonn."

Today's motor was a Jaguar of immense length. They had come too quickly. Bonn twice asked Rack to drive slower. The stander was desperate to go over seventy.

"What's the point of a car like this if we drive like a tart?"

Bonn wouldn't see reason. They turned into Kirkdale with only ten minutes to spare.

"We could have been here yonks since," Rack grumbled. "I've got to be your fucking stander, so I can't even go for a quick spin while you're shagging this geezer's missus. It's not fair."

"You are security, Rack. And please moderate your language."

"Christ all fucking mighty!" Rack burst out, hauling the wheel to enter the avenue. "There's only us here."

"Judgement forgot is habit condoned."

"What the fuck does that mean? This bloke only wants to talk first."

"Very well."

Kirkdale had grown inwardly like a thickening, but many grand houses preserved a former status. This was one. Bonn noticed the two conservatories stuck onto the house's sides, with oddly fenestra ed projections rising from the glass ridges. Somebody's notion n sophistication. He corrected the unkind thought. How could he know design excellence?

Rack drew the car into the drive, stopped at the unnecessary steps. Two concrete lions were stuck on the balustrade. Bonn alighted, went up and knocked. Rack drove down to the road and halted as the door opened.

"Are you Bonn?"

"Good afternoon."

"I thought you'd be older, more…"

Bonn entered. How could he account for his age to this fortyish decisive man, so bellied and heavily built, who was gazing at him with something approaching disbelief. Bonn thought, I am here in answer to an invitation. What explanations were needed? And how could such a man's preconceptions form, and on what evidence?

The house was sumptuous inside, larger even than its exterior suggested. He could hear music playing. Fauré? Delius?

"I've never done this before," the man said resentfully.

He seemed to expect some comment. Bonn was at a loss. His difficulties were always with the husbands in dommies, domicilary visits like this. Some women clients lived alone and presented fewer problems. The majority of domiciliaries had compliant husbands or "partners" in the trite term of the day. He decided to ask Posser, if a moment presented.

The man became blunt. "How exactly do you go about it?"

"How best pleases the lady, Mr Solpris."

Bonn sensed no unease. The man looked out past the portal window's lace curtain, checking Rack.

"Do many blokes ask you for this?"

"I cannot say."

At first Bonn had supposed that hiring a goer for a wife must be ruinous to a spouse's self-esteem. He had learned that that never seemed to be the case. Many, like this Mr Solpris, seemed simply curious, wanting details and arrangements of the trade. Posser had taught him stock replies that usually sufficed.

"I want just the usual, understand? Nothing different."

"I understand."

They were in the hall. Bannisters on the curved flight of stairs, a balcony, oil paintings on velvety walls. It was almost grand, but not quite.

"Tell me what she says. Know what I mean? I don't know if she's ever had it away with different blokes. See what I'm saying?"

"No, Mr Solpris." Bonn saw the other's astonishment, and wanted to be kind. "I cannot betray a lady's confidence. Should you wish such an account, you cannot obtain them from me."

The man leant close, almost outraged.

"I'm fucking paying you!" He kept his voice down. "You've got to."

"Then I regret I must leave, Mr Solpris." Bonn reached the outer door. "Please convey my apologies to your lady. I do hope that you will correctly explain the reason I could not stay."

"Wait." The man took a step away, returned, looked hard at Bonn's chest to avoid his gaze. "Do it. It's fine, all right."

"Only if you wish, Mr Solpris."

"Go left, then last on the right."

Bonn ascended the stairs, not looking back. He found a door ajar, knocked, and saw the lady.

The room was wide, surprisingly had two long picture windows showing an extensive garden. Two workmen stooped along herbaceous borders.

The woman was self-assured, perhaps in her mid-forties with grey dusting her brown hair. Slender, average height, in a tailored dress, she gave an appearance of calm control.

"How do you do? I'm Bonn."

"Do come in. I'm Emma. I think it's best that we use first names from the outset, don't you? Is that the only name you have? Do sit down."

"Yes, Emma." He sat opposite, where he thought she'd gestured. "I always assumed I invented it."

"And hadn't you?"

"I do not know. I discovered it means good for nothing, in French argot." He smiled. "Not as original as I supposed."

"Emma is my real name. I hate it. Don't you find that women hate their given names? Nobody at school wanted their own." She showed no sign of nervousness. "Are you not too young? I'd expected…"

Emma seated herself, made almost as if to reach for a cigarette then withdrew her hand.

"I suppose one ought to feel ashamed about all this. It makes me weary. I don't suppose you know how utterly crass a woman feels, having to resort to…" She appraised him with a crease of worry. "I hope you don't take offence. I've worked out what to say."

Before he could speak Emma continued quite urbanely, "My husband has another woman. Our daughter and son are in their first jobs after university. I am quite capable. I work for a canal company, leisure and waterborne traffic, Midlands and the North. I am no weeping wallflower."

She paused as if wanting some observation. He was unable to provide one. She nodded, permitting his silence.

"I'm trying to show myself that I'm not some inept little woman who's lost her way, hoping to buy a passionate dream-world for an hour. I need, Bonn…"

Emma raised her eyebrows, had she got his name right. He gave one nod, their mood that sparse.

"I need reassurance. He's with her most days, has been for years. Rich enough to accept the loss of productive man-hours, you see. We discuss it openly. I am neglected in that sphere. Can I call it that? My assurance has become a matter of concern. We need not go into why or how."

"As you wish."

"I've become desperate not to miss out on things." She smiled a little. "I normally wear spectacles. I chose to leave them off for this… interview, in case I came over as forbidding. I thought you might be put off. I see that I was mistaken."

He was not sure what she meant by this. A portrait of her in her younger days – twenties? – hung on the wall of the window bay.

"I asked Pierre would he allow me, well, this. He was astonished. I persisted. I had heard women speaking of these arrangements. I actually hired a firm to discover the whereabouts of such firms."

"The Pleases Agency is in the Yellow Pages."

"Now you tell me!" The joke failed and she winced. "Apologies, Bonn. One request, please. Would you tell me how, what is it you people might say, how satisfactory you find this? Afterwards? Inadequacy seems such a terrible word, doesn't it?"

"Simply wrong."

She considered. "Don't men find some women good and others not?"

He knew she meant herself and her husband's woman.

"I can only speak for myself, Emma. Women are bliss. They give paradise. I do not know why they cannot see this." Into her silence he said, "There are no degrees of ecstasy, nor grades of heaven. It is an absolute."

"Then why does a man ignore a woman he already has, and goes to a slut?" She was bitter.

"I shall show you what I believe, Emma." He saw her glance towards the open bedroom door and wondered if it was time. "I am here for you. Just say."

"I wanted to ask what is the worst that you've done to – for? – a client. Would you tell me?"

"I regret, no. Ladies have a right to my silence."

"Good." She rose, for the first time showing a little hesitation. "Then would you tell me what is the worst you might do?"

"Only what you yourself wish, Emma."

"That bad?" For the first time her smile almost showed through.

She led the way into the bedroom. He wanted to look into her eyes when the time came. Emma was interesting, a woman of attributes who should not go to waste. He turned to see her take off her clothes as he began to strip, and found her watch-

97

ing him. He felt as if he wished to smile but a good one would not quite reach his face. She smiled for them both and looked without misgiving. They slipped into bed almost together.

"Can it be slow, Bonn? Tell me."

Close to, he noticed that she wore make-up laid thickly on her cheeks, and her lipstick cracked slightly as she spoke. Yet artifice was present in us all, he thought. Therefore it is something to admire, not to mistrust. Artifice affirmed life.

"I like you, Emma."

She drew away as if astonished, staring at him along the pillow.

"Nobody has said that to me in years." She touched his mouth, his eyelids, his hair and then moved her hand along his flank. "I hope you are not going to simply pretend."

"I cannot do other than receive the delight with which you bless me."

Her hands felt him, touching gingerly, looking at her fingers. "Is this all right?"

"If you wish, then yes."

"Do you ever refuse, Bonn?" Who else had asked that, or something similar?

"Yes." He felt her mouth suck on his throat and shivered. "But not now."

14 | Honest – to be trusted at face value, whatever the illegality

"This event is a consequence," Brother Jason told Brother Paulo. "Evil comes in many a guise."

Brother Paulo was the keeper of records. As such, he was oblivious to anything not on paper. Once a known drinker, now an unknown one. He was stout, florid even, and given to smoking. Brother Jason classed him an addictive personality.

"Jecko by nickname in the Home, Rupert Scowcroft in our records."

Brother Paulo thought a moment. "Twice attempted…?"

"To leave, yes." Brother Jason paused. "My next point is delicate."

He stared into the garden. Deciduous trees make such a mess, leaves a mash in wet autumn rotting the boys' shoes. It was all cost. He encouraged Brother Stephen to insist on ground-covering plants, the way the old Queen Mother used to. Ignored, of course. Talk to the wall and a gardener.

"I understand, Brother Jason."

"But do you, Brother Paulo? The boy is a known trouble-maker. The Church … need I enlarge on how we are vilified by the modern press? How they take advantage of our silence to their libels?"

"The advertisement in Eire was a serious mistake."

"So it was."

Brother Jason steepled his fingers, lips thinned in anguish at the terrible memory. In Eire three years ago, the Church had unwisely been moved to take out a massive double advert in a national newspaper expressing profound remorse at the suffering its perverts had inflicted on children in its care.

"However," Brother Paulo put in, "we must acknowledge its fiscal shrewdness."

"That is so." Brother Jason was reluctant to concede this. "The Church would be bankrupted by now if all the threatened lawsuits had gone ahead." He considered the issue. "It must have had some effect, d'you think?"

"We've seen nothing since."

"Politicians," Brother Jason spat, rising to contemplate the outlook from his study window.

"The press has vilified the Church lately. One paper threatened to print the names of over seven thousand abused children. Thank God the politicians apologised and promised to pay the Church's debts."

"Our nuns in Nazareth House will cost the Church millions. It is so unfair!"

"This country's press is satanic, Brother Paulo. They've even blamed Mother Theresa's Missionaries of Charity in Calcutta for cruelty to seven-year-olds!"

He viewed the drystone wall surmounted by tangled wire out there, sundry Clematis and herbaceous borders. No effective confinement in that direction. A road ran by to the canal. No, control had to be enforced at source, where the boys slept, lived, were schooled. Any other policy was laxity and sloth.

"We seem to be overlooking, Brother Paulo, that Rupert tried to run before."

"He was caught, once inside the quad, the second time in the street. Broad daylight." Brother Paulo ahemed. "Two passers-by came to interfere. You recall the report I made of the occurrence?"

"Yes. You did well."

"Nothing came of that incident?"

"No, thank God."

"Then what else have we forgotten?"

"He is persistent, our Rupert." Brother Jason seated himself in his swivel chair. "Third time he escapes, to spread poisonous slander about the Church."

"Some children are beyond control."

"They shouldn't be!" Brother Jason slammed his palm flat on his desk. Brother Paulo was unmoved. "The little reprobate is evil. We have had such as he before."

"Damage limitation?"

Brother Jason subsided. "Where is he, I keep asking myself. It cannot be far. The police will be useless, fax the boy's face to social workers then forget about him."

"In the city?"

"Of course." The more he thought of it, now he'd said it openly, the sounder it seemed. "Wasn't he a local child? Parental abuse, cruelty, the usual?" He sighed. "The consequences of that suffering leaves behavioural traces in a child. Rupert has been disruptive and evil. In other circumstances…"

"Yes?" Brother Paulo waited. He couldn't possibly take a decision of this magnitude. That judgement was for the superior.

"I would suggest a limitation exercise." He sighed, gestured helplessly at the outside world beyond the wall. "To eliminate the problem. The Church is entitled. Our Holy Mother has resorted to serious steps in the past. It is a matter of survival."

"Indeed."

"Scandal is an instrument of evil, Brother Paulo. We are more vulnerable now than ever before. How long did those Christian Brothers in Canada survive that pernicious investigation in the 1980s? And that perfidious television exposure, all the documentaries. How long did…?" He halted, unwilling to go on. "The Church's hare is up and running. Irreligious folk see only darkness and perversion everywhere. They want evil. We, the Church, want holiness and light."

"They are unprincipled."

"The pernicious would not hesitate to resort to legal action on the slightest whim."

"We have avoided that in the past."

"We had considerable help," Brother Jason said pointedly.

"The Church cannot always be so fortunate. If it came to a final reckoning, Brother Paulo, where would your judgement lie?"

"Judgement? Mine?" Brother Paulo was shocked.

"A soul may be rescued from its own perdition by an early return to God. You understand my meaning?"

"Yes, Brother Jason." The decision was thus made for him, Brother Paulo thought contentedly. He was absolved by his obedience.

"After all, you are the one who discovered – we need not go into your means – a new source of revenue for us. It meant economic survival. You must take the credit."

"It was fortunate."

"Might we not say providential?" Brother Jason smiled, relieved the worst was over. "Your commercial arrangements with contacts in the city could provide us with a sure means of eliminating the risk that this malign boy Rupert represents."

"It will be difficult."

"Come, come, Brother. Surely not too hard for a man of your inventiveness? Think of the benefit! The Church would avoid iniquitous slander. The wicked would be confounded. We should in fact gain the compassion of the laity. For once," he added dryly. "I trust it could be arranged?"

"The price…"

Brother Jason flapped his hands. "There is always a price. Prices have to be paid." He thought a while. "I explained Rupert's defection to the kitchen ladies. Isn't there an oldish lady, does the vegetables?"

"Yes. They call her Marj. A widow, Mrs Enshaw."

"I had the feeling that our Rupert was of interest to her."

"Perhaps she knew the boy before we took him?"

"That's one possibility." Brother Jason lost his smile. "She is the second avenue for action, Brother Paulo."

"Yes, Brother Jason."

The superior watched the other leave.

In clear religious terms, knowledge was either in use, or not in use. Brother Paulo knew in which category his understanding had to remain. It was the one true essential for discipline in a religious order.

He wondered idly how Rupert, aka Jecko, would die. An accident, always a road accident. Folly to carry it out any other way. The protective shield constructed for Holy Mother Church had to be totally resistant, its origins and provision undetectable.

Good had to be protected from evil. Simple as that. It had been an unassailable law for two thousand years. Evil could not triumph, for the mere sake of one nuisance child. If the recalcitrant boy had been obedient, as several others in the Home, then he wouldn't be forced into this kind of reparative action. Evil must take the consequences of its own character in young and old alike. If that meant the termination of one pernicious brat, so be it. Holiness, after all, was at stake.

15 | Scurf – one of no account

Hassall stood on the canal embankment wondering what the hell he was going to do. The body had been shifted to the mortuary after more photographs than any film star.

"You have to curse your luck," he told Spellman, the Scene of Crime Officer with the sourest outlook in the force.

"You mean me?" Spellman chuckled, shaking his head. "You love the job, Hassy."

"Oh, I do, I do." Hassall looked at the evidence bags being closed, such as they were. "What d'you reckon?"

They had found a plastic envelope containing a few tablets in the body's pocket.

"Rollies," Spellman said. "Without a doubt. They're stamped out like the Euro coins now. Ecstasy. Some Yank invented the name. Little 'e', they write it. Rave ups are called roller parties now. My cousin's lass has one a day."

"One what?" Hassall looked his disbelief.

"One e tablet. Stupid little sod spends her week's wage on them. Mixed with a compound."

"What?"

"Like tobacco. Doubt if it's illegal, mate."

Spellman was a disgruntled man. He had two women assistants he couldn't get rid of. Both proved useless, one putting in for early retirement, working her ticket because she was a dud. Compensation written all over her. The other was capable but hated the work. Spellman kept asking her why had she joined. She only snapped, "I didn't think it'd be like this, did I?" and kept saying she wanted out. Hassall almost sympathised.

Rollers, rolls, Ecstasy, ... Different names for the same stuff. No more than a trace had been found in Deirdre Turnstall's body besides the morphine overdose. Hassall wondered if this canal cache was from the same batch. Could doctors tell?

For another two hours he sauntered with his gloved hands ready for action. He walked in plastic covered boots along the canal. He tried judging the distance by eye from the road. He tested the hoardings that fronted Liverpool Road and spent time watching the canal towpaths for anglers, joggers, strolling lovers.

Vane was talking, analysing, making comparisons with classical cases he'd only read of. Eventually he grew impatient. Hassall sent him off to repeat the interview with a dog walker who'd seen the body in the water. Miracles do happen, because a passing police car saw the man run distraught from the canal trying to flag them down. They tramped everything flat within miles to despoil evidence, of course, tried to reach the body with some clothes prop they'd found, careful not to get their posh uniforms wet.

Vane hated going over somebody else's questions, so it wasn't a wasted afternoon. The man's irritation pleased Hassall, who made him go back and check some more.

Hassall noticed some kids playing at the churchyard end of the bridge. He went that way, saw evidence of a cinder area and goalposts – old gas fittings most likely, with bricks for corner flags. Scuffed almost level, no weeds, therefore in daily use.

Some bloke from the *City Guardian* came questing. Vane would rue the interview when he read the paper's version of what he'd said, but he had to learn. Hassall kindly said, "You'll handle that best, her being gorgeous and all," meaning the corpse. Vane did the interview happily, thinking he was revealing nothing, poor sod.

Hassall walked the bridge, noting that it was useful to folk coming from Deansgate or plodding across from London Road mainline station. That meant they went to the housing estate, stack-a-pleb boxes in a small park. He needed somebody smart to stand and suss who came by from the ETOD, estimated time of death, to now.

"Here," he said to Spellman when he'd done his walkabout. "Your bolshie lass, whatsername. Could she do a job?"

"If she liked. Not if she didn't."

Hassall shook his head. "And still they draw the bloody money, eh? How about lending us a hand?"

"Staking out the bystanders, Hassy?" the SOCO said shrewdly. "Using my manpower, not yours?"

"My highly trained bunch of the city's finest," Hassall gave back evenly, "is all away on courses."

"Marvellous. Ask her. She's sulking in her motor."

Hassall called to Vane and asked him to bring Ms Wayford, if she was agreeable.

"I'm at a loss," Hassall told her when she arrived. She carried a clipboard, always a bad sign, and looked like her smiles would be too highly priced for elderly hoi polloi like him. "I need your advice, please."

"The prelim's been faxed, Mr Hassall."

"It's these walkers." He pointed out the difficulty, people crossing to the estate at all hours. "There's no way of predicting them. I wondered if you could suggest something."

"That estate?" She had a map ready, wise lass. "They come from one of three directions, but all funnel here. There's the reverse people, going from the estate to the Square, but they'll be relatively few."

"That's a thought." He hadn't considered those going the other way, not much.

"You'll need clickers, two at most."

To count numbers. "What kind of hours?"

"Ten, twelve. Best is continuous."

"Right." He grimaced. "Thanks. I'll have to see what I can fix up soon as the post-mortem establishes an ETOD."

"If you're stuck," Wayford said reluctantly as he made to resume wandering.

"Really?" He acted impressed, grateful. "Ta muchly. It'd be a real advance."

She almost smiled. "Not at all. I'll tell Mr Spellman."

"Marvellous."

An end terrace house abutted on the canal walk half a mile along. He strolled in his plastic boots. From there, a sombre street of semi-derelict terraced dwellings stretched a couple of hundred yards towards the church. Every second or third house was almost gutted. It was the lack of Wildfire that suggested that there must be a track leading off. Those tall red-flowering weeds settled everywhere. They released large floating seeds, floating like snow on summer days. Local children called them Sugar Stealers from some fanciful imagining, and chased them, who-ever caught most the winner.

No Wildfire weeds near the gutted end house, so Hassall went and tested the planks sealing the climb to the road. Solid, so no route there.

He crossed to the other side of the canal and looked, walked the length of it and back. Only at one place could he see a thin darkening of the soil. They'd gone in and out of the cellar, obliquely, away from the direction of the bridge. You normally look for the most direct route, not the most wayward. Clever.

Returning, he lifted a few layers of tall weeds aside, Knitbone and Dock, and realised the druggos were even cleverer than he'd first supposed. They'd always jumped the first pace, to leave no mark, possibly carried a plank to prevent indentations in the canal side. He almost fell into the recess. Good at hiding, so not children, who would simply invent some trick like that then for-get it after a few squabbles.

He followed the track, found the place where bricks were wobbly in the overgrown walling. He removed a good few, eighteen or so, and called Vane for a torch, but he was unavailable, doubtless analysing essentials with Ms Wayford. He borrowed one from a uniform and went on down.

Nothing in the cellar except an expended syringe, a thick

pencil and a thin length of linen, such as exercise maniacs and mainliners used. For different purposes, of course. He returned to daylight, dusting himself down, and shouted for Vane to come with Ms Wayford and give the end house a going over. He omitted to mention that he'd already been inside the cellar. That would only rile them both. He made sure they knew the sequence in which he'd laid the bricks down when removing them from the gap.

"Left first," he told them. "Furthest away from the wall last, okay?"

An hour later they came up with a cache of rollies, some seven thousand yellowish tablets in plastic.

He thanked them profusely for their brilliant detective work, and went to find Dr Burtonall.

16 | Stringer – a female street prostitute of a group allocated a particular beat

Clare reached her flat almost exhausted. The clinic had seemed particularly hard today. She shelled her jacket, groaning at the phone's winking light. She hated the message device with fervour.

She made tea and sat to listen to the damned machine, wondering if the water in Charlestown was more polluted than elsewhere. It tasted funny.

The first message was from a bookseller; her book on forensic pathology was in. Second was an old medical school friend, got a new teaching hospital post in paediatrics, let's meet and celebrate. Clare shrank guiltily in her armchair. She'd never liked the woman, nor trusted her. She instantly decided to pretend the phone had been on the blink, should Miranda – that *name*! – ring again.

Third, here came Clifford: time we met, a couple of divorce details, nothing important. Hoping she was well and dot dot dot. Another to ignore but without the guilt.

Fourth, Hassall's voice, clearing its gravelly throat, wanting to ask about Deirdre Turnstall. Vane came on fifth, same message, citing an assortment of mobile phone numbers.

Then her mother. She almost spilled her tea.

"I know you're there, Clare, so please pick up the receiver. It's time we had a little talk." Asperity ruled where Mrs Esme Salford uttered. An extended pause. "Very well. As you seem disinclined to exchange a single word, let's meet at the Weavers Hall. Shall we say ten-thirty tomorrow? I hope Victoria Square isn't too far out of your way. If it's inconvenient in any way, please let me

111

know. Dad sends his love. We're both well…" *Even if you can't bother to phone now and then.* Implied, unsaid.

Clare groaned. This meant Mother had been up to her usual manipulations to get Clifford and her daughter back together. Over coffee Mother would have a battery of blame words at the ready – Clare's divorce was "calamitous", Clare's attitude "total resentment". Was it a plot, Clifford and her mother ganging up to coerce her into reunion?

Never in a million years.

Maybe Clifford's call was a more oblique tactic on the same lines? Well, Clare would put an end to this once and for all.

She still had time before her evening surgery. Just one patient, a girl asking for a special interview. Clare held back problem cases to the evening, when she could allow more time. Physical ailments for the morning clinics, others in the early evening.

The problem was that Bonn was out there in the darkening city. Perhaps already walking into some hotel where some wealthy bitch had hired him. She swallowed her anger, threw her clothes off and went to shower. Time for something to eat, then see this patient. No chance of booking Bonn this late, not now.

She stuffed her hair into the shower cap, couldn't find the body moisturiser, swore inelegantly and stepped into the rushing water, chin up to the fast stream. See? Even this ele-mentary act sowed pernicious thoughts in her mind: when would she be able to stand like this with Bonn, simply taking a shower without her mind ticking away the valuable seconds to the moment he had to leave?

And when would she be able to say something casual on-the-spur like, "Let's have coffee together tomorrow, darling. Weavers Hall? It's really lovely now they've redecorated with those new fabrics…" (That *together* was a delight.) Instead, she now had to suffer her mother, who'd instantly work the talk round to a daughter who let her marriage "fall to bits", a favourite condemnatory catchphrase. The question of children ("Where's your chance of a family *now*, Clare?" etc, etc) and "living like a shop girl over some retail outlet…" would doubtless be high on the agenda. Impossible to explain that Clifford was a criminal, implicated in possibly two deaths.

She felt better after a prolonged buffeting, turned the water temperature down to chill, and stepped out refreshed. Only to see the red light blinking yet another summons. Irritably she dabbed the button and heard Bonn. Her heart almost turned over.

"Ah, erm. I'm sorry, you off duty. Perhaps I might ring at another time, if that would be…"

Click. Burr. That was it.

As if mesmerised, she made the instrument repeat it. No questions, just hesitancy, leaving her mind a mess of conjecture. She felt anguished for him, so unable to speak words outright. At first she'd been put out by his manner. Now, it was sympathy, mixed with anger at herself for having been relaxing hopelessly in the shower, something she could have done any time, leaving Bonn trying to speak to the useless bloody living-room.

Her sense of well-being vanished. She made some toast, defiantly coated it thickly with butter and honey. She tried the identification re-call but only got that infuriatingly smug phone voice telling her that the caller "withheld the number".

She got herself ready to see the girl patient, thinking just let her come for nothing, that's all.

* * *

The girl gave her name as Donna Reede. The surgery and office were empty. No Mrs Hast to sulk around the place slamming doors, thank God. Time the woman was replaced. Nurse Scanlon was already showing signs of discontent, and Mrs Hast was causing it.

"Come in, Donna. Do sit down."

The girl was a plump eighteen. She was moderately dark-skinned. Asiatic? Tidy, showing defiance.

113

"I think I'm pregnant," she said immediately, before Clare had even asked for personal details.

"Right. Could I take down your name, address, hear something about your job, family history, before we go on?" She smiled, trying to put the other at her ease. "Otherwise I'll lose track."

Clare was certain the address would be false, that the girl was another of the street girls, but medical protocol required this sham. Donna cited a tenement block beyond the canal down Liverpool Road. Clare had recently driven past there and thought it derelict. Perhaps it had been renovated. In two months, though?

"And your parents' address?"

"No. That's the problem. I'm nearly four months." The girl's defiance was blunter now.

"Give me your dates, please. You have a partner? Married, or have a boyfriend?"

"I'm a stringer," Donna said harshly, as if challenging Clare to be outraged. Then quieter, "My friend – Maeve, who came here to see you and got thrown out – she said it's all right to tell you up front."

"Please, wait a moment. Maeve?"

Donna almost smiled. "She picked Faye Ray for her card name." And explained, "We give a name. For the medical card, y'know? Like to the doctor, or police."

"Maeve. I remember. She's your friend?"

"She got the push because she made herself sick. She's gone now. You got her into hospital."

"I can't talk about another patient." Clare thought a moment. "You are a stringer?"

"The girls are mostly stringers. The others get seen off. Grellie's the boss. She brung Maeve." She clasped her hands, more defiance on the way. "I want to keep her."

"Keep who?"

"The baby. My parents will make me get rid of her, but I

won't. I'm going to keep her. I can do it." She became impassioned, urging. "There's other stringers, some a lot older, have kiddies. They get by."

"You keep saying 'she'. Are you sure the baby is a girl?"

"I went to a hospital near Manchester. I had the scan. There's a techie who does it out of hours. It cost. The baby has nothing wrong."

Clare was aghast. "You bribed a technician in Obstetrics to perform a scan?"

"Everybody does things for money," Donna said, matter of fact. "She – the techie – puts the scan photos through next morning with the rest. The doctors check lots. They don't notice one more." She showed her belligerence. "I've a right."

"Of course. But why didn't you come to see me? We could have arranged a scan and your antenatals. And you wouldn't have had to pay some technician."

"I got the pictures."

Donna passed over a manilla folder. Clare extracted the images. The foetus seemed normal, the serrated measures marked across the images in the new fashion. She almost smiled in envy. That new method of scaling would have been a boon when she was doing obstetrics. There was a terse evaluation on the accompanying yellow flimsy, dictated and signed by Dr Grover, the new senior Obstetrics registrar. She returned them.

"Fine. I'll bring you in tomorrow when the nurse is here. Then, all things being well, I'll arrange your antenatal classes and – "

"I'm going to keep her."

That again? "Of course. Nobody is urging you to do otherwise."

"There's two lots as might. One's my parents." Clare looked questioningly into the girl's angry glance. "I don't want anything to do with them."

"Is there a reason?"

"Religion. They might go along with it, if I'd got some

boyfriend to marry. But only if the baby was a boy, see?"

Clare laid her pen down. "No, I'm afraid I don't see. You mean, if it's a boy they'll help you, if it's a girl they won't?"

"That's it. My brothers are the same. They'll go ape when they hear."

"On what grounds?"

"Girls is no use." Her tone became bitter. "A girl is a maggot in the rice. You never heard that? They tell it us from being born. Boys can do anything, run businesses, get educated. Girls skivvy. Maeve said you'd help. You can talk Grellie into maybe letting me come back once I got the baby to a helper."

"Back?"

"To work." Donna seemed suddenly years younger, more vulnerable. "I can work as good as now, see? A baby doesn't stop girls doing their strides."

"Strides?"

"Jobs. One bloke is a stride, whatever way he wants it."

"How many of the stringers have children?"

"Don't you tell." Donna thought. "I'm in the red string. We work Rivergate, Market Street." Clare's head swam. Her own office had been there when first she'd worked for the charity. "Two girls got children. They do as good as the rest."

Tears welled up in Donna's eyes. She blotted her cheeks.

"See, if Grellie let me come back once I've had her, they'd protect me. Then she – the baby – would be safe too."

Clare listened as the girl went over the same explanation. Round and round, family obsessed with religious propriety and hating another girl in the family. Boys were everything to some societies, Clare knew.

The syndicate could protect this girl and her baby, if they let her remain on the syndicate's books. Otherwise she would go to the wall, possibly have to return to her merciless family with all the grim consequences that might entail. She heard the girl out.

"Tell me again, Donna," she said. "Take your time. We're in no hurry."

"I've got to be back on, in an hour."

"Take your time," Clare repeated firmly. "I'm with you now. Tell me how your parents would feel if…"

17 | Pods – street consignments of different drugs

Rack didn't like the Shot Pot so quiet. It wasn't natural. Okay, there'd been a death, but you hadn't to think of it as death. Accident was about right.

The snooker hall's quiet was down to these northern gits. For all their beer bellies and racket they went quiet at odd times. London folk – he was one – talked it as it was.

The lads were shoving and yacking same as ever, snooker their life, red then that blue, mind me arm, where's my lucky chalk, all that. But quiet was underneath. Rack hated the fucking quiet.

Even yardies learned it. Wherever they came from, Kingies from Trinidad, Bardies from Barbados, couple of Greeks, whatever, if they lived in the north, they caught it. The silence. Oh, they'd be laughing and playing as usual, but were quiet deep within, thinking all sorts you couldn't even guess.

He bowled in shouting insults, daft bets, tenner on the yellow, a fiver it doesn't even stay on the table. They laughed. Wavell from Wigan showed a mile of gold teeth, slapping his thigh and falling about, while Toothie howled that Rack, noisy bamba claat, made him miss the red. Their din disguising quiet.

Rack thought, any more quiet I'll cut their fucking hearts out.

He shouted, "Think I'd pay if I lost?" and got shouts from the Manchester lads, in for the knockout practice.

He reached old Osmund playing patience.

"Black seven, red eight."

"That'd be cheating, Rack. Go in."

Osmund was waistcoated, immaculate white sleeves, collar starched – who the fuck starched collars? His remaining hairs

119

lay slicked across his pate. Osmund never cheated, deplored the world's folly. Rack thought him barmy. Playing patience all day long, never tricking the rules. The columns of faded clothes rolled aside. Rack entered the vestibule, the door clicked shut. One wall slid aside, kidded nobody. Two steps of a corridor and he was in. Secret as a riot.

There sat Martina, beautiful blonde, eyes ice blue, pale as paper, at a desk that carried one blank page and a pencil.

No chair for him, which was all right. She was lame. You hadn't to look at her gammy leg.

"Deirdre, Rack." Straight out, so she was in one of her fucking tempers.

"Don't talk like Bonn, boss," he said irritabuly.

Only Rack called her boss. He never denied the stre girls' rumours that Martina was his cousin. It might be true, who knew?

"What happened?"

"Neighbour found her and did the ambulance bit. She'd got Dr Burtonall's phone number on her. She'll see the autopsy."

"Any result so far?"

"Don't ask me. Ask her."

"She did it herself? Not us?"

"Leave orff," he said with disgust. "Look. I heard some kid's looking for her."

A double wariness entered Martina's eyes. Rack looked away. Better all round if Bonn shagged her regular. Martina was being a right bitch too often lately.

"Maybe from that Christian Brothers place there's talk about."

"Who told you?"

"Joy and Rita seed him." Rack's fingers closed. Respect was down to him, nobody else. "I'll go into one if I get narked, folk not telling me when they should."

"I want all this sealed shut, Rack." Pause. "Find the boy."

She was another one, but women couldn't keep quiet for

long. Blokes could shout and holler at football, and still keep that horrible seed of quiet growing inside for months on end. Women only lasted a minute.

"Pods, Rack."

He sighed. His mamma was Italian, from some Mediterranean dump. She practically lived in church, lit enough candles to do the Ozone Layer, blamed him for not being the fucking Pope or married with ten bawling babbies. He said he was a computer expert for Imperial Chemicals to shut the miserable bitch up. Her being Italian meant that every pod crossing Victoria Square was his fault. Christ, scag was all Tijuana, Columbia, Turkey and China, not him.

"You mean the new stuff? I'd never heard of till last week. Miraa's in bundles. You don't need rigs. It's only smokes and chews."

"Rig?" she asked.

"Rigs is syringes, needles, rubber bands for your arm. Jesus, Martina, where wus you brought up? Kids know more."

"Who brings it in?"

"Dunno yet. Dunno where from, either."

"Find out. What happened at the Triple Racer?"

How the fuck had she heard about that? He pulled a face, properly caught out.

"Only a scrap between two Indian lasses. There's a biker called Hollo."

"One Singalese, one Bangla." She kept her eyes on him.

"Who knows?" he said airily. Indian would do for both. "I'm going there now."

"Grellie had to haul them off."

Martina meant he should have been there to handle it. More blame. He did his sigh.

"I was standing Bonn at a dommy. I can't be in two places."

"Bonn does take priority." She said it reluctantly, like lancing a boil. "Take Grellie. I want no more trouble."

"I'll tank Hollo, then."

"Not badly. There's a big demand for our Asian lasses, so many ethnic punters now. Keep it honest."

"Right."

Rack was already into ways of tanking Hollo. Serve him right. You tell some blokes, still they don't listen. It made him mad.

"Has the new stander shown promise?"

Rack thought, just listen to the silly cow, talking like a headmaster. Shown fucking *promise*? If Funnel didn't keep his goer safe, Rack'd have him binned, finito. Who wanted promise?

"Funnel's okay. Comes from Salford," he threw in for nothing. "Has a brother wants in as a stander. I told him no."

Martina was curious. "Is his brother unreliable?"

"Does full frontal, them telegram things where blokes strip off singing. Ponces. I want none of them."

"As you wish, Rack."

Best thing she'd said since he come in. "Is that it?"

She looked to one side, her habit when she was sly. Already made her mind up but pretending your opinion counted.

"We've had an offer to buy our working house. Some Leeds and Newcastle leisure complex." He said nothing. "Just for the brothel. Ever since the Aussies did that legitimising adaptive mortgage scheme in November 2000, to float that brothel quotation on their stock exchange, investors everywhere have been clamouring for similar schemes."

The syndicate's working house was a new operation for the Agency, next door to Martina's home.

"Turn it down," he said sharply. "They wouldn't stop there. Want me to warn them off?"

She thought, or seemed to. "No. Give them the chance to accept a refusal first."

"Is that what Posser says?"

She looked at him sharply. He looked away.

Posser was her father, now seriously ailing and having difficulty walking near his Bradshawgate house of a morning. He had raised Martina alone in poor circumstances, and begun the goer business singlehandedly. Prospering, Posser had taken over properties in the city centre, and now the Pleases Agency operated sandwich bars to snooker halls, restaurants and discos. The Bouncing Block gym down Market Street was one of his startlingly successful recent buys. It out-performed even the Rum Romeo, the smaller of the syndicate's casinos. The goers though were the cream.

Rack raised a hand to show he meant nothing. She let it go. Her reprimand narked him, because if he couldn't ask such things who could?

"Is Bonn all right?" Another side glance.

"Yeh."

"There's a special wants regular domestic visits for his wife." Rack knew that the Pleases Agency never took standing orders. Repeats, yes. Regulars, no. Every booking had to be newly made, individual. Martina's idea of security. "Tell Bonn, see what he says."

"Right."

"And Rack? No splashing Hollo and the two girls. Understand? And find the boy."

He left without saying a word and stood telling the lads jokes in the snooker hall for the best part of an hour. Martina would think he was doing it to rile her, but she'd be wrong. Bints didn't understand. She'd be thinking there's Rack, wasting his frigging time.

Rack knew better. Talk words that came out the same as ever, same things, same football teams, same bets won and lost, same nags, pathetic racing at Exeter, all the usual crap, was the one thing that ended all the fucking quiet. Took time, but boring chat saw it off.

That was what he wanted. Back to the old gigs. Before last week, when he'd had to tell Set to let Deirdre go. Bad decisions like that started all this quiet up, just when you wanted a bit of peace. Still, tanking Hollo would be a laugh, cheer a few folk up. High time Rack enjoyed himself for once.

18

Bark – reception desk, implicitly at an illegal establishment

"Police examinations are the bane of my life," Clare lied to her friend Dr Sally Cockcroft.

"Serves you right for being an ingrate."

They walked the length of the corridor towards the Department of Epidemiology.

"Surveys are always down among hospital ruins," Clare joked. "I feel really embarrassed. Paint flaking, windows won't shut, screens with holes."

"You should see the changing rooms for us surgeons."

"Palaces."

Clare felt like grumbling, something niggling in her brain about the girl Deirdre's death. She had several questions for Dr Pedersen, but he was in a Clinico-Pathological conference, fighting it out with Clinical Biochemistry's obsessional-neurotic pedants. Today's presentation was yet another variant Fanconi Syndrome, all metabolites of ever increasing technical refinement and diminishing trace quantities.

"Don't do them." Sally paused for a final word. She turned to enter the Surgical Unit. "They can't make you."

"I thought of it as a six-week job," Clare remembered. "Now look. A whole year, and three annual appraisals. Their damned numbers are growing."

"Police like you."

"That'll be the day. I can't stand their hearty jokes."

"They're scared stiff," Sally said wisely. "Find something off the scale, and out they go. Careers gone in a trice."

"The same for everyone." Clare was exasperated.

"They'll have been on silly diets." Sally laughed. "And started aerobics yesterday!"

"And when they pass the medical, they'll resume beering it up."

"You've realised!"

They parted in good humour, Sally to the afternoon list in Orthopaedics, Clare to the clinic set up in rooms on temporary loan from Epidemiology. It was barely professional. The walls were lined with reference tomes, the two handbasins were on opposite walls, and the instrumentation had to be wheeled in on trolleys borrowed from Cardiac Out Patients.

"Still," Clare observed as she greeted Nurse Lawless, also on loan from Cardiology, "this shoddy room probably allows Admin to spend more on their plush carpets."

"Flowers, wine, caviar…"

Though Nurse Lawless smiled and continued the joke, she had to be treated with care. She had a boyfriend in Clerical and Admin, and was sure to gossip about attitudes among doctoral staff. Still, Clare thought, pleased at having got her needle in even at a distance, it would do no harm to pass the word that Admin was genuinely hated throughout the entire hospital by those who actually did the work.

"How many, Nurse?"

"Twenty-six in actual numbers, Dr Burtonall. By weight, forty."

Clare laughed. "So overweight."

"They're swelling. Everybody's fatter than they used to be."

Clare glanced at Nurse Lawless. The girl seemed able to eat anything, yet remained slender.

They admitted the first. Nurse Lawless did the urine tests and weighing. Clare took samples of peripheral blood for erythrocyte sedimentation rate, leucocyte and erythrocyte indices, the usual tiresome cholesterols. She tended to place far more reliance on the clinical examination, though, for that was what stuck in the doctor's mind when minor details of white cell variations long since ceased to matter. Anyhow, laboratory reports could be referred to any time. But the alert features, a hint of dejection, the mood transitions, those could prompt questions revealing some incipient disease.

The seventh police constable showed hypertension.

Clare asked him to lie down, signalling to Nurse Lawless to time his period of rest.

"We usually trust ambient blood pressure," she said easily, not to alarm the young man. "That's the walking-about BP. Yours is a little raised, so we sit you on the couch to quieten down."

"Is there something wrong?" he asked anxiously.

"A slight increase could be due to a million causes. We take precautions – do the BP again, take blood samples, ask you to come back a second time. It's routine."

Nurse Lawless was already noting down the constable's name on new sample containers: serum creatinine, blood glucose, differential High Density Lipoprotein and total cholesterols, following the list down.

Clare smiled. "Don't worry just yet. You're the tenth we've had with this kind of blip on first screening, so you're in goodly company."

She joshed the man along. In spite of her seeming levity and keeping him back for a third sphygmomanometer reading, the blood pressure stayed above 160 over 90 millimetres of mercury. This in spite of four separate readings, both arms. She used the mercury-manometric cuff, then the electronic estimate and found the same. The electrocardiograph was left to Nurse Lawless while she herself went to check that the aneroid machine had been checked for accuracy. It had.

"We need to see you again," she told the worried constable. She added to allay his apprehension, "It's a small chance, but why take it?"

"Is it serious, Dr Burtonall?" Nurse Lawless asked when they were alone. Clare was entering up her clinical notes about the ophthalmic examination. She wanted Galbraith at Salford

Medical School to check her findings on the constable's fundi.

"It's not too bad but worth investigating further. I'll refer his repeat assessment."

She sighed. "The most difficult thing is confidentiality. We have to assume that he wants the results revealed to police authorities. We must ask him directly. He won't be pleased."

The next man was a sergeant. He was pleasant, looked fit, and stripped easily.

"Evidently an athelete," Nurse Lawless joshed.

"Brilliant middle-distance runner, if you please. Vane, Kenneth Milroy Vane."

He gave his police number, height, weight, shoe size and said that he liked Hitchcock films and sword-and-sandal epics.

Everything was normal, blood pressure a resounding 120 over 80. Pushy, but undoubtedly in the peak of health. Almost a waste of time and resources sending off the lab tests. Clare said as much.

"Where's the morbid anatomy unit?" he asked, dressing quickly. "I'm due there."

"For what?"

"Girl, B.I.D. One of ours."

He seemed brashly sure of himself, definitely inclined to get under a woman's skin. Nurse Lawless seemed quite taken.

"Isn't Mr Hassall here, then?" Clare asked, offhand.

"Should be," Vane said. "Thought I saw him."

"Aren't we expecting Mr Hassall, Nurse?"

"Yes. The senior officers come last."

"Maybe he's gone over there. He said he knows two of the doctors." Vane grimaced. "I've drawn him."

"What was she?" Clare asked lightly.

"Overdose. Open and shut case. Junkies, sooner or later they do themselves in."

Nurse Lawless watched the door close behind him.

"Must be great, having all that assurance. It comes with their job, I suppose."

Not quite, Clare thought, but said nothing.

"Next, please, Nurse."

They found one incipient early diabetic, a vastly overweight young constable who was also a heavy smoker. He was astonished to be referred to a consultant physician in Out Patients. It was not an auspicious start to her day.

She crossed to the PM suite, following the signs through Pathology. No sign of Hassall or Vane. They must be going over the dead girl's details with Reception staff or the emergency ambulance crew.

19

To Tank – to inflict grievous
bodily harm proportionate to
an unpaid debt

Jecko followed the two girls. It was easy. Trying to look like he
was actually going somewhere was the hard part, a kid on his
own. He managed it by ducking into doorways, hurrying
across at traffic lights like he was late going home. A motorist
shouted at him. He kept Joy and Rita in sight.

They made Victoria Square, which was great because there
was the railway station at the Moorgate end beyond the bus
station. Buses on the way out to moorland villages, plenty of
people wandering, some good, some bad. But no cassocked
Brothers, and no police.

The girls were tarts. He'd worked it out.

Twice they alarmed him by getting into cars, but they soon
came back. Joy took her time. Rita was quicker, once still wiping
her mouth with tissues and glad to get rid. Jecko started looking
about, scared after seeing her pause after dropping the wad of
Kleenex on the ground at George Street near the Greygate corner. She chucked the stuff, then must have thought oh Christ
and picked it up looking for a litter bin. She glanced about like,
was I seen? Jecko knew all about furtive glances. Somebody was
maybe watching out *for* her? That was dangerous, for him.

He began moving slower, aware of his stockinged feet,
scared of Board people. Bentie and Grock said there really was
no School Board now. Everything was social services, all as
evil. Women, Bentie said, were worse than the men sometimes.
In the old days there used to be the Board, strict old men in
waistcoats you could trust. A right fucking laugh, that.
Where'd they gone?

Rita waited for her friend, getting on for eleven, cinemas loosing and travellers from Station Brough making a mad rush for trains. Jecko felt he was beginning to show obvious when he'd to blend in. But he had no shoes. He hung around the caff, midnight closing it said on the wall, looking at the buses and café screen, like he was itching to get home somewhere. Rita and Joy got slack, only two jobs. How many had they done since he'd lammed off?

The bastard Brothers would go to the police. Oll, who came from round here, said they always did. He had a cousin who'd got took back to that place in North Wales there was that fuss about. Government did fuck all except send children back to another hell ten times worse. Nod to say you understood, okay? That's all they said when you shut up. Jecko was great at shutting up, better even than Smatter, a fat lad who did hunger strikes and made a rash on his arms just by thinking, so the Brothers would leave him alone.

Between two groups of tired people he saw Rita and Joy leave the public gardens and go towards Mealhouse Lane. He followed, a pity when he'd been going to try for some grub left at a table. The caff didn't notice his departure, except for one sleepy kid who stared at his feet.

The girls stopped at a jeweller's window facing Foundry Street. They eyed the traffic.

"...tell Rack?" Rita was asking.

"We'd best do that." Joy lit a fag, jerking the smoke up. "You tell him."

"Me?" Rita yelped, then quietly, "Wait." They turned, smiled together. A motor slowed, the driver giving them a long look. The car accelerated. Their smiles vanished. "Me? I'm scared. What if Rack says we did wrong with the kid?"

"We didn't. Little bugger was terrified. Had his jamas on under his clothes. No shoes. He was doing a runner."

"He wasn't ill, either."

"There's rumours about that place, innit?"

"Look, we tell Rack. If we keep mum and summert comes out, we're done for." Rita shivered. "I once nearly crossed Rack, my second week under Grellie. Just give me a look. Scared me shitless. I didn't sleep for a fortnight."

"We do it together, okay?"

That was all Jecko heard. They parted and he followed Rita past the bottom of Moor Lane. She went up a four-step house to the front door. It was like the place Jecko had grown up in, except he couldn't hear anybody rowing. He went to the back street and climbed into a rubbish skip, working out where Rita's house was. He saw lights come on, but dozed off easy enough.

*   *   *

Morning, he got some trainers. He did it by going into Timpsonly's Shoe Emporium in the shopping mall and sitting near a cluster of three children. One girl asked if he was being served. He pointed vaguely and told her his mum had said to wait. "She's gone to the loo," he said, bored sick.

Ten minutes later he listlessly tried on some rejected trainers, got up to wander, looking at the racks of footwear. When everybody was preoccupied, he idly drifted out. Beyond the massive water clock and the budgerigar cage he stooped, tied the laces, and was off.

It was then that somebody took hold of his shoulder and said, "This him?"

"Yih, that's him, Dag," Rita said.

"Yih." Joy was there too. "Don't lose him. Rack'll go spare."

"It isn't me!" Jecko cried, trying to wriggle free, but a thin weedy man in the crumpled smelly suit had a grip of iron.

The man grinned down and said something that gave Jecko a flicker of hope.

"Nice shoes, son."

"I didn't nick them, guv, honest."

"Course not."

"Don't send me back, mister."

Rita smiled at him. "It's okay. We won't."

Jecko risked asking, "Promise?"

He was scared. But who was this Rack?

The shoppers had thickened, one or two people looking. Women and babbies were about, pushchairs, whole tribes, old cocks lighting pipes, fat old ducks ready for a chat. There'd never be a better chance. Escaping, you went the same way they were going. Pull back, they grabbed harder.

"Theeyer's Deirdre!" he said, looking up at them. It was the only other tart's name he knew, the name he'd heard when she'd knocked on the Home's side door, frightening him to death in the dark. "She's my friend!" He pointed into the crowd.

Joy actually cried out in horror. "*Who*?"

The girls recoiled. The man called Dag weakened his grip to look.

Jecko moved like he was peering to see Deirdre. And suddenly darted forward, breaking free of that hand and running like a whippet, dodging, weaving, nobody faster than Jecko.

He heard shouts, ducked between two prams, hared through Fornley Modern Boutique, raising his hands as he fled the double doors into the precinct so the cameras could see he hadn't nicked nothing – they come after you – and slowed to a casual through the chapel yard where it was all grab grub and trinket stalls.

Nobody'd seen him. No more shouts, no Dag looking round trees. He sat on the bench in the triangular park. It was set back with high bushes. Kids floated boats on a pond. Buses roared along the opposite side. There was a tatty bandstand, empty, with loose panels supporting rickety steps. Good place to hide there. Had he escaped, or not?

Rita and Joy must know Deirdre because they'd yelped in surprise when he'd said her name. He'd follow them and find Deirdre. She was the one he could trust.

Maybe?

* * *

They held a conference in the Butty Bar. They couldn't go to the Vallance Carvery and Grill, nor the Volunteer pub. Rack and some of the goers tended to have coffee there.

"I'm fucking scared." No beating about the bush with Joy. "He knowed Deirdre's name."

"Did the little sod really say Deirdre?" Dag was doubtful. "Maybe he made it up."

"Deirdre," Rita said firmly. "The little fuck. Christ, I nearly died. Her dead and all."

"I nearly wet myself." Joy looked as Dag got teas. "We'd best not be long. Grellie will go mental if she sees us slacking."

"This hour?" Rita scoffed. "How many we do of a morning?"

"One or two's enough. The bitch fined me last month. Grellie's getting worse. Don't cross her."

"I don't want to have nowt to do with this."

"You got to, Dag. You collared the lad."

"Why me? Don't look at me."

"We got to," Joy said. Despite her youth she was the clearest of the three. "Rack'll find out anyway and then what?"

Dag said miserably, "We've got to say it as it were. All together, right?"

"Let's do it now." Rita tried for that hard stare Grellie used to put the frighteners on her stringers.

Dag's face grew in length when he was upset. "I'll join in once Rack's heard your bit, okay?"

They agreed that was the only way, and went to find Rack.

"We should have told him before now," Joy said. Rita and Dag threatened her, said shut up.

"Looks like self," the senior registrar told Clare as she entered the pathology division. "The signs are there. Funny, though."

The morbid anatomy unit at Farnworth General Hospital was fairly new, with its vertical laminar-flow ventilation and air-washing vestibules. You had to get used to the tacky mats, that sticky feeling under your white post-mortem boots, click-shlurp at every step like you'd started phoney Irish dancing. She found the continual draught on her face annoying, as the HEPA-filtered air drove down at Class One Hundred standard. Clare thanked heaven that technology was opposed by the parsimony of the hospital administrators. Admin had refused requests to have the laminar-flow units separately heated. Warm draughts in an autopsy suite would have made it unbearable, the only time Admin had ever done any good.

"Funny ha ha," Bruno commented.

Bruno was the principal PM technician. A refugee from some unknowable civil wars in Eastern Europe, he was leaving middle age with cynical humour and an unshakeable conviction that strict hierarchy was the only workable social system. All else was folly.

"Funny why?"

Dr Gerry Pedersen was a Scandinavian over for a three-year stint. Stocky, he seemed the exact opposite of the popular image of Norwegian manhood. Pleasant, though, with an admirable command of English. He'd brought a wife who was shopping mad. Clare had met Margaret Pedersen only once, and had left reeling. The woman's volubility and enthusiasm made Clare feel inadequate for not knowing the prices of blouses, skirts, shoes, God-knows-what else. Gerry Pedersen had commented afterwards, "Don't go shopping with Margaret. We've lost whole tribes that way."

"One massive overdose of heroin, right? That's what it seems. Yet where's the orange peel?"

Peau d'orange was more properly a sign of lymphatic obstruction, say in breast tissue adjacent to carcinoma, and was commonly looked for during the physical examination of a breast tumour. The term had been sloppily extended to include the pock-marked skin seen around flexures of the elbows and the blued stippled corrugations over the ankles, forearms, calves, sometimes even the neck, that were so evident in drug addicts. Medical slang, Clare thought ruefully, spoiled communication.

"None!" Bruno exclaimed triumphantly. "See, none?"

Clare said, "You're suggesting she wasn't an addict?"

"She's a known seller, Clare," Dr Pedersen said. "Her record's a stack thick. Came in with her. The police had it here within minutes."

Bruno shook his head. "No, sir. They never learn to write!" He guffawed.

Unsmiling, Clare scanned the girl's cadaver on the metal slab. No more glazed white pottery, everything had to be stainless steel in the autopsy suites these days. Slight, not quite cachectic but definitely thinner than she ought to be. Clare could see what the senior registrar meant. The antecubital fossa of the dead girl's left arm showed substantial bruising and one punctum where the needle had entered the skin to despoil the vein.

"But street girls who deal are always addicts, Gerry."

"You get the rare one who isn't."

"Like this one?" Clare was doubtful.

"She seemed to have had difficulty getting into a vessel,

maybe rammed the syringe in after a few shoves. I don't know. But it's a lone event. Look at her. She was a sucker, a breather, never a mainliner from what I've found."

So the girl smoked, inhaled, swallowed, but did not inject.

"Injuries?"

The pathologist gave a wan smile, taking Clare's point.

"No signs of a struggle, if your idea is somebody holding her down to administer the final massive dose. The police even brought the tourniquet."

Bruno held up a bandage. It had been twisted into a string. A pencil was held in the middle. He laughed with frank amusement.

"She hadn't even time to sharpen it, Dr Burtonall! See? She could have drawn us a picture, help the police even more!"

Clare looked blankly from Dr Pedersen to the technician.

"It's a B8 pencil, new," the pathologist said. And explained further when she still looked, "Artist's sketching grade. Nobody else uses one so soft. You'd have to sharpen it every two words."

"We'd have told Mr Hassall," Bruno said, laughing all the more.

His appearance was incongruous, dressed as he was in theatre clothes with green cap, splash mask, rubber gloves and a full frontal rubber apon that reached to the floor. As he walked, he had to kick the panel forward with the toes of his rubber boots to make any progress.

"Hassall? The police have already been here?"

"Nothing better to do," Dr Pedersen said, ineffectually joining Bruno's banter.

"He'll be in the Hospital Friends Canteen, Dr Burtonall. You'll recognise him. Pretending to read the Murder Investigation Manual."

Bruno found his latest crack even more hilarious. Clare smiled weakly, but was concerned. For somebody so senior as Hassall to be calling on a routine autopsy signalled something seriously awry. The senior registrar detected his visitor's changed expression.

"Hassall was with that new man, Vane. He thinks she's one of the street women, Dr Burtonall. That's why they had you bleeped."

"I don't think this girl's ever called to see me."

"Your charity caters for vagrants and street people."

"Well, yes, but they come and go."

It wasn't quite true, and Clare was aware of Bruno's sceptical glance. She kept detailed records of all the street girls. The regular stringers of the Pleases Agency, and the pimpers, who owed allegiance to their pimps. The prostitutes needed protection from street violence. Both arrangements seemed to work.

"Maybe Hassall heard something about this one. Mr Vane said her real name was Dierdre Turnstall."

"Mr Hassall will catch me for a chat," Clare said lightly.

"Saves writing a letter!" Bruno fell about.

Clare watched the rest of the post-mortem in silence. The samples of blood, tissue biopsies, the slow aspiration of cerebrospinal fluid, the sampling of brain, the sections of the weighed liver, washings of the gastrointestinal tract being bottled and containered, the removal of the calvaria followed by the aspiration of fluid from the eyes, the calvaria capping the newly created space beneath after the excision of the brain in its meninges – that slow tearing sound always making Clare's teeth grate – followed by the detailed examination of the uterus and pelvic organs...

She was glad when the final suturing took place, with the massive hagedorn needles and tough twine closing the peritoneal and thoracic cavities. She felt she had been holding her breath for almost an hour. Autopsies were always an ordeal.

"Of course," Pedersen concluded, "you'd never really know, would you, if the girl was about to come and seek your help. She might be booked for later in the week."

"You could ring some of your private secretaries and find

out!" from Bruno.

The pathologist chuckled. "Bruno's just irritated that you now serve Mamon instead of the plain old National Health Service! He thinks you have unlimited servants and are paid a fortune!"

"That's about right!" Clare gave back flippantly but her heart wasn't in it. She could never keep up with the false levity of these pathologists and the technicians' ghoulish jokes.

She was saddened by the piteous sight of the dead girl's bare feet on the metal table. Could anything be more moving? Yet Dr Pedersen's remark made her think. Had she ever seen this girl? Bonn might know of her. Yet how on earth could she ask a question like that, of Bonn? If he did know of her, what then? The presence of Hassall in the hospital, having presumably left the PM suite just before her arrival, was disturbing. She had had several tussles with that shoddy, seemingly bored and lost, policeman. They were on good terms, but she didn't want another duel until she knew more facts.

By the time she thanked Dr Pedersen and Bruno, she'd taken a look at the notes. Everything in capitals. Age twenty-two, Deirdre Turnstall, supposed origin Salford, no fixed abode. Clare might find Mr Hassall in the hospital canteen, knowing he could never resist the chance of tea and a scone, but where would that lead?

Postpone, she told herself with secret relief. Delay was a sin, back in the convent school: *Clare, are you neglecting your duties? Is this a righteous approach to life's responsibilities? Write out thirty times the following admonition from St Jerome...* That would be Sister Conceptua's stern corrective. Always from St Jerome, that irascible taskmaster without whose endless reprimands no nun could make it through the day. Well, Sister Conceptua could take a running jump.

She went to the hospital car park and collected her overnight bag of fresh clothes, then pleaded an emergency at the hospital doctor's mess where she showered. She didn't quite feel ready for Bonn, but postponement for him was definitely out. She couldn't even stand the thought.

By the time she was on the A666 she was back into herself, humming a tune from the radio. The traffic was light, and she arrived in the city centre with time to spare. She dialled the Pleases Agency, and made the first possible booking with Bonn. He was poor on questions, but she could easily supply those. He could provide some answers.

Troller – one who parades the street for hire (usually female)

The woman was so pale. Bonn realised they had been speaking almost half an hour. If they went on like this there might not be time. Yet was that her intention?

Ivy Eight-One-Four had shown no move to demand her purchased rights to sex. She began talking of her childhood, her work as a cataloguer in a technical college beyond Walkden. She wore a wedding ring. Twin set and pearls, tweed skirt, brogues, neat and quietly precise, Ivy had completed a Master of Arts programme in the Open University. It figured largely in her life. Earnestly she explained her difficulties.

Bonn made tea. They seated themselves formally. Her coat put away, she nervously established modes of address ("Do I call you by a name, please?") and gravely informed him that Ivy was not an invention.

"I understand that ladies invent names," she said. "That seemed so devious, considering what I wanted, I mean."

Bonn was at a loss but dared not show it.

With only scant memories of his own early life, he relied on fragments of the lives of others. He had heard a mother admonish her child's grandfather in the Asda Mall, "No, Dad, grampas are *never* frightened!" with a sharp correcting glance as she'd managed a child's pushchair. Her father had instantly caught on. "Course not!" the old gent said.

Therefore, it seemed to Bonn, there was a well-defined set of personal standards in close relationships that must not be transgressed. One acknowledged procedures, paths along which thoughts must progress, in family, in loves. Ivy Eight-

One-Four seemed to have come to terms with her plan. It concerned somebody close, in signal departure for her. She was what, thirty-seven or so?

"I like Ivy. The name is refreshing."

She was startled, suddenly brought back to the suite in the Royal and Grandee Hotel.

"Refreshing?" She smiled hesitantly. "My mother's aunt was old fashioned."

"I like that, too."

"I was ill, you see, Bonn," Ivy said, as if reluctantly conceding a contested point. "The doctors say I'm better. It came just at the wrong time. I was leaving home."

"I am delighted you are recovered."

She smiled ruefully. "You seem not to be just saying that."

He was always surprised that words could be taken as something or nothing, meant or unmeant, according to a listener's mood. "I would not have spoken else."

"Thank you." She frowned. "I've lost touch with my son. He left on his sixteenth birthday. His father went when Eric was ten."

Bonn found no words. Facial expression was another possible misfit. He waited, wanting to take her hand now she had come this far, but that might have caused her to remember the sordid nature of her purchase and alarmed her into leaving. It would have been his failure, not Ivy's.

"Eric's in the Forces. My illness made me take stock."

She glanced at her cup, now cold, and seemed to remind herself that it was for Bonn to see to things. He made to rise but she shook her head.

"During my convalescence," she continued, not rushing, going over statements, "I heard of the Pleases Agency. Two visitors were talking. I ought not to have listened but I did." She overrode her embarrassment with a defiant tilt of her head. "I began to think. They call exercises and all that kind of thing physiotherapy rehabilitation, don't they?"

Bonn did not know. She said into the space, "Well, they do. There I was, coming home from hospital to an empty house, not knowing if I would survive any length of time. For all I know my son won't ever come back. His father's gone. I suppose I lead a sheltered life. I've never been what you might call outgoing."

Had Bonn been good at questions, he might have asked one here, why hire him.

"As soon as they told me I could go home, I rang the Pleases Agency from a hospital telephone." She laughed self-consciously. "I had to ask a lady in Gynaecology for change. It was coin operated, that thing they drag around the wards."

Bonn had never seen such a device. He nodded encouragement, wondering if even that was a falsehood.

"I was astonished that anybody answered. I didn't know what to ask."

Sitting listening, at moments like these he wanted to know how the other keys responded. Did they come out with, "What do you want from me? Shall we go to bed now and see how you get along?" Or what? Perhaps he could ask Posser if there was some way for keys, the chief goers such as himself, to learn from each other, discuss tactics. Except that was social engineering, which was always false and based on sham constructs.

"Afterwards, I had time to think. The nurse called a doctor because my pulse changed. You don't think of these things, do you? Taking decisions, I mean."

He didn't know that, either. He could have enquired how she had explained her emotional upset to the nurse, but she might have replied with a list of details, and expected some informed comment. What then?

"I told myself it was no more than I had a right to. You do see? Is that being selfish?"

"Not at all."

"They say – magazines, women's journals – a woman has to re-learn things, don't they?"

She was becoming used to his silence. He wondered if she

saw it as ineptitude. Or perhaps she was accustomed to quiet while she thought aloud.

"Rehabilitation, you see."

She focused on him, her expression not quite one of sorrow. Perhaps she saw herself as forced into this hiring arrangement by circumstances against her will, some consequence of her husband's departure, her recovery from illness.

"I want to ask all sorts of things, Bonn." Ivy sounded wistful, implying that she couldn't. "Like, what sort of women come to your agency, how they do things, what they ask you. I suppose that's not allowed?"

"I do not betray confidences, Ivy."

"I believe that," she said seriously. "Thank you. It makes it easier for me. I feel I ought to be making conversation."

"You are fine, Ivy."

"It's for me, you see, Bonn. To see that I can," she added abruptly after a pause. "That I still can. I've been so worried."

"Leave worry at the steps." It was some saying from his ill-remembered childhood. She recognised it and smiled fitfully.

"You lived in a house with steps up to the front door? That's nice. They're all gone now."

"I forget," he said.

She seemed to gain heart from his evasion.

"I would like us to go ahead." She turned to him, knees together, hands primly clasped.

"To go ahead," he repeated, making sure.

"When you did your first, well, met your first, well, lady – for the Pleases Agency, I mean – can you remember it? All of it, what you did?"

"Yes." He was uneasy at this turn in the conversation.

"Then can you – we – do the same?"

"I take it you mean everything."

"Yes. In the same order." She searched his face anxiously. "Was she experienced? Or new like me?" She coloured. "To the Agency, I mean."

"I cannot say." He could not be franker.

"But you can go through it just like you did?"

She was so earnest, facing an examination on which so much of her future seemed to depend. Bonn wanted to know why she felt the need to be shown how some completely unknown predecessor had gone through the same process. Did she mean endured the same? Faced the same use, exploration?

He wondered if it was a lack of confidence. If she trod the footprints, as King Wenceslas's page following blindly through blizzards, then she must emerge safe. Was it no more than that? If that were so, then Bonn suspected that he was failing Ivy.

"Yes."

That first session was not so many months since. She need not know where he might vary, because he always lost control at the rapturous conclusion. It would be a test of judgement.

"I wish to ask what you want for yourself, Ivy."

"Can't you see?" she asked seriously, eyes switching about his features. "It's safe for me. If you will."

"I shall, Ivy."

"Can you tell me as you go?" she breathed. "Only, it would make it all sound sure."

Like a text? he wondered. It was strange. Absolute compliance would leave spoor to his first client's identity, which would never do.

"No, Ivy."

He felt sad that she had to resort to this, tracking a precursor, as if taking up the duties of someone missed in a previous generation. So many subterfuges in relationships, in ordinary encounters. And in hiring a lover.

"I shall do as you wish. I might inadvertently repeat the lady's name."

"Against your code of honour!" she said, lips parted and eyes shining.

That phrase would do, if she wished. He noticed that time was leaving the clock faster. There was still enough, if she could be drawn along.

"If you say, Ivy."

She stood when he rose, smoothed down her skirt and waited as if for his instructions.

"I would take your coat, Ivy, and put it away." He moved to her side. "You would be on my right. I would look at your hands a while, then closely at your face. I would take you by the left hand, like this. We should go slowly into the bedroom." They moved slowly, Ivy carefully seeing where she placed her feet and looking around as if at changing scenery.

"I would be saying how I liked your expression. You would tell me that you wanted the curtains left partly open, and I would see they were exactly as you said…"

Rack walked down Raglan Road. There, the city centre grew
dishevelled between ethnic bars and factory outlets for suits
and skirts, bicycles, toys, jeans. Ebbo was there. His one asset
was he looked a waster, dross on legs. Nobody would figure
him for a suspect.

"Ebbo, I want him runned over, geddit?" Rack came talking,
gesturing, secret as gunfire. "Hollo."

"When?"

"When he gets here, stupid."

"Right."

But if anything went wrong, maybe Ebbo missing the mark,
motor not starting, Ebbo would go to the wall. Ebbo had once
seen Rack nudge a bloke off a car park roof for being late with
an alibi, and alibis were no big deal, things you just made up.

"He'll come on a bike."

"What sort?"

"Give me fucking strength," Rack prayed. "One with frigging
wheels." He stopped, raised a finger. "Don't miss."

Ebbo watched him jaunt off singing, doing some pavement
dance, bowing to a couple of old doxies who laughed at his
capers, waving to some lole barman grinning at his bar door.
Now the problem: Had he to top this bloke Hollo, or let him
live, put him in Salford General with multiple fractures or
what? Ebbo was too scared to call after Rack and ask.

He shuffled off to see about getting a motor to do the job.
He thought maybe a dark blue.

* * *

Hollo thought Rack a right laugh. See Rack swaggering along the pavement towards the Triple Racer was like watching a street carnival.

The head stander came shouting to Grellie's stringers, calling insults, replying to others, the girls smiling and pretending he was a nuisance. You could tell they were listening, heads bent to check what he'd said soon as he'd passed to yell and wave from the corner.

The Triple Racer was a few steps along Bolgate Street, top end of Victoria Square. There, within reach of Fat George the newsman facing the Asda supermarket, Grellie's blue string worked the cars trying for the Warrington exit. They trolled Deansgate but not as far as Liverpool Road, shunning Bradshawgate North because that was where the working house – actually numbers 11, 15 and 17 – stood, terraced dwellings linked by covered walks at the rear. Posser lived at 13.

Which made it all the more remarkable that the girls somehow sensed when Rack was coming. Or maybe they heard the noisy sod, him a hullabaloo.

"Watch out," Askey told the bikers lounging under the awning.

"He's a laugh," Hollo said. "Noisy git."

"Laugh? Not today."

Askey vanished inside with a long frightened face. The other bikers glanced uneasily at each other while Hollo thought, what?

The couriers affected different games. Some juggled, played chess, others chatted. They were on stand-by for messages. When Askey called a job, they went like mad, bragging afterwards about the short cuts and illegals they'd done on impossibly fast runs.

"Hollo?" Rack shouted ahead. "Come here."

"Me?" Hollo was pleased and donned his gauntlets.

"Take this to Vaughans."

"Vaughans in Raglan Road?"

Rack skimmed him a leather folder. Hollo caught it, stuffed it in his pouch. It would just go.

"Askey?" Rack bawled. "Come here."

Askey appeared with his ledger, nervously looking at Hollo. "Vaughans you say, Rack?"

"What's this I hear, Askey?" Rack grinned, put his arm round the small bespectacled man and shoved him inside as Hollo took off on his whining scooter. "You letting Grellie's bints scrap over some cret?"

"I sent to tell you, Rack. It wasn't my fault."

Rack kicked the door shut so the glass rattled. The bikers outside looked at each other, which really riled Rack. They'd no right looking at each other like that.

"Who'd you send?"

"Jee. I told her, go and tell Grellie then Rack."

Rack couldn't believe it. "You ignorant burke. Jee, when she's scrapping with Yasmin over Hollo?"

Askey stared, thinking Rack wasn't getting it. "I made her promise, Rack. She promised."

"You ignorant pig."

The ageing messenger with the domed forehead, lookalike of the long-dead comedian, had tried to do the right thing. It had gone wrong.

"Sorry, Rack." He knew punishment was due, but there you go.

"Did you check that Jee told Grellie?"

"Yes, Rack." Askey's eyes shone with relief, bottled in his thick lenses. "I asked her and she told me she'd gone straight to Grellie."

"Bints is lying cunts, Askey," Rack said kindly. "They're all colour blind, makes them liars. Know why?"

"No, Rack," Askey prompted, knowing he was in for a long lunatic theory, but not seeing a way out.

"It's the way bints feed. Ever notice they like sweet stuff?"

*　*　*

A thick-set man waited to cross the road at the Raglan
Road traffic lights. A blue motor came and stopped just as a
scooter, some mad biker in the yellow of a licensed messenger
service, arrived.

The pedestrian started across just as the lights changed
and the scooter jerked forward. The blue saloon swerved, ran
into the two-wheeled vehicle sending the messenger flying.
The man shouted and tried to haul him away to the kerb and
safety but the blue motor seemed to rebound from the raised
pavement edge and almost turned turtle.

The scooter was crushed under its wheels. The biker lay
there, the helpful pedestrian trying ineffectually to raise him.
The blue car's wheels were still spinning. The helpful man
knelt to lift the biker, but the weight proved too much.

"Come and help for Christ's sake!" he shouted.

A couple of people went forward, including some tramp-like
character. They dragged the injured biker to safety and placed
him against the wall of a bar. He was bleeding badly.

Ebbo straightened and stood back, appraising Hollo's
injuries. They looked pretty terrible, lots of blood about, and
the legs were bent wrong, one shard of white bone projecting
gruesomely from the ripped jeans.

He walked away with the helpful pedestrian.

"That'll do, y'reckon?" he said.

"Good job all round."

Aye, Ebbo thought gloomily, directing the other into a corner
bar for a drink, aye, easy to say. But if Rack comes grumbling
everybody else will dive out of the fucking windows and leave me
to carry the can.

*　*　*

An hour later, Rack still talking in Askey's, a police motor stopped and a plod got out, walked through the flock of lounging bikers and came in. His eyes took in Rack, fixed on Askey.

"You got a biker on your list called Hollo?"

"Yes." Askey checked the clipboards. "He's out, Raglan Road. Went an hour since. Should be back – "

"Won't be. He's in hospital. Accident, junction with George Street."

"Goodness gracious," Askey said politely. "Poor lad. Is he badly hurt?"

"Multiple fractures, concussion. He had this."

Askey examined the haversack, puzzled. He turned it over. "This wasn't ours. The trucko – that's the parcel to be carried – was a tan leather zip folder, unwrapped. To Vaughans."

"Vaughans rang some time since," Rack put in. "I bin here an hour."

"That's it," Askey said gratefully taking the story up. "Vaughans said they got the folder. Hollo must have picked the haversack up on the way back."

"I'll take it in, then."

The plod took details down from the time sheet and left. Rack grinned as the motor pulled away.

"Good lad, Askey." He stretched and said, "You're fined three days, mate. Put it in through Fat George on the corner, okay?"

"Right, Rack. Thanks for being reasonable."

"Okay. Ta-ra."

They all watched Rack go, him bawling jokes and nonsense to the bikers, shouting quips, walking backwards along the pavement, a riot.

Askey gave a tentative smile to Nod, one of his scooter lads, who put his head round the door.

"All right, Askey?"

"Aye, son," Askey mopped his lofty forehead. "Could have been worse. Only money. Gross take, three days. I've to pay through Fat George."

"Want us to have a whip round?"

"No thanks, son. I should have checked Jee and didn't. Rack's right. I got careless. Too much of that, the world comes unglued."

"Rack's a rotten swine," Nod said, but saying that was only protective colouring, because he was the nark who'd secretly bubbled Hollo, passing word to Rack about Jee and Yasmin's trouble with the new biker.

"Now, Nod, none of that sort of talk. Rack's a good friend to us." Askey had to say that, because he knew all about Nod.

* * *

Hassall couldn't meet his snout except in some caff on account of his fantastic new thirst. Were there illnesses that began with this endless craving for fluid? Sugary juices satisfied it best. Even his wife's lemonade would do, and it was crap.

The place he'd chosen was the road navvies' caff, Waterloo Street near the church. Zimmer would be dead obvious there, to complain he was being harassed by the police during his elevenses, which was really good cover. Hassall gave a theatrical start, sat facing the little man.

"Wotcher, Zimmer. Well, are we?"

"Morning, Mr Hassall." Nobody was more mournful than Zimmer. He did the horses on improbable tip-offs from some cousin who worked in Escho's the bookmaker at Rivergate. "I done nothing."

"So you always say." Hassall asked the counter lady for a pint of orange juice. "I'll look like a flaming orange before long. I drink gallons of the stuff these days."

Zimmer looked up hopefully from his cold tea. "That's how my brother started. He's got sugar, has jabs every day. It rots your legs, sugar."

"I'm fine," Hassall barked more loudly than he intended. Conscious that the two hauliers breakfasting near the door were staring, he grinned to patch it up.

Zimmer was supposed to have some steel tubing in his thighs after an accident. He was nicknamed after the Zimmer Frame, proving that a casual joke could stick.

"I know nothing, Mr Hassall," Zimmer whined loudly, part of his act.

Zimmer got his news by osmosis, picking up tins, cans, plastic bottles, ferrying piles of unsold newspapers to depots. Zimmer would cadge a lift on a leaf. Everybody suspected Zimmer of nicking anything left lying around. Hassall thought it the best possible concealment, always under suspicion, nobody knew of what.

"Nick him, Mr Hassall," somebody called from the kitchen. "He's a shifty bugger."

Laughter among the clattering pans, Geraldine's bass voice booming out to get on with the work because the railway hooligans would soon be in howling for their dinners.

Hassall called, "Keep your hair on, Geraldine. Where's my squash?"

Geraldine was a broad sweating man, moustache and stubble, hair fungating from his waist, greasy apron awry, always breathless. He slammed down a jug of orange with a glass and wheezed away. Hassall never reported the nosh bar for operating an illegal book, which oiled the wheels.

Hassall poured and gulped. Was this thirst natural? He'd never drunk such volumes. He spoke softly.

"Anything?"

Zimmer spoke quietly between slurps. "Some lad's done a runner from the Home."

"That's nothing new."

"This one's caused a right fucking panic. Everybody's after him. The filth – sorry, Mr Hassall, the police – have been told, but Rack, Grellie's whores, the whole fucking square's on the kee veev."

"For some kid? Why?"

Zimmer said loudly, "Dunno, Mr Hassall. Straight up."

That was Zimmer's shut-out, no more on that. Hassall capped loudly, "I never said you did."

Zimmer whispered into his tea, "There's new stuff about. Drug, looks like them wrapped firebricks. Remember them?"

Hassall almost grinned. Firelighters, they used to call them, got from the corner shop in greased paper. Dust and chipped wood, but they'd start your grate burning on the coldest morning. Did they make them any more?

"Where from?"

Loudly Zimmer did his complaint, "Honest, Mr Hassall. Don't keep on..." while Hassall acted disgruntled, "Yeh, yeh." And so on, the lorry men head-shaking at the scene, everybody knowing Zimmer was useless and the head plod wasting his frigging time, really comical.

"They're legit," Zimmer said through his clacking teeth, Hassall watching for the top gum to show with every syllable. He ought to give Zimmer money for some of that sticky denture stuff. His old auntie used it. "It's cover for appies."

Appies? Hassall thought a minute. Appies, for apple cores? Ecstasy tablets were stamped with an apple, bites out to make a stylised logo.

"Some burke makes them in a mill."

"That herbalist down the canal?"

"Nar, not him. He's grass and veg, only incense stuff and women's period pains." Zimmer looked about because it had been a longer sentence than usual, and long talk spelled collusion. "It's no good keeping on, Mr Hassall," he whined loudly.

"Who's the burke?"

Hassall was shocked because he'd almost finished the jug and was still thirsty. He ought to see someone, but the cop shop quacks were as secret as a football match. Dr Burtonall?

"Dunno." More whining for publicity's sake. "I only come in here for my tea."

"Useless." Hassall left a note on the table and shouted so-long to Geraldine. "Zimmer, get some of that tooth sticker.

You're an horrible sight."

He shut the door on the two laughing hauliers and went to make an appointment to see Clare Burtonall. What had the snout said about sugar? But when you got sugar you were poorly, and he felt quite well. Okay, more tired than he used to, but everybody felt that. She'd do some tests, prove there was nothing wrong. It would be a relief to tell his missus. She'd been on about it lately, go to the doctor's, make sure. He was due at Dr Clare's anyway, for a routine.

23 | Bunce – money, illegitimate profit

Sixteen years under his police belt, Hassall decided to run his job with secret compliance. He was no rebel. His desk looked untidy, but that was simply a sham. He looked tired – as all bad sleepers – and dressed off-the-peg ordinary, unlike some. No commendations, no medals, nothing exceptional. He'd grown up in this city.

No serious promotion for Hassall.

The younger end, arriving from Police College, were trendy and dressed chic. They scoffingly called the pol-col The Palace of Varieties, after an old music hall they were too green to have known. Jokes like that showed they'd been there, done that, got the spew-stained T shirt. They talked slang, shouted Ten-Four from dated Yank TV cops and robbers. Pathetic.

They knew the numbers of police forms off pat. Their language was abysmal, fuck and frig every second word, like English couldn't cope without crudities. Their jokes were standard *This wog wants to be this jockey, see* ... about coloureds, immigrants, women's anatomy. They were desperate to pick up chat of what they hoped were harrowing cases. Everything was a "case". They read tabloids. They were overweight.

Like himself.

But they got divorced every five years, mostly. They talked of shagging and used police vans to trip between pubs when a pal passed some police MCQ where half of them got tipped off with the answers from mates in the know.

Now he'd drawn Vane, a clean exercise freak who told him his percentage of body fat before saying hello. Vane had been engaged four years, "getting round to it". Brash git, Hassall thought. He said hello, asked did Vane get to the post mortem of Deirdre Turnstall.

"Yes. I got the copy today."

Hassall said, "Got wheels? Come on."

They went to the Bouncing Block gymnasium.

* * *

It was up steps, ornately coloured iron railings, the entrance under a hooped awning in Moor Lane. They went in and stood there while a receptionist in translucent white took down a man's details. She saw them, and said brightly that they would be seen shortly. Her teeth dazzled. Vane was impressed.

"Course, railings were only blacked when Prince Albert died," Hassall told Vane. "Before that they were all bright colours."

"Oh. Right."

"This place belongs to a syndicate." Security cameras blinked red here and there. "It owns several places in the city centre. Escho the bookie in Rivergate, the Palais Rocco bottom of Quaker Street. Lots."

"Right."

Ten minutes of claptrap conversation, nobody had come. Vane mentioned what the pathologist had said.

"One dose, forearm, lots of bruising. Tourniquet improvised. Girl really was named Deirdre Turnstall, small-time prostitution. Evidently a non-druggie, but OD'd a ton."

Hassall waited. Twice he glimpsed exercise machines when swing doors opened down the corridor, folk pumping iron and pedalling. The air was scented faintly of chlorine, sounds of echoes and splashing. He'd heard they'd had their swimming pool extended. There was talk of an Olympic standard pool in some new leisure complex, but where? The city was crammed.

"I saw that Dr Burtonall. She said where's Hassall. I passed the medical."

160

Knighthood, then, Hassall thought. He'd postponed his until Tuesday. He was worried his blood pressure was playing up. His missus kept telling him to go. "And I don't mean to the police doctor," she insisted. Chance'd be a fine thing. Clare Burtonall was hell of a sight worse than old Doc Horrocks.

What was this fine specimen saying?

"What do you reckon of that Dr Burtonall?"

"Her training, her manner? What?"

"Divorced, isn't she?"

Fancied his chances, it seemed. "Dunno."

"Reckon she'd take to a copper?"

Hassall looked his growing impatience at the receptionist. The less of this conversation the better. It always got back to the nick canteen: *Hass the Crass reckons that Dr Burtonall'd do a turn, straight up, told me...*

The receptionist had started on a newcomer, smiled her sparkling smile and prettily waggled her fingers to beg one minute more.

"Who knows?"

"Her ex is a big investment bloke, the lads say. She's at the hospital, and does charity sessions for city vagrants."

"You know more than me, then."

Vane was replying before he realised that Hassall had moved along the corridor. The receptionist exclaimed in alarm. Hassall opened one door, then a second, a third, apologising as he went. Massage rooms, steamers, people stripped and limbering. He reached the end, the receptionist trotting up asking him to please wait a second, sir.

"It's all right, miss. I'll find them myself."

The office was along a side corridor. Hassall entered. A hulk was there in tears, stripped down to a gilt loincloth. Without a word Hassall crossed the carpet and seated himself. Vane, baffled, stood with the receptionist wondering what was going on.

"I'll take it from here, love. Off you go."

"It's the upstairs," the hulk said, sniffing.

He was immense. Vane looked from Hassall to the hulk. It was a mad day. He was already forming up the tale for the lads in the social club. *Hassall the Vassal goes in this room and there's this fucking naked ape sobbing his fucking heart out, no kidding…*

"What about it, Frally? Looked all right to me." Hassall rolled his eyes to Vane, signalling don't take on.

"We've not seen the fucking flock wallpaper, though, have we, Mr Hassall?" the hulk spat in a temper. He wore eyeliner. His hair was gold. "Green and magenta?"

"What's wrong with that?"

Unaccountably the hulk stifled a laugh. He rose and crossed to the wall mirror. He let out a screech at his reflection. Hassall casually scanned the pencilled diagrams on Frally's wall, muscles shaded with cryptic notes.

"I'm a *mess!*" The body-builder dabbed and did things with tissues. "I'll tell you what's wrong, Mr Hassall. Sooner or later Miss Martina'll come hobbling up those stairs and take one *look* and I'll be begging for coppers – " he sniggered at the pun " – on Station Brough. *That's* what's wrong."

"Did you know Deirdre, Frally?"

"Deirdre who?"

"Don't," Hassall warned, frowning. "Not with me, lad. Deirdre Turnstall, deceased, spinster of this parish."

"No. I'll check the records if you like."

"Do it, then." As the hulk made for the door, Hassall said, "Don't leave the room, please."

"The records are in the clerical section, Mr Hassall."

Vane started up, "I'll get the girl, bring them, shall I?" Hassall gave him a stare. The hulk returned, stood doing his face before the mirror, from a handbag of cosmetics.

"Poor little tart," he told Hassall conversationally. "Nothing to look at. Well, those *legs* of hers. Cracked on she was only sixteen. Twenty if she was a day. They all do that."

"She ever in here?"

"No. We've strict orders to keep them out. Her bloke Set did some private judo lately."

"Got your own team, folk say."

"Wouldn't know, Mr Hassall. I'm strictly physique and health." He smiled roguishly at Vane. "Can't you tell?"

"You not a karate man, Frally? Kendo and that?"

"Certainly not! What d'you take me for?" He turned back to the mirror, tilting his head. "Fighting's degenerate."

"You teach it here, though?"

"Not me. Mallon's in charge. He positively *grabs* whole *acres* of the place for it." He glared down at Hassall. "Is it *worth* it? For a few sweating blubberguts? If you ask me it's abnormal."

"Who's the girl on the reception desk?"

"That's Nesta." Frally sniggered. "New. Brains of a gate."

Hassall rose. "You're sure about Deirdre? Never here, eh?"

"I'll ask around if you like, Mr Hassall."

"Ta. Much obliged." He reached Vane, who stood wondering what had been decided. "Let us know if you find she was. Otherwise don't bother."

In the corridor Hassall told Vane to go on. "I want the loo. Wait outside. Only be a minute."

Vane spent the time chatting to Nesta, joined Hassall when he returned along the corridor. Outside they walked to the parked motor.

"I was finding out who this Martina is," Vane told Hassall. "Nesta didn't know her."

Hassall stopped to shake his head in disbelief. "I told you to wait outside."

"Thought I'd do something useful, Mr Hassall."

Hassall resumed walking. "The whole wide world knows who Martina is. Going to the pictures with Nesta, then?"

"No." Vane was lost. He clicked his key at the car doors.

"You won't, either. Unless Martina wants you to. In which case you'll arrive with a cast of thousands."

He sat in the passenger seat. He hated driving.

As soon as they reached the bypass he reached in his pocket and hauled out a number of cuffs, belts, lengths of linen, and a B8 pencil bagged in plastic.

"I nicked them from the locker lines."

He held them up to the light one by one. You could use them like a tourniquet, if you'd a mind. And twist it tighter with a pencil. Junkies did that down the canal among derelict terraced houses.

24 | Firm – a group of goers
     | under the control of one

Food was dead easy because of the number of caffs and crowds in a rush. Jecko nicked two purses, one off an old lady in the bus station, another who was trying to find change going into a shop. Grab and dash. You couldn't do it often, especially in the same area. He ditched the purses in different litter bins in the park where old soldiers played chess, chessmen big as Jecko.

The money gave him fast grub, that you hadn't to eat for your health but everyone did, so how fucking clever were they? He bet that half the folk scoffing burgers and bacon sarnies were food inspectors. They tell you one thing – don't eat that, don't eat this – then gorge themselves stupid on whoppers, pizzas, double hammers.

Sleeping was no trouble, either. He dossed in rubbish skips because they were warm, and once in a looted motor in Foundry Street. He didn't go there again. Wouldn't, not ever. There was a disco further along, Ball Boys. Pansies showing off, screaming, though they didn't seem menacing, not like some pigs he could name. He'd left the derelict car early, glad to be out of that place.

For breakfast that morning he dared the Butty Bar, junction with Mealhouse Lane, before it was light. He liked it in there, sleepy girls serving porridge, fried eggs brown curled at the edges, toast thick as books. Well, he had liked, until the counter lasses started whispering and doing that thing with their eyebrows that acted like they'd been nudged. It meant they'd rumbled him so he scarpered.

He got grub from the Hotel Vivante kitchens in Walmsley Street up the Moorgate corner. Two waiters deliberately left good nosh out on trays, proper trays, hot with tissues on just like in a shop. A couple or three vagrants didn't mind when he showed up and shared in.

So there were good people about. But none of them would be half as good as Deirdre, who'd seen him practically shitting himself in the dark corridor, trying to escape that night, while she handed her heavy basket in to Brother Anthony. She hadn't given him away. In fact she'd made something up, said something she didn't have to just so the car lights wouldn't reveal him.

She'd saved his life. Only friends did that.

You didn't save somebody's life if you didn't like them, did you? You didn't help somebody unless you wanted to see them again. That meant he and Deirdre were pals, like. He would be her friend and she was his.

Grub and money and kipping weren't the problem, in this city where he'd been a prisoner for so long with the Christian Brothers in the prison they called the Home Orphanage.

No. The only problem he had now was finding Deirdre. She'd find him somewhere safe. She'd come with him, and they'd live together, like. He would be nine next year, which was practically old enough.

He'd been back to look at the Home. In the dark, from a distance, quivering and ready to flee. He'd seen the lights go out, heard the clonk of the last Angelus bell. The sound had made him run like the wind though nobody was after him.

He'd seen some bloke, a man smoking stinking fags, wearing pale shoes like he was making out they were proper trainers but were only leather. The man hid at the corner, and sent some girl Jecko'd never seen before to knock at the Home. She handed in a heavy basket, and that was that. It wasn't Deirdre.

That was the night he really set out to find Deirdre by asking one of the street girls where Deirdre was. He pretended he had a message for her, boxing clever.

* * *

"A what?" Geeta asked the boy.

Zoe said, "Bugger off, cheeky little sod."

That was Geeta, always amiable with kids. She was even nice to thieving brats who stole her stuff, like they knew the silly cow'd be a soft touch. Zoe kept telling her, but would she listen?

"Who'd you say it was for?" asked Geeta.

Once, Geeta had her take nicked by some schoolkids near the textile museum, and didn't scream blue murder, just said *oh, well, that's kids*. Reported it in to Grellie straight as you like, and without rancour did three extra shifts with the green string for that load of wankers at the Granadee TV studios. Grellie fined her two weeks' extra money, going purple and lashing out at everybody for a whole day over it. The girls played hell, but forgave Geeta, the silly cow. She was simple.

"Get on home, you."

Zoe clipped his ear, except he was too fast and dodged a pace off, stood belligerent. She felt for her purse in her slip belt. Still there. Some kids carried razors, slit anything for a penny.

"I've a message," he said again.

"What message? Who for?"

"Deirdre. Know where she lives?"

The girls heard this time and went pale. Zoe felt it worse and crossed herself. Jecko blanched at that and took off, darting and veering among the passengers on the Station Brough.

"Did you hear him?" Geeta said, trembling. "Did he mean her?"

"We've only one Deirdre. Right?" Zoe said.

"Unless there's new cunt on the Station Brough we don't know of."

"Find Grellie." Zoe was now seriously frightened. "Fuck this for a game, Geet."

167

A motor slowed, but Geeta signalled to Pearl and Corrie, two new girls in off the Rosslare boat, to take up the slack. One made a chopping gesture, edge of her right hand across her left wrist, agreeing yes but only if Geeta would let them keep half of the slub, the money they got for each stride.

"She's fucking soon learnt when she can push her sodding luck," Zoe said bitterly to Geeta. "New off the gangplank and she's doing deals."

"She's young," Geeta said philosophically. "Not worth a war."

"Find Grellie," Zoe said. "First things first."

Grellie was outside the Volunteer on Deansgate, in view of the stringers working the cars for her blue string. Blue was seriously under strength. A convention of architects and investors assembling at the Amadar Hotel had drained Grellie's numbers. She'd had to pull nine – nine working girls, like they grew on trees – three each from the other corners. The red string at Rivergate, south-west corner of the square, had begun to complain and ask for all sorts of rewards until she had to get wild. She was getting a headache, every girl out trolling thinking she was Queen Muck until she got straightened. Some days it was like they all decided to have a go. Once they thought they were doing other girls' work there was always hell to pay.

"Grellie. Please."

Grellie turned and glared at Geeta and Zoe. "What're you two doing over here?"

"There's some kid, Grellie."

"Geeta." Grellie was tired, now so angry she could hardly see for rage. Anybody else provoked her this evening, she'd go into one. "Both of you get back and do your strides. One more bleat out of anybody else I'll – "

"It's maybe that kid, Grellie."

Vira was Grellie's second at the Deansgate corner. A second was a girl who acted like a deputy, deciding things when Grellie wasn't around, hoping to Christ she got it right and Grellie wouldn't ballock her for making wrong judgements. Vira wasn't normally so brave that she'd interrupt, so it must be something. Grellie rounded on her.

"What kid?"

"Rack passed the word through Vivienne at the casino to keep an eye out for some lad."

"Why?" Grellie was now really incensed. More urgent news she'd not been told of?

"Nobody knows, Grellie." Vira said it uneasily, ready for a backhander even in public.

One of the blue string chirped up. "It's true, Grellie. I was there when Vivienne passed word out. It was through Tania in the Vallance Carvery."

"And you've all kept looking since?" Grellie snarled.

"I have," the girl Eileen said, bravely keeping on. "I saw a little scruff nick a pair of trainers from Timpsonly's Shoes the other morning. Nobody noticed. He'd no shoes to start with."

Worried, Grellie considered the girls' faces. She'd have a quiet word with that clumsy cow Vivienne for being shoddy with her messages, the whole world knowing something and she, street boss, left ignorant.

"Zoe. What about the lad?"

"He come up and said he'd a message to give to somebody and where'd she live."

"I didn't hear at first," Geeta added. "Then he said her name."

"Whose name?"

"Deirdre." The other girls paled and began to withdraw. "It's true, Grellie," Geeta insisted. "We must've scared him off, because he suddenly went white and hared off."

"What scared him off?"

"Don't know..." Zoe crossed herself. "I did like that, like you would."

"It was that set him running, Zoe," Geeta said. "I saw his face."

169

"You sure he said Deirdre?"

Geeta and Zoe looked at each other for support, nodding yes. Everybody was looking at Grellie, it was now her shout, a big decision to be made and them all in the clear just doing as they were told.

"Eileen," Grellie said. "Go and tell Vivienne we've news of that kid. Go now. And tell Askey I need to see Rack straight off. Vira? Take over here. I'll agree to whatever. You two come with me."

*   *   *

Bonn was on the balcony of the Palais Rocco with Rack looking down at the mogga dancing practice. The pianist was Joland, a skeletal ex-junko who did hotel foyer work, tea-tinkling every second day.

Bribery being what it was, Joland was an informer for Rack who depended on swift news. Joland was best at sports news of corrupt football deals and Olympic officials from the Continent. He had eight or nine languages. Finished up doing remember-this-oldie while dancers learnt and relearnt the Frug, the English Waltz, the Charleston, the Cake Walk ("Would you believe it, ladies, it came in during the autumn of 1900? You gents will all *remember* it, tee hee…") but earning well from Rack's IOUs.

Bonn looked down at the dancers. They were paired, none in elegant dress, just as they'd walked in. Today's instructor was Felicito.

"I wonder if he pretends," Bonn said to Rack.

"Course he does. He's never even seen Spain."

"It is a puzzle."

"No, it's frigging natural, Bonn." Rack leant over, pointing. "See Mateo? He's scared of flying, scared of ships. So he's never been anywhere. Judges expect it. Know why? Because dance judges can't walk proper. Know why? They all got expelled from school. Know why? Because…"

Because, Bonn thought. He was worried about a mobile phone.

It had been left in the room, startling him, after Clare Three-Five-Nine had gone. Prettily boxed, a card saying *With love* but no signature except a CX. Clare with a kiss.

He would reject it, and give offence. She would be upset. He suspected that, were he to read the manual and learn to operate the gadget, the first he had ever handled, it would give him some fond message, perhaps with a number for him to call whenever he had the opportunity. The stringers all round the city square carried them, talked ceaselessly while waiting to be picked up and used by car punters.

"Listen, proles," Felicito was warbling, posing in his spangled sheath. "Mogga dancing is six bars of one dance followed by another, then another, all to the one melody. Get me, darlings?"

"Yes," the dancers chorused, taking steps while he prattled.

"Very well. Joland, dear, make some decent noise for these poor clodhoppers. *One* and *two* and…"

A girl approached. Rack looked round. Bonn pulled out a chair for her to be seated. She perched on the edge, looking at Bonn.

"I got a message. Grellie says can she see Rack."

"I'm here, you stupid cow."

Rack was kneeling on a chair, elbows on the balcony rim to peer down better. He got narked when people talked only to Bonn like he wasn't there when the fucking message was for him, not Bonn. "Did she say what for?"

"No," Eileen said, her eyes still on Bonn. "Some kid."

Rack turned and sat. Martina had said something, and he'd told Toothie and Laz to do something about it but nothing had come yet. "What kid?"

"Two girls come from the opposite string. Tellt of some lad. I saw some kid nicking trainers in the shopping mall, but dunno if it was him. He said he'd a message for Deirdre, and asked where she lived."

"The kid said that?"

"Geeta and Zoe looked scared."

"Shut it."

Rack sat, eyes far away. A waitress approached, notepad out and pencil poised. Rack's gaze hardened. She hurried on by.

"I've never seen you close to before, Bonn," Eileen said. Rack clouted her. She swayed slightly with the buffet but was unfazed, just shifted slightly. She was amazed that Bonn dressed so ordinary. The way the girls spoke, she thought he'd be glitzed up, turned out like a star. He wasn't, just dressed average. Except he looked at you special, seemed sort of hesitating inside. Eileen felt Bonn's eyes. She'd never felt anybody's eyes before when somebody was only looking. It made her feel odd.

"I apologise for that," Bonn told her. "I'm sure it was accidental."

"It's all right, Bonn." The girl was pleased to say his name, secure while Bonn was there speaking right to her.

"Deirdre, though," Bonn said.

"I knowed her. She went with Set."

"The child." The words took a time coming, Rack glancing from one to the other, clicking his fingers, itching to do something.

"I can't make you out," Eileen was emboldened, Bonn speaking like words were weighed out in something truly precious, but to her alone. A crowd of women went past, all looking. "Do you mean I've to tell you?"

Rack leant close to her. "You," he said, low. "Tell Grellie I'll be at the Carvery in ten minutes. Get gone, you gabby cow."

"Right." Eileen acted like she'd scored a million points against all odds. "Ta-ra, Bonn." She paused in spite of Rack because Bonn wanted to be told of the boy. "The kid only looked a shrimp. I've a brother his age, eight, no more than nine."

"Thank you for your information, miss."

"Eileen. I'm Eileen. In the blue string."

Rack rose threateningly and Eileen fled, looking back at Bonn from the top of the stairs.

Bonn cleared his throat. Rack thought, Oh, Christ, here we go.

"Rack. I feel you could have been less blunt. The girl was only trying to help."

"Bonn, mate," Rack said wearily, like how many fucking times did he have to go over simple things? "She's fucking trouble. Bints that age, trolling their arses off and loving it, they're always trouble, see? Know why?"

"I was just disappointed you spoke thus to her."

Thus? Who says thus nowadays? Rack struggled to hold himself back from a torrent of abuse. Some tarty little bint starts chattering to Bonn when she'd been told to shut it, yacks about some girl who got herself rightly topped, bringing word of some little bleeder who might blow the whole fucking gaff, and Bonn gets upset because he hears his stander call her a gabby cow? Un-fucking-believable.

"I'll go, Bonn," he got out.

"Rack." Rack waited.

"Spit it out, Bonn," Rack said in his jokiest manner. "You've got that singer's missus, six o'clock at the Royal and Grandee Hotel."

Bonn remained silent. Then, "I apologise. I kept you back without adequate cause."

"Right. See you half-five, okay?"

"Very well."

That's another thing, Rack thought, marching off, doing his swagger, imagining he was a gunfighter in Dodge City. Normal folk say okay. Bonn says very well, when nothing's very well at all.

He started whistling as he launched himself down the bannister. All problems were limited. Keep them in the city centre, they were easy. A kid was no different. If he's nicking shoes, Rack thought, taking up Joland's melody and starting to bawl it as he passed the ticket kiosk, then he has none, right? That means he's done a runner, right? That means he can get stuck back where he came from, right?

Easy peasy, he thought, and went singing towards the Vallance Carvery. It took logic, like what he'd got and other people hadn't.

"Clinical Biochemistry gets all the best resources," Clare told Hassall, making sure that Ron Randle would hear. She gave a start of theatrical phoniness. "Oh, hello, Ron! You know Mr Hassall?"

The two said hello. "Dr Burtonall's usual jest," the clinical biochemist commented. "Taking advantage of her wealthy position. Quacks are paid more than scientists. Did you know that?"

"Yes," Hassall said. "And do sod all."

"Man after my own heart. How can I help?"

"Was it Ecstasy, Ron?" Clare asked.

She turned as Vane came in, not even breathing hard from running up three flights of steps from the hospital car park. He gave Clare an engaging grin, nodded to the men.

"Yes," the clinical biochemist said. "Methylenedioxymeth-amphetamine to me, MDMA to the uninitiated, e to its friends, Ecstasy to its victims."

The biochemist was a stocky tubby man of thirty or so, five children and a bellicose wife whose aim was to emigrate to the USA. He researched toxicants and drugs, but glumly made do with clinical biochemistry to make ends meet.

"All the tablets?" Hassall asked.

"I sampled four per cent, random. No other drugs mixed in to speak of. Did your people find any dabs? The glassies looked promising."

"No fingerprints on the plastic."

"Our people are still going through them," Vane put in.

"This drug, then?"

"Well, Mr Hassall, you're talking of a drug that's standard at every rave party. It isn't new, despite the rumours."

Randle led the way into his office cubicle, from where he could see the length of his laboratory. Seven laboratory technicians were working at benches. A radio played crashy music. The visitors found places to sit among piles of books and papers.

"It's actually a pretty old chemical," the biochemist began, looking through a tome for something to show them and immediately giving up, relying on memory. "In 1914, Merck took out a German patent for MDMA. They only synthesised it as an intermediary, an unknown compound possibly on the way to something really worthwhile. Very speculative, the way all drug firms do. Silly rumours abound about Germany's motives, of course, because our humdrum world loves a sinister plot, even if it's non-existent. The Americans had a go at it some fifty, sixty years back and never got anywhere. It was in the eighties that it crept into large scale concerts, park raves and suchlike."

"Does it do any good?"

"Whole nations have to decide that." Randle shrugged. "The Saudis ban it, under terrible penalties. Yemenis chew it most of the afternoon and buy it over-the-counter."

"Does it kill you?"

Vane gave a complicitor's smile to Clare, a forgive-my-senile-boss's ignorance glance that made him her ally.

"It's semi-lethal, in a way. Mostly, young folk die of adulterants, other substances that drug pushers include from ignorance. And of course from overdoses. Dr Burtonall will have to go on from here."

"Serotonin's the key," Clare took up the explanation. "It's naturally present in the body, especially at nerve endings. A synapse – junction between two neurones – gets triggered by the release of serotonin. That's a normal response. Receptors get hold of the serotonin on the second neurone – think of a piece of jigsaw fitting only into its receptor piece – and off the stimulus goes."

"Ecstasy blocks it?" Hassall asked. He had noticed Vane's smile, quickly dowsed.

"No, Mr Hassall. The opposite. Ecstasy causes a nasty spillage of serotonin wholesale from the synapse neurone. All that free-floating serotonin makes the recipient neurone think it's yippee time. The neurones are damaged in the process."

"Is it then that the youngsters die?" Hassall heard Vane's stifled chuckle. "Some say it's a habit drug, and pretty safe at that."

"Sometimes, yes they do. Of heat stroke, perhaps. Of massive blood coagulation, sometimes. The temperature soars. The victim can't cool down and the blood can't work properly. Neither can the organs that depend on a normal blood supply."

"It's a worry." Hassall got up. "Can I close the door? Bloody racket out there, innit? All them machines, songs making it worse." He returned, stumbling over a pile of volumes. "My problem, see, is why do some party ravers get better and go about saying it's the king pleasure drug?"

Clare suspected that the senior policeman had read it up pretty meticulously.

"Because, Mr Hassall, they get a good supplier who doesn't adulterate the tablets. Who really does supply them with a small concentration of clean e, and who doesn't sell the ravers more than one at a time."

"Wise parasites box clever, you mean?"

"That's an exact analogy, Mr Hassall. The pusher develops a regular clientele. He can sell time after time to the same youngsters. He preserves his buyers."

"Who won't give him away, or their supply would dry up?"

"You would know more about that than I."

"Can it be made?"

Randle nodded. "Any BSc could manufacture it from basic substrates. Some do."

177

"Can different batches be traced?"

"Hardly," Ron Randle frowned. "We can distinguish between two batches by reason of contaminants, and the stray trace elements in clean samples."

"Sounds very guarded."

"You might want it testified to in court."

"That's it, Mr Randle," Hassall admitted. "Caught me out! Can you do the test for us?"

"Yes, certainly."

Randle said his so-longs, then asked Clare to wait a second. Clare hung back, mystified, but allowed Hassall and Vane to go ahead.

The biochemist lowered his voice. "What are they up to, Clare?" And at her blank stare explained, "The samples have already been referred to the Public Analyst. George Makings and me were at Manchester University together. He rang me about this business. I suppose the samples are from that Turnstall girl?"

"Yes." She gazed after the policemen, looked away almost in time as Hassall glanced back. "I'll phone you. Run the fractionation, though. What'll you do, HPLC?"

"Depends. High pressure liquid chromatography's a good start." He smiled ruefully. "I've a research assistant whose first thoughts leap to electron spin resistance and molecular dipole moments, before ever he looks at a sample's colour!"

Clare laughed in sympathy. "My old chief in Cardiology grumbled just the same. He complained that his registrars felt for a nice artery to do arterial cardiac catheterisation before even feeling the pulse!" They fell silent.

"Coming, Dr Burtonall?" Vane called loudly over the lab din.

"Look, Clare," Randle said uncomfortably. "I'm a bit uneasy. Chatting about our subject's fine, but it makes me wonder what else we're being used for."

"Me too, Ron."

"Shall I give you a bell?"

"Please. See you soon?"

"Right."

Clare rejoined the others at the head of the stairs and together they went to the car park. Vane admired Clare's motor as Hassall walked on by.

"Dr Randle a particular friend of yours, is he?"

"I've known him a couple of years. A fine mind."

They reached the old saloon car. "Lovely old motors these, Clare."

"It has sentimental value." She didn't know whether to be short with him. She hadn't invited him to use her first name.

"Maroon's pretty distinctive." He smiled. She was conscious of his wish to be thought engaging and felt partly amused, partly pleased. "I'd give a lot to own one."

"On your high police salaries, I'm surprised you'd choose one this aged, Mr Vane."

"Ken to friends. Promise me you'll give me a ride?"

Before she could make some evasive reply he'd gone towards Hassall with a cheeky grin.

She smiled and got in, started the engine and drove out of the car park, wondering what exactly had happened there. Let's remember that he was a patient, she chided herself, checking the traffic flow before pulling out. One does not establish friendships with patients. Nor does a doctor have the right to take a patient for a spin in her car however keen some motor aficionado might be.

Whatever would Hassall think, if she did take Vane at his word? Her own age, more or less. Presumably unattached. Well placed, a good bet for promotion, and evidently well thought of … Stop it, she chided herself. No more of that.

She thought of the body in the mortuary. She would call Dr Pedersen as soon as she got home.

Syrup – an illicit deal based
on pay for itemised service

Along Mealhouse Lane, up from Victoria Square, the Rum
Romeo Casino stood. It was merely several terraced houses
knocked into one beyond a preserved façade. Its exterior made
no promises. Dull russet awnings wore gilt letters made to
look faded. A bouncer, his suit straining its stitches, stood
unmoving. People went in, few seeming to leave. No cars
pulled up, though many slowed before moving off.

Inside, Martina was pleased at the crowd. It was always a
good sign when the tables were rimmed with punters this early.
She entered the gloaming from the Foundry Street alleyway,
hating the thought of anyone seeing her limp. Magda was on
the bark, the reception desk that had the function of punter
clearance. Good conscientious girl was Magda, size of an egg-
whisk but the tenacity of a hound. And she was settled, as
Martina termed that docility she found essential. A settled girl
was no trouble, did as she was told.

Not like Nadine. Martina smiled to herself as she took a
seat far from the crowds round the gaming surfaces. She signalled. The lights in her corner dimmed even more, proving
that the experienced Laura was watching. Music was never
deafening in the Romeo, thank God. The Palais Rocco would
have been impossibly raucous. Loudest was the Ball Boys
Disco. Blood could flow there. Here, the clientele turned a
blind eye to any fracas.

"Martina. Like your suit."

Grellie plumped herself down opposite, shaking out her hair.
Too tight, Martina recorded with satisfaction. Done like

that, Grellie's shining hair became less of an asset, though glossies were saying page-boy was back in. Yet who was she to judge, when it was Grellie out there on the street bossing the working girls, doing her strides with the best of them? No telling what the punters wanted in a girl. Except, Martina thought in rueful judgement, perhaps there was, and this street leader knew best.

"Thank you."

One thing, Grellie was no ingrate. The supreme difficulty of any organisation was, first find an honest lieutenant. Someone to look you in the eye and tell the truth, as near as maybe. In acknowledgement, Martina did not praise Grellie's hair, sort of tit for tat.

"I asked you early, Grellie, for news."

Grellie told the Cantonese waitress a soda water. Martina had been given bottled Pennine water without having to ask. They both observed the girl's movements among the tables for a moment. Grellie pursed her lips when Martina raised her eyebrows.

"No, she's too new, Martina. I want evidence about her first."

"We don't want to lose her. A bonny girl's worth a lot, if she's right."

"As long as she's no risk."

"What risk?" Martina asked sharply.

Grellie inclined her head to signify the tables away from the bar. Waitresses moved slowly, never pausing to watch dice roll, the cards show or balls come to rest. Croupiers were in action at five tables, unusual this early in the day. The bar was hooded in shadow, its lights blacked by drinkers' shadows.

"Gambles, does she?"

"Her boyfriend does. Horses, football."

"Chalk?"

"Who knows?" Grellie could afford to be irritable. How on earth could she suss out a girl's dependence on cocaine so soon? "She's not even been here a week."

"Find out." They waited, smiled as the waitress placed the glass. "Thank you, Ah Ling," Martina said pleasantly, and was gratified at the girl's sharp intake of breath. Martina knew her name!

"Nadine, is it?" Grellie asked when she safely could.

Martina sighed, so quickly into the next problem that Grellie again wondered how much of her boss's response was sheer acting. Sometimes Grellie felt a complete absence of rapport, weirdly like talking politics to a punter while he was in delirious mid shag.

"Is Nadine taking on spare tools?"

"On the side?" Grellie stared at her soda water. The lines of refraction fascinated her. She had once told Bonn this, proud of remembering the right school word, refraction.

This was the first she'd heard of Nadine's side work. Something was seriously wrong. Martina of course should get to know, but second. Street stringers, and Nadine was one, were down to Grellie.

"Her feller put her out two, three times last week. Some sports meeting."

"In the city?" Grellie said in disbelief.

"I'm unsure."

At least that was something. Grellie stared at Martina, uncertain. Did Martina really know every frigging thing, down to the streets where Nadine had done a couple of knee-tremblers, and was she simply playing dim to let Grellie off the hook a little?

"I want you to see to something after you slap Nadine's wrist, Grellie."

"What?" Grellie almost wanted to tell this cold blue-eyed bitch to stuff her job.

Martina said nothing. Nadine approached, swinging her handbag. A smiling twenty-one, dark dress, boots with looka-me heels, shoulder length hair, a maddening pillbox hat her trademark. She received appraising glances from the punters, and scored at least two averted faces.

"Martina, Grellie, you sent for me?"

That defiance, Grellie thought, proved the cow really had been playing away. She felt her nostrils tug, slowly placed her glass. Nadine pulled out a chair and sat, smiling. Martina remained silent.

"There's nothing wrong, is there?"

"Stand up," Grellie said.

Grellie controlled her shaking hands. She wanted to strangle the cocky bitch. It wasn't like they didn't know the rules. Christ sakes, Rack all but had Martina's laws stamped into the pavements.

"What?" Nadine stared, straightening but not obeying.

"Get up, you scavenging tart."

"What's the matter?"

The girl rose, going pale. A passing couple glanced across and quickly moved on.

"You played away, stupid little cow."

"I didn't!" the girl squealed, backing away. "Honest to God I never!"

Grellie inspected her glass for motes. Instantly Magda signalled and Laura, dutying the rear exit, came with every appearance of casualness and grasped Nadine's arm.

"No noise, Nadine, or I'll stab you. Y'hear me?"

The tall besuited woman was older, a frothy blonde with gold bangles, teeth, earrings, rings. Her eyes stayed fixed on Grellie for clues what to do.

"What've I done?" Nadine was frightened, looking from face to face.

"Stay near, Laura." As Laura drifted idly a few inches beyond earshot Grellie said in a barely audible voice, "Your feller sent you trolling. You get punished, simple as that."

Grellie spun the pause out until the girl was sobbing.

"You've a job to do first. Wait over there."

Nadine retreated to stand against the wall. A sudden scatter of applause made all heads turn to see somebody lose or win. Grellie let Martina speak. It was high fucking time the bitch did, she thought in anger.

"I want Nadine to do a job, Grellie. Find that boy who ran from the Home."

"That Rupert? He's been seen about."

"Called Jecko. Maybe eight years old, they say."

"Who say?" Grellie demanded harshly, stung.

"Police."

The last thing Grellie wanted was that bitch Nadine to see her taking orders, even from Martina.

"How long have we got?"

Martina was thankful for that plural. As long as Grellie remained loyal, things need not become nasty. If she turned against the syndicate, though, everything would be different.

"Black urgent."

"Why use Nadine when you've got Rack?"

Martina avoided answering for a moment as another roar, this time of dismay, sounded from the central gaming table. Blackjack, probably. Roulette players stayed silent, poker and dice players were one prolonged steady mumble of grievance.

"Nadine will be desperate. Tell her a tale and she'll do anything to find the kiddie."

"And after?"

"That'll be then, not now. Do it."

Grellie beckoned Nadine, who hurried over and stood. Less cocky, Grellie saw with satisfaction.

"A boy called Rupert Scowcroft, nickname Jecko, did a runner from the Home. You know it? There's police notices out. Don't do a thing until you find him. Follow?"

"Yes, Grellie."

"You draw no wage, no money, nothing. Pay your own way. Find him and tell me instant, got it?"

"Yes, Grellie. What if – ?"

"Night or day, any way up, find him and tell me. Nobody

else," she added, one in the eye for Martina.

"Yes, Grellie. What if I don't?"

"You do nothing, sweet fuck all, until you get him. You don't breathe or sleep. Tell your scurf that he's up for grabs. Same for you, same for him."

"But he's rough, Grellie." A muted wail.

Grellie let the bitch see her smile. "We know how rough he is. No noise, Nadine. If I hear a whisper that you're on the lookout for the boy, it's the wet walk home for you. Understand?"

"I understand."

"Now go. Nadine?" As the girl turned back, Grellie put a finger to her lips and said, "Shhh!"

Martina watched her go and said quietly, "You're good, Grellie, give you that."

No use saying thanks to Martina so Grellie just got up and left by the rear entrance. Laura stood in the shadows to see her off the premises without hindrance, then resumed watching for Martina to sign for her motor. She wondered what it was between those two, like cats ready to scrap.

Opposites, she thought, finding a satisfactory explanation, needed no reasons to start a riot. It just came natural to some women.

*   *   *

She lay back, arms behind her head, to watch him dress. It gave her an extra frisson of pleasure, easy warmth now with all her early urgency gone.

"I often wonder about men's shape," she explained when he caught her and paused.

"We are normal," he replied gravely, resuming, his back lean and taut. "Women are different."

She laughed, then sobered, remembering Deirdre Turnstall.

"Did you know the dead girl, darling?"

186

He hauled on his trousers, stuffing in the shirt and clipping his belt, casting about for his shoes. "The dead girl."

He turned to look. Even caught out, as he was, his eyes strayed down. Breasts again, Clare thought. They were like infants, Bonn more of a child than any male she'd ever met, yet possessed of the most disturbing complex gravity.

"Deirdre Turnstall from Salford, twenty-two years old. Dead of a massive heroin overdose. Was she a street girl?"

The bed tilted as Bonn sat beside her. She felt the weight change, something moving in her heart. It always happened, this feeling of being close to tears at the distress that came. He was about to leave, maybe to serve some ugly bored cow with more money than sense. It was so unfair.

"I do not know, Clare."

"And you wouldn't tell me if you did?"

Another protracted pause. Watching him from her supine position, she suddenly understood how light obsessed portrait painters, one slight sheen along a body's contour establishing a creature's entire beauty. Bonn denied that a male could be beautiful. They'd had this out. His argument was that women were beauteous, men were simply plain shapes and that's all there was to it.

"No," he said finally. "I should respect her confidence."

"I want you to find out about her."

She explained about the heroin, the curious evidence of the improvised tourniquet.

"Deirdre seemed to have died from clumsily injected heroin. One massive overdose. A pusher," she ended, trying the unaccustomed words out as she went on, "not a user."

"One usually implies the other, Clare."

"Don't be so sad, darling. I'm sorry I asked."

She opened her arms to him and he laid his face on her shoulder. She clasped him. Her watch on the bedside table showed that she had ten minutes of him left. She would tell him that his money was in her handbag, in an envelope. It was quite a ritual. He would step across to bring it. Even if she told him to open her bag, he would refuse. She had lost all inhibitions about paying him, honestly feeling that they were unified in spite of the transaction. She felt that they had become one, like married people became a single entity in law, behaviour, trust, convictions.

It had never been that way with Clifford, so why now?

"You have a reason for asking."

His voice was muffled, his moving mouth hot on her neck. She wondered if she could phone the Pleases Agency and demand another hour, but knew it was out of the question so late. They wanted notice, reasons unstated.

"She wasn't suicide, I'm sure. Somebody killed her."

He nuzzled her, quickly moved away. It was time. She gestured. Obediently he fetched her handbag and stood waiting as she undid the clasp and gave him the envelope. She thought, I'm simply giving my man a few notes to ease his day; perfectly allowable when a couple is one. No more the anguished dithering, whether to leave money uncovered on the window sill, or under a doily, and trusting him to find the payment. She could even joke about it, when the time was right and it would not offend.

"Where is your guardian? What was he doing? While we're here, I mean."

She knew he was followed and protected by an uncouth dark-haired yobbo. Flashy, noisy, given to vanishing and making sudden reappearances. She had seen him, knew he was known as Rack.

"Sufficiently close."

"He would leap out of the chandelier if things went wrong?" Sarcasm was silly, but it came out.

Bonn almost smiled.

"He would never allow matters to reach the point where that became necessary."

"I don't think she was on my list," she told him. Awkwardly

he laid the envelope aside. Were they trained to conceal the fee quickly, slickly, and was he too embarrassed to let her see how he did it? "Most of the street girls are, including the brothel. And the goers." She now knew that the charity for which she ran the surgery was financed by the Pleases Agency. It had been a harsh realisation. "I'm afraid her death might be something…"

"Thank you." He picked up the envelope.

She hoped he would stay a moment longer, perhaps ask when she would want him again, ask about her clinic, maybe even suggest they meet away from the Agency's tyranny. He never did.

"I won't let it rest, Bonn," she said as he moved towards the door. "The poor girl deserved better. She deserved life."

He raised a hand, and was gone. She heard the door click shut and cursed herself for having bungled the last moments. It was sickening, becoming a hopeless routine. She dabbed her eyes with a tissue. Bonn had left exactly on half-past ten. She was now alone, also exactly on time, his time. Or, more correctly, the Pleases Agency's time, as bought by her, the client, and as permitted by Martina's rules that governed the syndicate.

No more wet eyes, Clare told herself in sudden rage. No more mere hoping. She would take charge of her own life. She had done that once before. She had rid herself of Clifford. Divorce had been hard, yet she had done it. Determined, a woman could do anything. There was no other way to possess Bonn.

The dead girl might be a way to gain access to the Pleases Agency. She dressed quickly, deciding to leave her bath until she reached her flat.

On the way out of the hotel ten minutes later she paused and rang Hassall from the phone booth in the foyer. He was absent, probably gone home, but she left a message asking for an urgent appointment at nine-thirty next morning.

27 | Neffs – stolen or fraudulent goods

He had the feeling he was being hunted.

Six nights he'd been escaped. Five times now he had stood in the darkness outside the Home, and twice seen that girl hand over a basket. Never Deirdre. He was frightened that she'd left the city for good. She wouldn't though, not Deirdre, who was his friend and would stick by him.

She'd seen him about to escape, and had saved him. What she did on the spur of the moment was like, well, like St Veronica that the Brothers talked about in Holy Mass. Deirdre was a saint. Maybe she was looking for him?

Whoever was following him wasn't Deirdre.

He'd gone into the loos at the bus station, seeing some bloke out of the corner of his eye. Thin, pausing to light a fag, stooping like it was windy. That instant, Jecko ducked into the loos and hid.

You did it by opening a window like you'd gone through it. Then you clung to the back of a cubicle door, leaving it ajar. That way, your pursuer walks along, sees every cubicle empty, looks at the small window, and runs out.

Jecko did it. The hunter came in, nobody about, and muttered, "Fuck." And ran up the steps. That was it. The rest of that afternoon Jecko went round the Textile Museum with a crowd of kids his own age. Got a free nosh out of it, the Museum canteen ladies reckoning they'd miscounted, the teacher only thankful she'd got her number, sod an extra.

It was a good day. He heard something about Deirdre in the Butty Bar, where he'd gone when it started raining. It

191

was crowded.

He bought a giant cheeser, loaded it with tomato sauce, and sat in the corner.

Two girls came in, grumbling about the weather. They shook their hair out, tautening their plastic hoods into a string, claimed teas and sat. One smoked. People tutted but she didn't give a toss.

It was then that the darker one said it about Deirdre.

"Deirdre's at St Runwald's Tuesday."

"Have they finished with her so soon?"

"Meg from the Bradshawgate working house was telling me. Two o'clock."

"Poor cow. I thought doctors took their bleeding time, cases like her. Farnworth General's always slow, idle sods."

"It's the police, pretending they're Sherlock Holmes."

"Love her heart."

Jecko was thrilled. Wet through and steaming, coughing whenever he moved, even so he was excited. Deirdre must be in hospital. Was she in trouble with the police, for not telling on him? His heart overflowed with love. The police, all bastards, had tortured her *and she'd not told them a thing!* You could keep St Veronica. Deirdre was best.

He heard them out, piecing together the bits he caught.

"Sally asked Bonn if she could go. She's in the green string. There's been so many fucking arguments it's a fucking bear pit over Greygate these days."

"Bonn." The darker girl breathed the name like it was her boss, maybe even more. She groaned quietly. "What'd he say? Deirdre went crazy every time she saw Bonn."

"He said of course she must, if she was moved so to do."

"If she was moved so to do!" The dark girl smiled, looking at something in the distance. Jecko craned to see, but she was only looking where there wasn't anything. "Who else talks like that? What I'd give!"

"Don't let Grellie hear you say that, Loretta." They bent

192

heads, conspirators.

"You feel the same, Polly, you bitch," the girl called Loretta said. "I wish I'd the money for Bonn, that's all."

"Go halves, you and me share?"

They tittered, glanced about to make sure they weren't being overheard. And then Polly's eyes fixed on Jecko, who didn't look away fast enough because Loretta signalled to the counter girls, touching her earring twice and tilting her head. Jecko didn't know what it was, but the counter girls immediately looked straight at him and one lifted the flap to come through, trying to look like she was about to clear some tables but aiming for Jecko.

He scraped his chair back so loudly everybody turned to see. He shoved through the door, almost flying into some old man tapping in with a stick and medals, knocking his concertina out of his hand.

Ten minutes later Polly was talking to Rack.

*   *   *

Jecko knew he'd had a miracle escape. He spent a safe hour wandering the shopping mall beyond the Weavers Hall. He was hungry. He bought fish and chips in a newspaper, went to sit in the children's play area where nurses kept children until their mothers and dads came back for them.

Nobody bothered him there, though all children's names had to be given in to be written up on the wall near the Pong Shoot and Smiling Clowns, and his wasn't.

Deirdre was going to be at church on Tuesday. That Polly said so. Two o'clock. They were Deirdre's friends, because they were sorry for her because she was in hospital. Polly'd said, "Love her heart," so they were on her side.

Hospital, though. Which hospital? He didn't know Deirdre's second name, so he couldn't ask if she was getting better. They'd only say, "What's her full name?" He wouldn't know and then they'd arrest him and take him back to the swine.

What else did they say? Something about church. His stomach turned over. He almost spewed up his chips at the thought of church, cassocks, cottas, the Christian Brothers, incense, their vile punishment machine called God.

St Runwald's. Deirdre was going there, two o'clock Tuesday.

He went to the public phone box, got Directory Enquiries, and asked for St Runwald's church number, please. A mechanical voice gave it him, didn't care if he heard or not. He remembered it, rang it straight away.

"Hello? Is that St Runwald's?"

He was shaking, kept looking about checking nobody was watching. The mall was busy, everybody pushing through because they closed the end doors at seven today.

"Yes. Can I help you?"

A woman's voice. He felt relieved, except, chilled, he suspected maybe she was a nun and they might be worse.

"I'm ringing for Mrs, er, Spencer," he said wildly, reading the name of the shop facing. "Tuesday at two o'clock. Is that the right time for Deirdre?"

"Deirdre Turnstall?" the voice said, full of sympathy. "Yes. The vicar will – "

He slammed the receiver down and left, smiling. Deirdre Turnstall! His heart sang. Now he knew her name he could go and see her in hospital. Hospitals couldn't turn you away.

| **Badge** – permission to street deal illegally in women, drugs, or stolen items

Twice yearly a small fair moved onto the waste ground at the end of Turton Street by the canal. It settled on the cinder plot close enough to the city centre to attract a crowd, proving a blessing to the tenement wives on the housing estates.

Rack took five per cent for the syndicate.

Olivio Bassani was the fairground supremo, and salted off a quiet tenth of the remainder of the revenue, in cash. He received receipts for services, unspecified, from Rack's paper expert Camilla, who had an uncle who worked for museums and banknote people. She did Martina's accounts for the Café Phryne, the genteel tea rooms established for the Pleases Agency's lady clients.

The system had worked well since Rack had arrived.

Bassani's Travelling Fayre provided carousels, daredevil slides, a feeble Ghost Train, fast food, fizzy drinks, and a few side shows including booth wrestlers to challenge after a few pints and goading bets from friends. Olivio welcomed Rack, "Here again, Rack. Culture and glam, free from Bassani!"

"Crap more like." Rack eyed the roustabouts sweating at their canvas and roping poles. "Where's the Starship, then?"

Olivio shrugged. "Electric fault, bit of an accident in Warrington, another in Lancaster."

"A death?" Rack knew there had been two, teenagers caught in twisted metal, lack of maintenance the verdict yet to come. Bassani's Mighty Delight Fayre was up against it, would probably fold, so Olivio had to be watched this time more than usual.

"Nothing to speak of." Olivio beckoned with a twitch and led the way to his trailer. It stank of cigar smoke and sour toilet water. "Siddown."

"Money, Ollie."

Olivio poured himself wine, gestured Rack to drink. Rack remained standing, listening to the various commands outside. He'd come without honches, maybe a mistake.

"Look, Rack. You and me go back, eh? I'm a bit strapped for the first few nights, okay? I want some slack, maybe a badge."

A badge was permission to deal in illicits, anything from illegal imported drugs to women, designer neffs – imitation garments and accessories – items usually controlled by Rack's distribution system.

"You asking me for a badge?" Rack knew it had to come. Ollie owed transport dues, petrol to wheels, and rent up and down the country. "Tell me you're having a laugh."

"It's bad, Rack." Olivio scratched his belly. "Worse'n you'd think. I lost my Brenda over it." He blotted an eye, gulped, poured, gulped, refilled.

"You poor sod," Rack said, wishing he was recording this so he could have a laugh telling Ollie's sorry tale to Martina and Posser.

"Ten long years. She had to go. Economy, see?"

Brenda was a West Indies lass, very costly on the gold-bangle front. West End taste, East End nous. Beautiful, but careless with blokes.

"I've stinted, Rack," snuffled Bassani, watching Rack to see how his utter heartbreak act was doing. "Saved like a maniac, and still I'm short. I've lost so many blokes from bad takings. How about it?"

"How about what, Ollie?" Rack asked as if puzzled, also acting away. He'd have been a terrif actor doing West End shows. He had a good voice. He made people stare in the streets when he'd had a few, singing. Round here they appreciated a tenor.

"You and me doing a quiet syrup."

"How would that work, Ollie?"

"Things aren't so good any more, Rack. Like, a few million fags in real genuine cartons from Holland, Belgium, the French. Shared boxes with a bit of chalk, maybe Nam Ninety, some ganja, Guaddy Gold. That was then, Rack. All from the south, the Chunnel. It was like printing fucking gelt."

Cigarettes smuggling was an old game, with hash and some heroin, and drugs from the Caribbean and Vietnam had done Europe proud.

"That was then, Ollie."

Rack never liked shaking his head. He often wondered why. Vibes, he reckoned, from his ignorant Mamma who still loved Sicily, brains of a spud. He often practised at his mirror, could do a good frown. He did one now. He had the stare of a hero.

"See." Olivio pointed a finger, gun-like. "It's this new stuff. They say it's legit, no laws against it yet. Am I right?"

"Dunno what you're on about, Ollie."

"Okay." Olivio did his greast slow nod. "That's cool, Rack, pretending you dunno. I reckon I could shift a load, with the old Eckers, MDMA, right? The kids use the two together."

"What new stuff, Ollie?" Rack honestly didn't know what the fuck the fairground owner was on about but pretended the opposite.

Smirking knowingly, Olivio took a breath and went for it.

"Look. You and me split half of whatever load you give me. I retail it to the kids on the fairground. You provide the stuff, my people sell. Night on, night off, confuse the constabulary. How's that?"

"What about my rent?"

"It'd be *instead* of your five per cent, Rack." Olivio was instantly distressed. "I'll give way on the split, settle it."

"No, Ollie." Rack pushed away from the trailer wall and stepped to the door. He didn't open it, and said, "Money first, Ollie, by this time tomorrow. Then we do your deal, okay?" He had no intention of keeping the bargain. People like Bassani, who the fuck'd they think they were?

"Okay, Rack," Olivio said miserably.

"Borrow from your pals who know so much, Ollie," Rack said brightly. "There's one thing more, though."

Then he swiftly opened the door and jumped lightly out, to see a bloke slipping round the side of the trailer. He thought, well well. Too dark to see properly, but he had an idea who to strangle while asking. Or vice versa.

"What, Rack?" Olivio stood framed in the trailer doorway.

"Forgot what I were saying. Night, Ollie."

"Night, Rack."

Rack felt irritated by events. Time he sweated something out. He thought of the porn studio. Hadn't heard a cheep out of them. People were taking the mickey. It didn't do. Let one lot diss you, soon they'd all be at it. His spirits rose, and he went off whistling.

*   *   *

The movie was almost done. Man Beast Hump was working steadily in Steela while Ironia caressed both. Gary circled, Ray trailing leads and adjusting lights while Bondice signalled.

"Keep going," Rack said from the doorway.

"What the fuck," Ray said.

"Keep going," Bondice ground out, thumbing an order to Ray, expel this wart, but to Gary she gestured keep going, keep going while it was just as she wanted. The girls looked round at the interruption. Only Steela showed alarm, Ironia only puzzlement. She was supposed to gob Hump as he pulled out of her partner, but had she to continue or not?

Rack strolled in, barely seeming to nudge Ray yet Ray folded with a loud whoomph as the air left him and he crumpled, gasping for breath and clutching his midriff.

The performers looked at Bondice. She gave a nod of res-ignation and said to cut the action. Hump wailed like a cat as

Steela moved away. Rack eyed his distress sympathetically.

"That happened to me once," he said. "Not twice, though. Put fucking years on me. Here, you."

"Me?" Gary said. "What's going on, Bondice?"

"Smash your camera."

"What?"

"Like this." Rack flailed a two-pound hammer at the camera Gary held. Blood spurted from the cameraman's fingers as the camera flew against the wall, splattering glass making the girls screech.

"Okay, you got it," Bondice said. "You're Rack, right? The message? I'll deal."

"Your cans," Rack said. "That's what you call tins of film, innit? All of them."

"Look." Bondice strove for calm. She'd been in this situation before, and the camera equipment was all Gary's. She could buy her way out even at this late stage, this thug a cretin. "Look. I'll do a deal."

"They in the other room?"

"I'll agree what you asked. Let's go for a beer. Want a girl while we settle the gelt?"

"I could have been an actor," Rack said, working on the rest of the equipment with the hammer, looking about for different pieces. He found the line of Gary's lenses and filters and tapped each one with the hammer. "It's easy, if you've talent. Right? Stay there, you three."

He glanced at the groaning Hump, then at Steela and Ironia, judging the girls against Grellie's stringers. Not bad.

"Your cans. All of them."

"Look." Bondice felt the first stirrings of panic. "The deal's still on, right? Am I right in this?"

"Phone your bank," Rack said. "I want two years' takings, gross. Got that?"

"Two...?" Bondice stared. "You're out of your fucking tree, lover, you think I'll pay that kind of gelt to scum like you."

She glared about, wanting Ray, Gary, Hump to mob the bastard in his crazy get-up, green eye shade, jeans, striped shirt and enormous cufflinks, fluorescent boots.

"Got your phone? Transfer the gelt or you hurt. You two pillocks, get the cans in here pronto."

"Stop him!" Bondice yelped, rushing at him.

Rack batted her to the floor and kicked her for stillness.

"Shut it. Do as you're told. Bring them in."

Gary moaned, clutching his battered hand. "My fingers are broke." Ray was still crumpled, wheezing, on his knees.

"Use your good hand." Rack was still searching for camera equipment, smashing each bit he found, keeping an eye on everybody. "See what happens when you don't pay heed. I sent word often enough, didn't I?" He stooped over Bondice. "Didn't I?" he yelled.

She gazed up at him, like this couldn't be happening to her. She was a woman and he'd swatted her down. Her nose was bleeding. Rack violently kicked her leg. She screamed.

"I said didn't I?" Rack bawled, raising the hammer.

"Yes! Yes!"

"Speak when you're talked to, you ignorant bitch."

Casually he searched for more gadgets to destroy while Gary went into the next room and fetched cans of film. A quiet bloke in working clothes accompanied him as he returned.

"That all, is it?"

"Yes, Rack." The man looked at the girls.

"Keep your eyes in your head, Akker."

Rack had run out of things to smash. He cast the hammer at Ray with a mutter of annoyance. It struck him with a faint click as a rib cracked. He shouted briefly, instantly subsided as Rack glared.

"Rung your bank yet?" he asked Bondice. She reached for her phone, painstakingly took it from her handbag and dialled. Rack passed her a slip of paper.

"Transfer all the takes to this number, right?"

He waited, humming, while she gave instructions. She needed spectacles to read the destination bank's account codes. Steela and Ironia watched, trying for cover on the bed. Hump was spent, sweating and breathing heavily.

"Done it? Right, mate. You." Rack pointed at Ray. "Smash all the phones you got. Use the hammer."

He nodded approvingly as Ray destroyed the cell phones.

"Now her left leg. The cow won't have handed it all over. Bitches like her always think they can get away with anything. And get the knee."

Ray babbled and Bondice wept but Rack beckoned the workman forward.

"If he hasn't done her on a count of three, do his shoulder."

"Right, Rack."

Rack spilled the film spools from the cans while Akker stood over Ray as the assistant dropped the hammer gently on Bondice's knee. She screeched and tried to crawl away, pleading and gasping promises, bribes, anything. Rack sighed, gave Akker the nod to do it properly. The three actors sobbed and wailed while Akker smashed Bondice's knee. She had fainted as Akker battered Ray's shoulder with three swings of the hammer.

"Right," Rack said, glancing round as if seeing everything was as tidy as he wanted. "Fire it, Akker. I'll be in the Volunteer until sixish, okay? See you."

"Okay, Rack."

Akker stood over the tangles of film and looked round at the others, all staring at him in disbelief. He brought out a gold cigarette lighter.

"Ready everybody? You can stay or go. As you like. On a count of five. Ready, steady..."

29

Goldie – one of indetermi-
nate colour or doubtful loyalty

It was the day following.

"I wonder what we'd have been to each other in different circumstances," Clare said, dressing slowly to extend time against the clock's impossible odds.

Bonn took an age to reply. She felt a mite irritated. Was it so necessary to ponder as he did? Had they not made love moments before, Clare would have been exasperated. She checked her stockings for ladders, tutted at finding a pluck.

"Perhaps the same."

She turned to watch him throw on his shirt. He didn't really care about clothes, though most youths did, she knew. Young male patients were worse than women, meticulously folding their clothes in her surgery. Not Bonn.

"Would we?" she asked. Her turn to think. "If you were a clerk or a taxi driver, how would we have started? What might we have said?"

He sat on the crumpled bed to consider this. Finally, "I think your allure would have been as it is now."

Her heart lifted. He must mean that he had been instantly drawn to her. She could recall only the annoyance she'd felt at his continued apologetic look. It had been in the hospital grounds. Bonn had saved a child from an irate male swan, dragged the little girl from the water away from the angry bird's beating wings. She'd treated broken limbs from a disturbed swan's attack before now.

"But how would you have begun? Asked me out or what?"

He shook out his trousers, stepped into them, hauled and

clipped the belt, careless still.

"I might not have."

"Might not have what? Dared speaking?"

"Probably, no."

She hadn't felt any convincing urge to see him again after the first encounter, had she? And she certainly couldn't have predicted that the determined conviction she now felt towards him would become likely. In fact she'd been only faintly disturbed, almost as if with a clinical interest. He had seemed enigmatic, she merely curious.

Her shoes were suddenly there. She must have kicked them off earlier, but Bonn knelt to put them by her feet. She moved her toes and obligingly he slipped them on her.

"Let me look."

She took his head in her hands, examining his features closely.

"Did you know, darling, that symmetry is almost an imperative in psychological attractiveness between men and women?"

"No." Even that took a full minute.

"The male is influenced mostly by the woman's external appearances. Women aren't, not quite so much."

"I do not follow."

She felt a furious urge to mimic in cruel falsetto, *I do not follow*, to try to madden him, but she would only wound and he would withdraw. Who knew what harm that might do? Her hands still held his face, feeling his skin, examining him minutely.

"Charles Darwin wrote that." She tried to smile. "Women respond to males of high status who command vast resources." She kept her tone light. "It all seems to do with reproductive efficacy, from prehistory. The cave thing."

He listened while she told him about facial symmetry.

"I cannot believe that everything is determined by looks, Clare." He wanted to say more. She waited. "I feel that perhaps you know too much about the human."

"People always think that." The notion annoyed her. "They assume that we doctors aren't human. They're wrong. We have feelings."

"Please do not take offence."

"Male hormones make the jaw extend so that the man's lower face is proportionally larger than a woman's. The woman gets a larger lip volume, making her mouth more appealing. See? Those facts can't be challenged, darling. Neotenous, is the in term for juvenile characteristics."

"Women do not have childlike shapes."

She almost laughed. Her attempted explanation was becoming difficult. She pouted, placed her mouth on his a moment.

"True. But fat goes where it is ordered to go by body chemistry, and that decides a person's contours." She stood, arms out. "Look at me. Not quite the hourglass figure, but getting on that way. The waist-to-hip ratio is a hormone thing."

It was suddenly less amusing and she couldn't go on. Deposits of fat in the woman's gluteofemoral areas were used up in child-bearing, especially during late pregnancy and when providing breast milk for a new babe. She had heard several colleagues argue whether a high waist-to-hip ratio – essentially meaning a thicker waist – possibly evoked some dim primitive memory in the male, implying for cave dwellers that a woman might be old or already pregnant and so of less value to competing tribesmen in prehistoric times. It was disturbing. She wished the conversation hadn't begun.

Not only that, but modern dieting fads among women all seemed directed at reducing the waist-to-hip ratio and abdominal stoutness, suggesting atavistic impulses to display health and possible fertility as courting offers to a seeking male.

She resumed dressing, quickly averting her attention and openly checking the time as if suddenly reminded that she was due elsewhere.

"It's in the eyes, Bonn," she said, smiling, taking position before the mirror but unable to avoid watching his response in the reflection.

"Beauty in the eye of the beholder."

"That's it. The retina isn't just a simple plank of ganglion cells. They overlap in concentric circles. The edge between light and dark cause a particular excitation. All around, adjacent cells become dulled, while they are terrifically stimulated and tell the brain cortex so."

"Contrast," he said, surprising her. She'd assumed she would have to spell it out.

"That's it! The brain detects contrast and sees it as alluring. So we women …"

She waited, prompting, to see how far he could reason.

"Put eye shadow on," he concluded gravely, "to make your eyes more distinctive."

"Yes! The Ancient Egyptians knew it. Chinese Dynasties knew it. White faces, dark eyes. Pale and interesting to Jane Austen's generation meant exactly that."

"And now the neurology."

She smiled. He'd sensed her aversion to the previous conversation and was helping her to turn it around.

"The limbic system, if you want to look it up, darling." She was almost ready to leave. "In the deepest recesses of the subconscious limbic system, pleasurable sensations are created when you see contrasts in a woman's features."

"I do not believe that attraction is so mechanical, so reflex."

"Women know it instinctively, bring it to surface consciousness. Those hundreds of magazines are about nothing else."

He was dwelling intently on her words now. She became worried. What on earth had she started?

"The different halves of the cerebral cortex do different things," she said, making sure she'd left nothing about the hotel room. So embarrassing, to have to return for a handbag or purse. What on earth would the receptionists think?

"Left and right."

"Yes. The left is language, the right facial characters. The woman is better at left-brain things. The man at what shrinks call visual-space aptitude."

"Actors' best sides."

"Psychologists rate the right-hand side of a woman's face the more beauteous to humans. The left isn't so lovely. In men, there's no difference." She was smiling now, confidence restored. Bonn rose, and together they went to the door. "No face is perfectly symmetrical. The left side – the uglier! – is more expressive than the right, in everybody."

"I wonder if they teach actors that."

"Babies can spot an attractive face at twelve to thirteen weeks. So we all know it without having to learn. And don't ask!" she warned as they paused just before leaving.

"Ask." He frowned.

"Ask if knowledge about sexual matters is a deterrent to a woman doctor."

"I had no such intention."

"I know," she said, surprising herself, because she had known that nothing would be further from his mind. "I think you're unique."

"As you, Clare," he said gravely, and opened the door into the corridor for her.

She'd intended to embrace him before departing, steal a moment as usual, but she suddenly found herself merely saying goodbye. She would have turned to look, at least exchange confiding glances, but a noisy couple were already in the corridor heading for the lifts.

The door closed quickly and inaudibly behind her. Bonn was always so careful and self-effacing. She might have stayed here alone, as solitary as she always felt when leaving afterwards.

It wouldn't do. More especially, she told herself angrily, my giving him nervy lectures on the physiology of sex between genders wouldn't do either. What on earth did I go on about it like that for? It concerned her hopes for herself more than anything. Foolish.

Foolish to talk with him in such a fashion. There must be no more of it. She'd been really uncomfortable going on about

207

fertility characteristics and attractiveness markers. Cut it out, Clare, she cautioned herself. This business is strictly financial and social. Keep it as entertainment, if you can. Her real difficulty was that she had so few clues to Bonn's thinking. She must find other ways to him. He already reached well into her.

She headed for the clinic. Her phone bleated in her car, a message from Hassall asking to see her. Why did he want to see her? She must face him down. She was doing nothing wrong.

Rack drove Bonn to St Runwald's presbytery and parked, listening to Radio Four crap while Bonn knocked. Rack had still to do over two of Grellie's lasses who'd begun milking punters free, but that was background, like breathing. He worked out a theory of churches while Bonn stood in the rain waiting. Rack reckoned church was a government thing, backed by mafias. Else why so much bingo?

He didn't like the thought of Bonn going to see these folk. Mamma was bad enough, praying to fucking candles night and day and wanting him to do the same, daft bitch.

The door opened and Bonn did his speech. He was a friend of Deirdre Turnstall's and asked about the funeral. He was admitted by a silver haired lady.

"I'm afraid Reverend Arkwright is out on visits," she told him. "You could wait, but he's at Stalybridge and Miles Platting today."

"Thank you." He did not sit. "I trust there are funds for her service."

"I haven't heard, but then that isn't my place."

"I wish to reimburse the parish, you see."

"Thank you. Reverend Arkwright will be pleased."

They stood awkwardly. "Some child rang to ask. I had the feeling he'd rather forgotten the message." She smiled indulgently.

"A little boy," Bonn prompted.

"Yes. Two or three days ago. The reverend had only just pencilled the date in. For a Mrs Spencer, the lad said."

Bonn cleared his throat. A direct question was worth it in

the circumstances.

"How did he speak of her, please?"

"Deirdre, he called her. Deirdre. As if he knew her. I'm sure he said for a Mrs Spencer. Perhaps a neighbour, or some one hard of hearing. I looked for the name on the parish register, but we don't have a parishioner of that name. He seemed pleased." She smiled. "Like my grandchildren, delighted to have done something right."

"And you answered him."

"Yes. I told him the service for Deirdre Turnstall was on Tuesday afternoon at two o'clock."

"How exactly did he ask?"

The housekeeper became wary, things were taking an unexpected turn. She would have to give a summary of this visitor to the vicar and was becoming unsure.

"He said when was Deirdre's service. Just like that."

"He didn't use the word funeral."

She thought a moment. "No. Service, he said."

Bonn thanked her and left. He signalled patience to Rack and went to read the church notices in the porch a while before returning to the car.

"Some lad rang the church. I think he'll be here on Tuesday."

"How the fuck did you work that out?"

Bonn said, "The housekeeper told me."

"Just like that?"

"Nearly." Bonn stayed Rack by a gesture. "It's the best we can do. He intends to be there. I'm sure of it."

"Okay, Bonn. But Martina will be fucking furious if somebody doesn't tell her."

"I shall be sad if anyone goes to ask the housekeeper any further questions about the child. She knows nothing more."

Rack said after a while, "Right."

He couldn't bear one of Bonn's long reproachful silences. Worse than any ballocking. He decided to keep to what Bonn said, though it went against the grain.

"You tell Martina you said not to, if she goes fucking nuclear, Bonn, right?"

"Right," Bonn said. He reclined the seat and closed his eyes for the journey back to the city.

*　　*　　*

Bonn called in to ask Askey to pass on any news of the missing boy to him. He saw the messenger's face blanch.

"I was told Rack would clear everything, Bonn."

"So I hear." No rebuttal, though. Askey was still in the dark.

"Ta for the stair lifter thing, Bonn."

The diminutive clerk accompanied Bonn to the pavement. At the warped tables, bikers fell silent as Bonn passed.

"The gratitude is all mine, Askey."

The bikers watched Bonn walk off.

"How'd he reckon that, Ask?" Nod wondered, mystified. He knew that Bonn had paid for the installation of an automatic chair for Askey's handicapped sister, save her climbing stairs. "What's wrong with somebody saying ta?"

Askey shrugged. He was worried about Bonn's request.

"She said tell Bonn she was pleased, so I did."

He went back inside, wishing he could get out of the contrary orders he was lumbered with. Tell Rack first about the missing lad. Now tell Bonn first. If he obeyed Rack, then Bonn would be sad. If he obeyed Bonn, Rack might break Askey's legs or burn the Triple Racer, the firm he'd built up over a lifetime. He didn't know which would be worst.

But he knew he would tell Bonn before Rack. He poked his head through the hatch into the fading light and reminded the bikers to keep on suss about that running lad, eight years old.

The riders said right, okay, Christ's sake don't fucking keep on.

"Just don't let him by, that's all," Askey said miserably, and lowered the hatch. It would go wrong. He just knew it.

* * *

"Diabetes, Mr Hassall."

"I've got the sugar?"

"There are basically two kinds," Clare said. "One comes on torrentially, as people say. It's more associated with young folk. The slower sort can sometimes be controlled by diet, with maybe oral medication. The first sort's stormy, needs insulin injections and diet."

"Is it...?"

"Normal life expectancy in your case, Mr Hassall. That's if the patient behaves!" Clare smiled to make it kindlier. He was almost distracted. "Do your police regulations allow you to stay on with a metabolic disease?"

"I suppose I'll have to go before a board." He hesitated. "Will you come and testify?"

She was surprised. "Don't you have your own police doctors? I know two colleagues at Farnworth General who – "

"So do I," he said bluntly. "Sorry. It's a bit unnerving."

"I'll give you a load of pamphlets. There are really marvellous societies, support groups, all free of charge and willing to help. Or you can come back to me."

"Thank you." He felt stiff. "I don't quite know what to ask."

"The horror tales are not all true, unless you become helpless. If you take charge, you should get along fine. There are complications, as with any disease. I'll run over a few things to watch for. Then go home, tell Mrs Hassall, and come back to me soon as you like. I'll want you to get on regular monitoring. You'll need somebody to give you once-overs."

"Was all that questioning necessary?"

She had interrogated him closely about his family history.

"Sometimes it has a family bias. There're reports of hamlets in the Middle East where diabetes is commoner than not having the disease. Overweight, inaction, they're major contributors

212

to the adult-kind diabetes. It's increasing, of course, seeing we all eat too much and don't exercise so much."

"Is it curable?"

"We have no magic wand, Mr Hassall. The excess sugar in your blood gets eliminated by the kidneys, hence the thirst – you need enough water to excrete it. Think of it in simple terms like that. Manage yourself within the limits the Diabetes Clinic sets, you should run your full course."

"Is it genes?"

Clare sighed. "If you want me to say that somebody's spotted a new gene, and we can simply rub it out, no, Mr Hassall. It's not that simple. Fatter people are four times more likely to get your kind of diabetes than those who keep their weight within reasonable ranges."

"Why this clinic?"

"Heart, vision, renal problems, circulation, neuropathies, all can follow uncontrolled illness. It's our aim to lessen their likelihood." She smiled. "You'll meet scores of people who're fitter than most of your police in the clinic, Mr Hassall, all doing well on sensible foods and brisker activities. It isn't a training schedule," she said, trying to encourage. "It's an adjustment. And don't think of yourself as a doomed invalid. You're nothing of the kind. You're entering a different life pattern. Bring Mrs Hassall if you like."

"Thank you." He moved to the door, holding his hat. "One thing. Will you still be in charge of the reference checks?"

"On the police? Why, yes," she said, surprised, "unless you've heard something to the contrary."

"No, no. Nothing." He smiled, nodded, said his thanks and left.

Clare looked at the door, heard him say goodnight to the new receptionist, and leant back.

Was there some warning in his remark? She thought of Ken Vane. Surely Hassall couldn't have intended his casual question to mean that he knew of her chats with the young officer? And where was the harm anyway?

Yet there was no reason for Hassall to have brought that up just as he was leaving. She'd had no clues from the police about a replacement doctor for the hospital series. Those tests all stemmed from her own work, begun a year or so ago.

Uneasy, she thought of Ken Vane. She liked him, though he was full of himself, and very different from Bonn. But she was allowed, she thought defiantly. Heaven's sakes, why make things so complicated? There was a kind of simplicity to seeing Bonn, while meeting Ken was somehow tangled. She couldn't speak freely with Ken Vane, and she could say anything to Bonn and knew it was safe.

And conversation was so different. She got answers, immediate and amusing, from Ken, whereas Bonn suffered long silences before a reluctant reply that sometimes drew her in deeper, sometimes against all wisdom.

She sighed. Probably Hassall was just trying to distract himself from the news of her diagnosis. That was probably all it was. Anyhow, what had happened? Nothing, that's what. Yet.

Clare often found that daytime annoyances were more justifiable. During the night even slight irritations fanned themselves to unreasoned anger, that could take control of sleep.

In the dark hours that night, the image of Deirdre Turnstall's body kept recurring. So small, dissected on its stainless steel slab, the water runnels kept assiduously clear by the laconic Bruno while the pathologist whistled with irksome tunelessness, driving her mad. She found herself awake, trying to identify the melody. To shut her rambling brain up, she decided that it must be something from *La Boheme*, as if night thoughts mattered.

In the same mood of self-rebuke, she phoned the Pleases Agency next morning, using her mobile phone and found that Bonn was booked up. She felt outrage. What did that mean, for God's sake? Surely he couldn't be consorting with inadequate women the entire day, could he? Wasn't he allowed to have a meal, a rest? Dismayed, feeling abandoned and quite lost, and conscious that she was revealing her disappointment, she demanded to know when he would be free.

"That would be tomorrow," the quavery voice trilled. "Does madam have a preference as to when?"

Clare rudely disconnected. "Yes," she said viciously to her living-room. "Yes, you senile bitch, madam certainly does have a preference as to when. Madam pays your wages, you daft old bat."

For a few moments she sat fuming. Who exactly was the client here? Whose money supported these people? She wasn't some bimbo, to be told to wait, like a Victorian wallflower at a coming-out ball. God Almighty, she was a highly qualified professional woman who paid the Pleases Agency through the nose, and had a perfect right to prompt service.

She had a special bond with Bonn, and he with her. Wasn't that enough? She broke a cup and saucer by carelessly trying to adjust their position on the coffee table, thus ruining the whole set. She wanted to blame everybody for that, too.

Bonn ought to make them give her concessions. He was too weak, a typical man. Where was the harm in simply putting her through, allowing her a few words with him on the phone? Surely she had a right? This was intolerable.

The Palais Rocco might be a chance, except it was too early. Waiting in a hotel foyer might work. The thought crossed her mind, but what on earth would she say if he arrived with some strange woman, another client? And the abject misery of loafing about, pretending she was a legitimate hotel resident would be shameful. The despicable image almost made her lose control. Sister Conceptua in the convent had been adamant about etiquette : *A young lady must always consider whether she is lowering herself in social intercourse, for in the evaluation of others lies apparent worth, girls; never forget the dangers of impropriety...*

The ludicrous recollections of her useless convent education calmed her. She worked out possibilities. There was one place worth thinking about.

The Café Phryne. Using that little establishment, she'd successfully reached Bonn before. Her exasperation growing, she decided she was perfectly entitled to call in for coffee, perhaps, get the counter girl to accept some message. The bloody place should earn its keep.

Thirty minutes later she walked into the Café Phryne, and took one of the alcove tables.

*   *   *

It was quiet, only a scatter of a dozen women at the tables. Effete wasp-waisted young men wafted sinuously about, confiding the café's menu in whispers. Clare was impressed however by the décor, always convincingly different. The theme this morning was bookish learning. Floral pages from illuminated manuscripts were displayed among real flowers in the wall recesses, so cunningly lit that the brightness seemed created by the displays of writing materials, scrolls, leather volumes and arcane parchments. Cleverly inviting, such skill.

Carol, holding her position as the café manageress against a score of rivals on Martina's staff, coolly hid her recognition of Clare's arrival. The doctor, she knew, was addicted to Bonn. This was not the first time that she had come in quest of her hired lover. Carol attended to her register by the entrance.

A waiter arrived to take Clare's order. He was perfectly shaped for dancing, impossibly slim with his phoney gentility.

"What would madam desire?" he asked as if in strictest confidence. "I recommend the torte this morning. Grifton loves doing those. Madam would not be disappointed."

"Yes, please, Angelino." Clare read his name on his waist-coat. "Rather strong Turkish."

"As madam pleases," he said icily after an almost imper-ceptible pause, and eeled away, lips set thinly in disapproval.

Clare glanced around. This was the time, she knew, that had she smoked she might have taken out a cigarette and have it lit for her by a dozen eager waiters. She sighed. Elegance suffers when pollution fades.

She approved of the absence of bamboo, the ubiquitous decoration that supposedly represented perfect adornment of any hotel, restaurant, public forum. The Café Phryne's display was restrained, its intentions clean and sparse. The girl was worth her weight in promotion, Clare thought. No wonder they kept her on. She smiled, seeing in one recess opposite a carpet page of the Lindisfarne Gospel, outstanding in its dark

217

reds, russets, gold and muted ochres. The accompanying flowers were brilliantly chosen, freesias infrequent, green fronds and ferns almost absent. A lovely series of set designs. She tried to work out if there was channelled lighting. Had the girl used reflected daylight from some impossible prisms?

"Good morning."

Clare looked up, startled. The woman must have only come from a couple of tables away.

"Good morning," she said uncertainly.

"May I sit down for a moment?"

Uninvited, the woman sank to the chair opposite and placed her elbows on the table. She was middle-aged. Clare recognised a face-lift, saw the slight tension of the skin over the facialis and the orbicularis oris muscles. A skilled cosmetic surgeon had done the second of the lady's two operations, Clare thought grudgingly. Private, highly paid. Her clothes were the best of Lavoisier Chic's season.

Was she a patient, Clare thought with swift dismay, about to discuss Farnworth General Hospital?

"I take it you are here for the same purpose as I am," the woman said, smiling. "My friend and I were just wondering if you might like to meet, to discuss our encounters. Compare notes, that sort of thing."

"What sort of thing?" Claire asked blankly.

"Our … meetings. You *know*. A friendly get-together. We could meet regularly, perhaps. It would be a kind of sharing."

"Sharing?" Clare was hopelessly out of her depth.

"Experiences. It seems such a good idea. You're bound to have a totally different slant on your … on your special times. It would be so interesting, don't you think?"

She leant closer then quickly withdrew as the waiter arrived to distribute Clare's coffee and torte. He flourished a serviette, and demanded if the newcomer wanted to be served. The woman let him glide away.

"It's only the same as shopping, really, isn't it? You like this one, I like that one. We compare notes, prices, how … rewarding each encounter actually was. And how beneficial!"

She laughed, glancing round her shoulder at her friend, a plumper older woman who was smiling encouragingly in Clare's direction.

"I'm afraid I haven't a notion what you mean." Clare waited. Waiting could be a weapon in these circumstances. She refused to let any sudden realisation dawn in her eyes, giving nothing away.

For an instant a faint doubt showed in the other's expression, quickly followed by anxiety. She glanced round for support.

"Some of us – well, really just me and my friend – were wondering…"

"Yes?" Clare smiled, eyebrows raised. "Is this something to do with the ex-patients' group?" She allowed the pause to extend before adding, "My rehabilitation unit at the hospital?"

The woman paled slightly. No more confidential smirks to her friend now, Clare saw with satisfaction.

"I think I must have made a mistake." The woman rose slowly. "I'm so sorry."

"Only, if it is," Claire coursed on with growing enthusiasm, "you might like to ring a number I could give you. They meet Thursday afternoons. They've begun a new fund-raising campaign…"

The woman rejoined her friend after a burbled apology, leaving Clare in control.

She had the coffee and part of the torte – far too sweet – then left giving the intruder a bright good morning. She said nothing to Carol.

The interruption had disturbed her. She emerged into the market, crowded and boisterous at this time of day, and started along the narrow pavement towards Rivergate. She had only gone a few paces when Vane joined her.

"Slumming, Clare?" he joked, nimble on the kerb. "They're all rogues here."

"Colourful, though, Mr Vane."

"Have you relented?" he asked, deliberately slowing his pace to get round the stalls.

"Relented?"

"I asked you out. It needn't be in the city. Somewhere outside, like the Pier. It's up-market nowadays. Not that you'd remember it from times when it wasn't."

She smiled. The man was agreeable, and at least it would be somewhere different, something new. She felt suddenly tired, wearied by the endless tension of loving Bonn, the sordid struggle with the frail-sounding crones at the Pleases Agency. Did that give her justification? Heaven's sakes, it wasn't a life-long pact, was it? Not even a date.

Loyalty was the most draining conviction, especially loyalty to the unattainable. She was arguing to convince herself. That had always been her tendency, persuading herself out of boredom.

Yet why not? She might hear something from Ken Vane that she might otherwise never learn. And information might help Bonn.

"If you promise not to go on about police procedures," she said lightly.

"Really? Great!" His enthusiasm was infectious. For a moment there she felt that she had done the right thing.

They settled on the same evening, about seven. She insisted that she would drive herself to the restaurant.

"Spoilsport!" he complained.

She laughed. They parted at the corner of Victoria Square. She walked on to the Weavers Hall shopping mall with lightness in her step. The reasons she had discovered for agreeing to meet Ken Vane were fairly sound, so she knew she had struck a blow for freedom. From what, she couldn't imagine. She must think, and work it out afterwards.

32

Honcho – one who enforces order (esp. at a place of illegal activities)

Martina sent for Bonn at eleven-thirty that morning. Rack wanted to come too but Osmund in the Shot Pot said Bonn was wanted alone. Rack stayed among the snooker tables, cueing and shouting, disrupting games down the length of the place.

Bonn was fetched in a panic by two girls from Grellie's yellow string at the Moorgate corner. He had walked quickly, not pausing even when signalled by Grellie from the bus station. He entered the cubicle and stood as the miniature space closed, wondering idly about secret cameras. He read the ancient newsprint curling on the green beige wall. It was a full minute before the buzzer rasped. He pushed the side wall and went into Martina's office.

Nowhere to sit. Plain empty desk, but for one sheet of paper and a virgin pencil. And the beautiful Martina.

"Your Clare Three-Nine-Five consorts with the police, Bonn."

He said nothing. Part of Clare's work involved forensic medicine. It was bound to, seeing that she coped with itinerants, addicts, and the Pleases Agency's working girls. What could one say?

Martina was cold. He recognised signs of a blazing temper. In other circumstances, he might speculate on paranoia as an adjunct to power, but not now.

"Are you being deliberately stupid, not answering?"

"I heard no question."

She held anger back. Why did he use her name so sparsely? Another person, even the appalling Rack or the quiet killer

Akker would have added her name, if only to mollify. Bonn eked words like blood. He was intolerable. She decided to give him facts, tie him down.

"Your friend was in the Phryne. She met Vane in Market Street. They arranged to go out. Carol saw them. Harry Tath at the pottery stall passed word to Fat George."

Therefore it must be true. Bonn was puzzled. Accidental? Or Vane deliberately making the encounter seem so? Which suggested the policeman had been waiting, sussing out her movements. Amorous intent, or something to do with crime, were two possibilities. Was there a third?

He still had nothing to say. His "friend", though? And "his" Clare Three-Nine-Five, when she was by definition the Pleases Agency's customer? What words would suffice when Martina was in a towering rage? Martina had to be deflected from the consequences of her own actions when she was like this, or she might give some order that would be utterly ruinous. No going back, no emendation. She might then be left there, isolated and aching.

He would have to deflect her from what might prove irreparably damaging to her.

"I wish I could help," he said. It sounded pathetic, miles short of argument.

A wife of a multiple stores owner from Southport had been a client the previous week. Pattie Six-Two-Three was hooked (her term) on golf, and tried to insist that he get the Pleases Agency to allow him to accompany her to Lytham St Anne's, where there evidently was some golf club. She had been furious when the Agency refused her. "They've got to heed you, Bonn!" she'd cried in outrage. A formidable compelling figure, she was used to getting her own way – also her own description. She had already told two golfing friends that she was bringing a special young man as her new golfing partner. She simply couldn't turn up without Bonn.

Her truly violent argument had begun almost half an hour

after dressing. Bonn had stayed more or less out of it as she stormed on. She had even gone so far as to dial the Pleases, of course getting nowhere. Bonn guessed that she drew the tremulous Miss Hope, no logician, who had obstinately stuck to her few permitted sentences in reply. Finally Pattie struck him across the face, sinking on the couch in a sulk. Recovering, she announced that she was never going to use the Pleases Agency ever again and that she would blacken its name, and as for Bonn ... et cetera. She slammed out, and later sent Bonn flowers to the Pleases Agency address. Rack had been incensed, seeing the mark on Bonn's face, and went on about it to Martina, wanting to at least smash a car or two. Martina still had not ruled on it.

Thinking the tumultuous episode over, Bonn sensed that Pattie Six-Two-Three's fury was increased by his inability to argue along. It was not an entirely new experience, yet somehow stayed beyond his understanding. It would be repeated, such being the extraordinary nature of women. What chance did one have? He knew no tactics, no stratagem that would have satisfied Pattie's odd mood. Just as, now, he had no means of appeasing Martina. It might be that all women, perhaps, sooner or later wanted a riotous argument and this was simply Martina's episode.

Bonn wished that he'd come from a real family, where a father and mother and perhaps a brother or sister might have explained some of these essentials. Might Posser know more about it? But to ask the old invalid smacked of pathetic incompetence in the arts of life. Pride had to be overcome in Martina's interests. He decided to ask Posser, perhaps when Martina was doing the books one evening.

"You can help," Martina said.

He pondered this.

She hardly ever took her eyes from his. Was that her manner when speaking to others?

Martina was rumoured to have spent some time lately with

223

TicTac from Cheadle Hume, a recently promoted key. TicTac was a smiling ex-footballer with engaging mannerisms. He ached to be an ocean racer, which Bonn vaguely supposed involved powerboats. Some of these extraordinary craft were moored in the city's marina. TicTac had one, mostly to serve as a focus for chatting enthusiasts. He attended drama festivals. Twenty-four, TicTac had served his early days as a younger goer in a team of three centred on Warrington. His police record for breaking and entering had been expunged after costly negotiations by Fazackerley and Culcheth, Martina's lawyers.

That rumour had been spread by Grellie, Bonn knew. And Grellie might not be disinterested.

He wondered, though, if Martina looked so intently into TicTac's eyes when she passed the time of day with him. Or was her intent quizzing manner reserved only for single-minded interrogation of an employee she suspected?

"Then I shall," he said.

No name yet, Martina thought hotly. He stood there, infuriating her with his endless patience. Her anger was fueled by his incomprehension. It was like talking with an imbecile who couldn't rise to any challenge, any abuse simply beyond his ken. He was bovinely stupid or on some astral plane. Either way, Bonn was becoming a liability. She wanted communication, not a series of guessing games.

She took up the pencil and savagely scored the paper. Bonn stared. This was original.

"One, you must discover the relationship between Vane and Clare Three-Nine-Five. Two, I want an explanation for your visit to Tootal's the herbalist down Liverpool Road. Three, why are you so interested in Deirdre Turnstall's death?"

"I shall try to discover why Clare Three-Nine-Five is seeing Mr Vane," he said evenly. "I shall endeavour not to cause her offence."

"Her feelings don't matter," Martina said harshly. "Just do

it. And if she takes umbrage, who cares? She can go some-where else for her … for her consolation."

"I visited Mr Tootal to ask about herbals coming into the city. I wished to find out if somebody could be using the girls as mules – I believe that is the term – or as some form of con-duit of which the Pleases Agency is unaware."

"Is that likely?"

"I do not know. Mr Tootal was not really very forthcoming." Bonn saw the swift change in her expression and added, "From ignorance, not secrecy."

"Do you know him?"

"I had seen him once or twice before."

"Does he know you?"

"Only by sight." He strove to find a way to say it, finally came out with, "In another existence."

"No news, then?"

"There is a preparation called miraa that Mr Tootal knows." Bonn told her of the herbalist's suppositions.

"And Deirdre?"

This was more difficult. He looked at the window. That was all you could do, in Martina's restricted space, simply let your gaze happen on the glass, for it was covered by an adherent opaque paper and overpainted. It might have looked out over the Phoenix Theatre's cinder car park. So many inquisitive people there, was that it? Or, more likely, was the window blanked out by a girl unwilling to expose her lameness? He caught himself wandering, came to.

"I think we sometimes – I mean myself alone – ignore the tragedies our activities represent, Martina."

Her name at last. She felt worn out. He could have spared himself this trial by greeting her without his irritating reti-cence. Christ's sake, he lodged in her dad's home. Okay, in a garret of his own choosing, but they often had meals together when there were opportunities to talk and be at ease. They had been close once, in a particularly bad time of need, but now they seemed farther apart than ever.

"Meaning we don't help our girls, or our goers?"

His hesitations were not hesitations. They were filled with senses, fluctuations of thought, fleeting impressions, selections made of choices and reasons before speaking, all the time weighing whether they might give offence.

"Yes," he said, shocking her.

"I resent that! It's been Posser's rule to stand by our own." She spoke grimly. "We've adhered to Posser's rules ever since I took over."

"I too resent it, but it must be faced. Rack does well, but he cannot be everywhere."

"Why didn't you tell me? Or tell Rack? Instead, you go off investigating on your own. It's stupid."

"I know, Martina." He took his time before saying, "I thought I might help without causing trouble. It's the child, you see."

"The boy? That runner?"

"A child has no power, has it?" He adjusted his words. "Has he? I have heard nothing. Yet he cannot have disappeared. This large city is merely a massive village. If we could explain Deirdre's tragedy..."

"Then we could see the killer off? That what you mean?"

"You would not be cruel, Martina."

He felt an almost aching compassion for her, so beautiful yet so hard pressed by events, a person struggling against being so newly young.

"Then do what?"

"Perhaps understand, Martina," he said sadly. "It might help us."

For some inexplicable reason he thought of Clare. As if at some psychic prompt Martina linked her fingers to indicate the interview was over.

"I'm calling a meeting at the Barn Owl. I'll send word. Meanwhile, get on as I said. Tell Miss Faith to give priority to

226

that Clare. One other thing. I'm not having my people struck by clients, Bonn. That Pattie Six-Two-Three, Rack will see to her."

"That will not be necessary, Martina."

"It is utterly vital," she countered with satisfaction. "She has sent flowers again. They will be returned tomorrow, in a way she cannot fail to understand."

He left, and went to sit in the watery sunshine of Central Gardens by the old men playing chess. Several of Grellie's girls walked past. Usually they would have spoken or tried to engage him in conversation, but today they simply walked on by. He said nothing to them.

*　　*　　*

Martina heard Bonn leave. No chorus of greetings from the snooker players to signal his passage, as would have happened for, say, Rack or Grellie. Her nook of an office tended to vibrate from any din, so she knew. It was as if Bonn was pre-saged by some aura. Or were they simply embarrassed by someone seemingly so vulnerable? Or was he perhaps a person simply beyond everyday comprehension? It wasn't his position as key, for other keys came and went on the whole informally and caused little disturbance.

She tapped the drawer, and Osmund entered.

"Please bring Rack. Ten minutes."

33 | Hem – affordable or credible lies

Odd how tired Marj's feet got in the first few hours in the Home Orphanage. Not quite so queer, the bent old lady thought, as how they recovered once the boys' dinners were served. Her feet had become a trial lately, but by teatime she was floating on air. That meant her feet were dead and bloated.

It was different when she reached her minute terraced house at the top of Mozart Street. Prising her feet out of her shoes was like delivering twins, thick toes at all angles. Once, she'd had beautiful feet, soft skin and her toes small and straight. Shoes did it, over the years.

The afternoon washing up in the Home kitchen was done by Clifton, a chap with hardly any English who crooned daft songs and jigged while he worked. Nice enough, brought his cousin in to help him with the heavy pans, solid iron for cooking impossibly large amounts. Women couldn't lift weights like those. Clifton and Courtly did their work then left, talking of football, gambling odds.

Marj didn't know how much longer she could go on. Her job was the same laborious work she'd done for decades. Younger women weren't conscientious nowadays. Strange to tell, she now found serving most exhausting. She lost track of who'd been given what, sometimes gave out no veg then gave twice to the next boy in line. They played her up, of course, little devils, swapped plates to confuse her, their laughter and chatter only going silent when Brother Jason came by. Sometimes, another Brother who was monitor for the day called for them to stop larking about and get on. Brother Jason never said a word.

The dark hours didn't help, nights drawing in by eight. Having to depend on the street lights by quarter past made her feel almost physically sick, the world turning to autumn with winter looming cold over its shoulder. The city became frightening then, wet and slippery, traffic appalling and street unknowns lurking against dank walls. Rain made haloes of every lamp now that she had bad eyes. Awkward to see, though her journey took her along streets she'd known all her life. She could still read, given a decent book with a proper story, not one of the war things where it was all shooting. The telly was a godsend.

Once, she'd never have thought the city could scare her. Life was jangly yet smooth in the old days. Jaunty was the word, even if people didn't have any money. Now, look at the price of things! And the fright of things.

She often found herself hesitating even turning into Raglan Street. Where once buildings hummed and crashed with machinery, and echoes were thick with a thousand voices on the evening shift, the tall structures were now silent, closed of a night. In her youth mills were like giant brilliantly-lit liners sailing through a black night sea that was the town. Now, it was all an abandoned fleet of marooned hulks. You walked past hoping the next street lamp would soon come.

Only a handful of neighbours was left, the rest gone to the Soft South or passed away. In Mozart Street ten of the terraced houses were still lived in, the rest boarded up waiting for the City Council to decide.

It was here, as she turned off Raglan Road, that she always paused to look behind. Several times she'd walked on into the brighter area, pretending to see if the corner shop was still open, afraid of somebody following her down the dark. Usually it wasn't anybody. Sometimes it was some sour-faced youth. One alone was a risk, two were a menace, and three to be well clear of. Older men weren't dangerous, with their steady regular paces, hands in pockets. Irregular steps, though, meant youths on the prowl. No bobbies strolling in their wet street capes nowadays, torchlamps on breast chains, pointed old-fashioned helmets, familiar with bluff jokes.

She paused and looked behind.

Some kiddie was there, just as she'd felt, staring at her. Stocky, burly lad, maybe eight or so, but even children like him were a threat. People said it was drugs. How on earth did children that age know drugs?

The boy must be on his way to the pictures, or to them arcades filled with noisy machines where kiddies stood mesmerised. She peered through the drizzle but suddenly the boy had gone. In a shiny plastic mac, no hat, trainers. For a moment she wondered if it was Jecko, her favourite in the Home, who'd gone missing. She was only guessing, her eyes not up to it. He was sure to be found soon.

Please, she prayed, Virgin Mary Mother of God, keep the child safe and lead him secure to where he'd be fed and get a place to lay his head.

Shops began at the far end, cars crowding the traffic lights, two pubs and a cluster of youths chanting some football song. She crossed over so she wouldn't get confused at the intersection. Things had changed since she was a girl. There'd once been an old mission hall by the paper shop, hymns Tuesdays, Thursdays and all day Sundays. 'You Must Be A Lover Of The Lord' was standard, with tambourines and stickbells, and then the Temperance Parade last Sunday of every month with the Band of Hope. Her favourite was 'Come Join Our Abstinence Band', when all the children, a tin cup of Abstinence on a string, marched down Rossini Street clapping in time. It was fun. Try telling kids that these days they'd look at you like you'd gone daft.

She liked Jecko. A brute of a lad, for hadn't she seen him kicking some other boy until they both bled and had to be taken to Brother Jason for punishment? Yet most days he was quiet. You never lost your knowledge of children. Silence in a child spoke loudest. It shouted of something evil shutting him up, masking his senses. Not that a loud demonstrative child was always happy, no, but talkativeness gave you some chance of getting to know what was wrong. Jecko's silence was like a wall. When he got like that, sometimes in the dinner queue he would look away, take whatever food he was given.

It was only sometimes. She liked Jecko. He deserved better than whatever the kitchen staff cooked for him. He was like her Bill, even her Doreen. You never lost your knowledge of children.

She knew Jecko was working himself up to running away. She'd known it when he paused that final day at dinner time. He'd looked at her and tried to say her name.

"Mar," he'd said. Then got it out, "Marj."

"Yes, luv." She'd waited, smiling, serving spoon hovering for more mash, more gravy. "Beans, then," she'd filled in for him because the boys down the queue were starting to shove.

That day it was Brother Ambrose, elderly and forgetful, who served as verger for the Home chapel behind the walking cloisters. He was hopeless controlling the boys. They always took advantage of the old man now he'd become doddery. He still taught Latin, somebody said.

She reached her door. Lights were on in Mrs Holmwood's front room. Tom Holmwood, the eldest, would be home soon. Comforting to still have one burly man there of an evening. Farther down, two other houses showed lights against their curtains, and she could hear a TV serial beginning.

Later than she thought. She was slower now.

One more glance behind before she turned the key and pressed the Suffolk latch. Nobody.

She went in, closed the door behind her, making sure she put the bolt across.

She took off her coat – amazing how heavy coats were. She never remembered clothes weighing anything at all, when she was young.

Soup tonight, bread and that quick spread instead of butter

232

and anyhow it was cheaper. She had a piece of fish left over. Hotted, with an Eccles cake for afters, a nice brew of tea with sugar, would do her tonight, until she dozed off in front of the telly, then cocoa and bed. Some days, she didn't really feel like having anything. It was hard to work up much of an appetite after that kitchen.

It was while she was doing parsley sauce – it came in packets now – that she heard a noise in the yard. No gardens in Mozart Street, just a cobbled square with slab-slate walls linked by iron clasps from the 1820s. An outside loo at the end by the ash midden. Though who had coal fires nowadays?

She paused to listen.

Once, she would have opened the back door and shouted down into the blackness, "Who is it? Are you all right?" Now, she knew better. Mrs Ecclestone from Taylor Street had been mugged, such a horrid word, only two weeks since. The police had come knocking, telling everybody not to open your doors at night in case. They didn't need to say in case of what.

The noise again, this time quieter. Somebody nudging the dustbin. Metal, it gave a clang, very faint but there. She still had her hearing, but no telephone. She used the phone box at the end of Maudsley Street to phone Doreen at weekends. Bill kept on about getting her a phone for herself, right here in the room, but where was the sense in that? All that cost, and people you didn't know ringing you up, pestering you to buy insurance and motor cars, as if anybody had the money. No, phones weren't sensible. Anyway, she could always run over to the Holmwoods, who were on the phone. Tom even had one he carried about.

Clang. Somebody was in the yard.

Her house was old. Two up, two down, a loo and a bath in what used to be her pantry. The doors were solid heartwood, the latches iron. The windows had small speers you could fasten at night. She couldn't imagine anybody climbing up to her windows.

She knocked on the wall, an appeal for help from the old days. Two knocks back, almost instant. She heard a shout and went to the front door. Mrs Holmwood was peering out.

"I heard somebody knock against my bin, Bertha."

"I thought there was somebody, Marj."

Bertha Holmwood was a shrivelled woman who'd had four children, all gone now. Spectacles, hair drawn back in a bun, that same old pinafore, wouldn't make a bookend.

"Shall we look?"

"If you like. Harry'll be home in an hour."

Two doors opening was wise, one not so clever. Whatever happened, there'd be a witness. Marj locked her front door and undid the back door latch, looking into the dark yard. Bertha's light sliced the night across the black-grey walls. Nobody.

"They must have run, Marj," Bertha called. "I'll tell Harry not to bother."

"Right."

That was their deception, that tough Harry was on his way out to search for intruders who might molest old women. There was no Harry, of course, not any longer. They played this scene once or twice a month in the lantern hours. It felt silly, but you could never tell.

Yet she began to think as she started her tea. She watched the television, anything except news. She didn't want to hear anything about wars, people hurting each other. It was a horrible world.

The question wouldn't go: what if that little lad was Jecko? But why would he follow her home? Yet maybe it was him and he was frightened, wanting help. Maybe, she thought with a pang, he was hungry?

The image of any little lad sitting out there in the dark hoping for something to eat became unbearable. She looked at her meal, how far she'd got with it. She still had some corned beef. Sometimes she did that with oven chips, bread and that spread, making quite an easy meal when she was tired. With pickle, if that was to her fancy.

She could make a couple of sandwiches, maybe put a cup of hot tea with milk and sugar out there on the top back step, just in case? It had looked extraordinarily like him, but then her eyes...

Dangerous to open the back door. No way of getting somebody to come with her, go round the end of the street then down back Coe Street. No, she'd have to judge it.

She busied herself making some corned beef sandwiches, thick doorsteps of bread, and put a mug of tea in the middle of the plate, sandwiches round the rim.

Careful, she switched the TV off and picked up the poker, last used twenty years ago. Quietly she slid the bolt. Fast as she could, she cried aloud to frighten anybody out there then opened the door and placed the plate on the step, immediately back in and shooting the bolt with shaking hands.

Her heart was going so fast she quite lost her breath. She listened.

Absolute silence. She calmed, scolded herself for too much imagination – her mother always said that – then slowly resumed her evening. She was in time to catch the evening serial, that folk nowadays called soaps.

The story wasn't very good, and she clicked the channels looking for a nice love story but none came. She heard no more sounds in her back yard.

Come morning, the sandwiches were gone. The mug was empty, so no cat, no stray dog. The old latched gate at the bottom of the cobbled yard was still bolted and latched.

But, Marj thought, boys climb.

34 | To Blam – to injure, to attack, a person

"Today's the day," Clare told her mirror.

Lipsticks had a mind of their own some mornings. Just when you wanted slickness, the right shade, everything went askew. Twice she tried to do her eyes. First attempt, she looked like an Egyptian courtesan, the next something out of a teenage disco. She surrendered and left herself pretty plain. Professional, she mouthed at the mirror, so take that, Miss Martina.

No surname, she realised, skimping breakfast, her heart not in taking the advice she doled out to the street girls: Breakfast's the most important meal of the day – statistics, common sense, feelings of wellbeing, longevity for goodness sake.

Miss Martina was who, exactly?

Clare went downstairs, far too early. Morning appointment, half past nine on the third floor of the Weavers Hall. Miss Martina's secretary had been coldly assertive. A new voice, so who was *she*? When Clare had said that she had a clinic to attend, the voice became colder still.

"Then please apply for another appointment, Dr Burtonall. This number is available at eight-thirty each morning."

Clare angrily conceded. She agreed to alter her clinic to fit in with Miss Martina. She felt she was a supplicant, Martina the monarch, the city her fiefdom.

And here it was, the meeting.

* * *

The venue was at Rivergate, south-west corner of Victoria

Square. Martina was already seated at the head of a mahogany table, almost in tableau with three smartly tailored girls and three young men looking in from the stock exchange. Acolytes, nothing more, possibly for colour. A grey-haired middle-aged woman sat beside Martina after welcoming Clare in and inviting her to place herself opposite the pale young woman.

"I'm Beryl," she said brightly. "Miss Martina has approximately twenty minutes."

"Thank you. The matters can be simply resolved, I believe, but I need your permission."

"My permission?" Martina said, like what's-all-this-at-your-age.

Clare was struck by her beauty, those blue eyes. She remembered telling Bonn about facial symmetry as a marker for attractiveness. Martina's was a countenance to turn any man's head. No ring on the third finger, no paler indentation where one might be worn regularly. Symmetrical, the face full yet narrowing, lovely full mouth, cosmetics restrained.

Martina made a sign and the acolytes left in silence, the smiling secretary closing the door behind them.

"Yes. You are the head of the syndicate that controls the girl stringers who work in the city. I accept that I am employed to care for them medically."

"You've been treated well?"

Clare was startled. "Yes. Of course."

"Have you gone short of anything?"

"No."

"Then why ask my permission?"

"Two girls have come to me with medical problems, and I need to promise them your support."

"You are their doctor. Therefore you have the problem, not I."

"Can I mention their names?" On Martina's nod Clare added, "Faye Ray is one. Donna Reede is the other."

"I know them, and why they went to see you. What is it?"

"Faye Ray I want to send to an anorexia clinic. She will

238

recover, in the right circumstances."

"Might she not?"

"One in five die if untreated, Martina." Clare tried not to sound indignant at the other's coolness. "I am excluding a series of other possible diagnoses, but I'm pretty certain it's anorexia nervosa. I'm doing a series of laboratory tests. Faye agreed to my telling you."

She passed a list across the table. Martina read it aloud, to Clare's surprise pronouncing every medical term correctly without hesitation. Clare wondered uneasily if the girl had already seen the list. But how?

"Why are you showing me this?"

"Well, the expense for one thing. Faye has had the disease for some time. I usually do a scan for bone density, hypopituitarism, Addison's disease, malignancies, and do a computerised tomographic brain scan to exclude intracerebral tumour. There are other tests – liver function, absolute erythrocyte indices, blood urea. I'll want to exclude human immune-deficiency viral diseases, plus tuberculosis among others. The problem of inflammatory intestinal diseases is one that – "

"Details are your problem." Martina slid the paper across the polished surface. "Money is no problem. Get on with it."

"But committing her to an expensive clinic will be so costly! At the moment she's in a National Health Service hospital."

"Do what you like with her, doctor. Next?"

Clare controlled herself. The girl was almost insulting, having the gall to glance pointedly at the clock on the panelling.

"Donna Reede is the second girl's recorded name."

"And?"

Not quite drumming her fingers, Clare observed angrily.

"She's pregnant four months. Her family would insist on an abortion if they knew, for reasons of religious or ethnic orthodoxy. She is unmarried, wants to go to term and have the child."

"So?"

Clare took the quiet question, suppressing her response to

the other's rudeness. Yet the girl's gravity was actually less than offensive. Clare wondered if all these problems were nothing new, heard a dozen times before, while her visitor thought she was bringing complex medical novelties.

"My question is, will you allow her to return to work later? She's frantic that she might be unprotected after the baby's born. She says her brothers will come after her."

Martina leant back. "Doctor, why have you come here? I'm a busy person."

Clare felt herself redden. "Because I'm not in a position to promise that you will have her back. She seems as terrified of your people as of her murderous family."

"Expense again?"

"Not really. I hope that if I prescribe medication, investigations, treatments, you will finance them, and be considerate."

"You were told that when you began to work for my charity."

"But can I guarantee that the girls will be kept on after recovery?"

"No."

"Then I need to know the limits to your ... charity, Martina."

"Very well," the beautiful girl said. "Anything medical, yes, for as long as it takes. Anything about employment or social, no. You will please send a summary of the employment implications."

Clare waited for more, in a lengthening silence. Was that it?

"Thank you, doctor, for your time."

Martina gave no signal, but the door opened and the six young executives entered, taking up their former tableau positions.

"Thank you, Martina."

Clare rose, Beryl rushing eagerly to open the door for her and saying how nice it was to meet her at last and could she find the way out and did she need a car back to the clinic at Charlestown. Clare quickly said goodbye and walked to her parked SuperSnipe.

That was Martina. Third encounter, and Clare still knew

nothing about her. Miss Opacity. But she'd won! And tonight she'd win with Ken Vane. She needed nobody, the super professional with total independence.

She felt empowered, capable, able to deal with anything.

*   *   *

In the panelled room, Martina sat alone while Beryl led the entourage away down the back stairs. They were only window dressing, brought in from Mr Fazackerley's offices. She phoned.

"Grellie? Martina. Where are you?"

"Wait."

Silence, then after a few moments Grellie's voice came on. "Sorry. I've a client. I'm in the studio flats over the Phoenix Theatre."

"That Faye Ray, in hospital."

"I know about her. Yes?"

"Allow her six months of sick, then bin her."

"Right. What if she comes back cured?"

"Bin her. And Donna Reede."

"I know her. She's in the pudding club, the girls are saying."

"She can come back two months after delivery. What string's she on?"

"Her? I put her in red, at Rivergate. Is that okay?"

"We'll make up the numbers somehow. Red's gone short lately."

"Tell me about it," Grellie's voice grumbled tinnily. "Can I ring off? I'm already behind. I've a dib waiting."

Martina closed the connection and belled for Beryl to wheel her out. She hated the thought of that Clare, or anyone else, seeing her lameness. She still wondered if she'd done the right thing, hiring a woman doctor who was besotted with one of the keys. Doctors after all were ten a penny. Wouldn't a male doctor be less complicated?

The syndicate wanted a doctor who could make up her

mind instead of coming running for permission every minute. The cow should earn her keep, or go.

Yes, definitely time for a change. She decided to speak to Posser this evening, and get rid of the dithering bitch.

35 | Clag – trouble

"The ship was only launched this morning," Ken Vane said. "Who'd have thought? Have you seen photos of what this part of the city was like only six years ago?"

For once Clare felt really free and off the leash. The marina had been reclaimed from the industrial slums. Now, its waters, straight off the Pennine Chain, fed into the great ship canal connecting the city to Liverpool's Mersey.

"Launched last week," she corrected, leaning against the aft rail, feeling the breeze.

He grimaced. "Caught! I'm the detective here, understand?"

"It's still an achievement, Ken."

"All the crooks in the North must have gathered like vultures. They can sniff government money."

"My ex-husband was one." Her smile lessened it for him. "Don't worry. His reputation's not quite unsullied."

"I heard." He became slightly serious, a change she welcomed. She wanted to see his several sides. "How's it been?"

"Since the divorce? Fairly tranquil."

"No engagement in the offing, then?"

"Nothing serious." She included him in that category. Take that, Sergeant Vane.

The small pleasure cruiser held a few score passengers. The ship's vibration was hardly noticeable as it glided slowly across the lake. It was a lovely setting for a supper, the sinking sun slowly losing the city's grime and finding traces of fresh colour in the sky.

Why her wariness, though, in this casual, surely quite

natural, encounter? He'd entertained her with anecdotes of police training college, magistrates' ineptitude, calamities on street duty. Whether by luck or judgement, Ken had avoided mentioning anything medical. She finally abandoned her unease as the cruiser made its turn and started for the quayside.

"Who'd have thought that we were sailing in the very heart of the grimmest city in the whole North?"

"Not me." He gave indicated a distant high-riser. "My cousin lives there. He's a doctor too. Looks after a sports team."

"Medical?"

"Yes. A little older than you, though." He grinned, boyish. "Fifty-two."

"Cheek!"

They talked pleasantly of changes in the city. Clare thought, the question any moment from now will be, what next? Do we go for a "final drink", whatever that might mean? Or do I let him drive me home for "a quick coffee"? Or is it going to be a buss on the cheek followed by a heartless and unfelt promise to "do this again"? She noticed the dark smudge in the gloaming as the pleasure steamer veered to its new course. That was the city's darker area where Victoria Square held to its ancient past. It was where Bonn plied, and where Martina's rule ran with the iron invincibility of feudal law.

"I'll introduce you to him," Ken said lightly. "As long as you don't talk about anything medical. I'm squeamish, see?"

"Aren't we all?" Clare said.

"Nothing like Hassall, though," he astonished her by adding.

"Hassall, squeamish?" She hadn't thought. Hassall had never shown the slightest temerity, and he'd attended several post-mortem examinations in her company.

"He sweats at anything forensic. You should have seen him down by the canal. We found a ton of Eckies."

"You mean e tablets?"

"Mind you, he missed them in his search. I found them

with a police woman. She was keen to work with old Hassall, God only knows why. He thinks the cache is something to do with the fairground." Ken gave a wry smile. "Like, the city has no drug problems until the fair comes to town!"

The notion of Hassall being careless and timid didn't match Clare's impression. As if sensing her withdrawal Ken began a tale against himself, his clumsiness when handling a weapon for the first time.

"Worst on earth, me," he said disparagingly. His self disparagement made her feel a whole lot better.

They left the ship laughing among the disembarking crowd. She invited him in for a coffee when they reached Charlestown. It was four hours before he had to leave, on early duty the following morning. Her confidence soared. She felt free, relaxed and finally in charge of every aspect of her own destiny.

To **Straighten** – to discipline, usually by violence

Hunting the running boy was sending Nadine mental. She felt she had been trolling the city centre for weeks. Until Grellie and Martina put her on suss, she'd thought she knew every inch of the city centre. Now, she kept coming across some dive, some nook, a minor business she never knew existed. But as yet no sign of the boy.

After another hopeless day, Nadine did a stride from habit, taking the money straight to Grellie who was working the Greygate corner and looked truly fed up to the teeth.

"You doing like I said, Nad?"

"Yes, Grellie," Nadine said, the perfect ingrate. "Just I wanted to help Zoe out. She's in strife with that Nantwich fucker. He's always Monday night, brings money in an envelope. Know the one? Complains about not getting a receipt."

"I know him," Grellie said sourly. She wished she hadn't given up smoking just to please Bonn, but she had so it was no use griping. "Mad as a fucking hatter. Tells his zodiac from the number of shoves. That him?"

"Mmmh. Last week he was Aires, tonight Scorpio, crazy bastard."

"As long as he pays and does no damage."

"There's the little fucker!" Nadine suddenly hissed and was gone.

"Who?" Grellie quickly moved into the shadows two doorways down but Nadine had vanished.

That more than anything worried Grellie. If Nadine could be gone in a fucking flash, how often did stringers turn invisible when they saw her coming? The bitches were getting too streetwise for their own good, and that was a fucking fact.

She corrected herself. Too many abusive words. Too much "swearing" for no other reason than irritability. Bonn wouldn't like it. Maybe he expected Rack to pass word down to the girls and the working house, everybody keep your mouths clean in public?

Yet what did happen between Bonn and his clients? Surely to God they must give out some vicious expletives when they started to wet? What if they wanted him to talk dirty, the way a woman sometimes did? She'd like to ask him, but knew there'd never be a way, unless she somehow managed to get Bonn for herself.

*   *   *

The hurrying girl had the sense to make out she was running to catch up with a friend. She'd seen the little swine duck into a doorway of a derelict pub covered in fly posters, one darkened panel hollowed into a knee-high tunnel. She trotted on by, shouting, "Vera! Vera!" until she was well into Union Road and stood still, panting, looking back.

Trouble was, the lights were behind her. Silhouettes showed against street lamps. Give him a glimpse and the little bastard would be off like a ferret and she'd still be in shtuck.

She was in real trouble. The way she'd been drubbed in the casino, Nadine knew that now it was life or no life for her, never mind how Grellie put it. Martina was the dangerous one, cold as a fucking frog, heart like Pennine grit. Grellie could often be reasonable, see practical sides to punishment – work for nothing a whole year, even, but serve your time out till she said that's enough and it's all over. Fair. Nadine was a working girl like the rest, after all. You'd get a clean break from Grellie, who knew what it was like to slog your arse off in drossy doorways day after night. A friend, sort of, even though she was boss and could have you done over, Grellie still understood that sometimes a girl got herself strifed up.

Not Martina. Cunning as worms, she. Cut her in two, you got two enemies back instead of one. The lame cunt had never struggled on her tiptoes while some drunken burke shed into you, winter rain piping down your neck and still hours to go before you'd earned your nobbins and you could go home and sleep.

No, no change from Martina. Nadine shivered. Mercy from her? In a pig's eye and a million years.

Sorry for herself, she almost missed the lad nipping like a dark-coated ghost beyond the end of the street. A passing tram gave him away, sheening its lights along his wet shoulders as he flitted towards Mozart Street.

She cursed, went on her toes, running close to the wall, pausing on tenterhooks as a motor swished wetly along the road, waiting a sec in case the little sod had halted in a nook to check. Then she ran, ran like a hare.

Mozart Street was one of three parallel streets, back ginnels to each fronting the slate-walled yards. She used to know them, had been born in Wapping Street, knew the names of people past. What was he going down there for? The streets were almost derelict now, "in course of being reclaimed" in the words of the city Council, meaning on the way to yet more ruination. She paused in the darkness, not knowing which way and having to guess. Two or three lamps only, ancient gas lamps, only a few curtains leaking yellow light. Once, forty-six dwellings fronted the terracing. Now, semi-ruins.

No sign of the kid. Yet she was sure it had been him.

The back ginnel?

She ran down the street, hoping to Christ he wasn't hiding behind some steps, and got lucky. She made the cross ginnel and went panting harshly to the corner, unable to see a thing except for the faint shine from Coe Street's lights against the wet.

The street child's trick was to stoop, and use the meagre

249

reflections from a wet pavement to watch for a moving shadow. This way, she glimpsed him, no more than a thickening in the darkness against the sky glow. He paused a full minute then was absorbed into the sombre grey of somebody's yard.

Nadine counted to a hundred but he didn't reappear. She counted a hundred more and still nothing. Somebody walked past the top of the street, clumping in working boots towards the station. Nothing for it. She would have to walk past the yard, then she'd know. Plenty of empty houses, maybe four of every five, the City Council still living on promises of reclamation, some time, never.

Quietly she walked up the narrow back street. About the right spot, she paused to listen. Two houses showed lights. She judged the slate walling.

And she heard a door latch go.

It could only be him, maybe waiting, getting a hand-out from somebody there. Maybe he'd got relatives? Not if he was from the priests' Home Orphanage. No, the girls were all on about the little swine. He'd done a runner. Martina wanted him, so that was that. She walked back to the main street, counting the yards, and got the house number where he'd vanished. Forty-five.

She almost sang out loud as she walked into the lights of the city square. She didn't reply to girls who called out. On a mission, soon to be in the clear, making her number again with Martina and Grellie.

No sign of the head stringer. Nadine wasn't going to give her priceless news to the likes of Sonia who was bucking for Grellie's deputy in the green string, or Nance who was always sickening for something and trying to get out of doing her strides, the cow. None of them, no.

Martina had said get word to her straightest. Something must be up because the girls were all looking wary, either huddling in the coming drizzle or smoking and irritable. She headed for the Deansgate corner by instinct. Near there, the messengers of Askey's Triple Racer lounged among their mad-painted bikes.

"Seen Rack, George?" she asked Fat George.

He shook his head, flogging his papers, racing tips, phoney parking cards, dud football tickets, ten per cent to Rack and no comeback.

But there was Louse, pretending to read some tat, not even knowing it was upside down.

"Seen Rack? Grellie?"

"Rack's standing for Bonn. What?"

She shrugged. A message to Louse was as good as delivered.

"That kid, Rupert. I got him."

Louse looked at her disbelieving. The poor stupid cunt telling him with nobody else around for yards. Where'd be her proof?

"Want me to pass it along?" he asked, quiet.

"He crans up in Mozart Street. Number forty-five. Just seen him."

"Well done, Nadine," Louse said, folding his paper. "I'll find Rack or Grellie." He smiled at her in the gloaming. "Reckon you're quids in now, eh?"

She smiled, so grateful now she was in the clear.

"Ta, Louse. Martina said soonest."

"Like lightning," Louse said, and walked away from the poor bitch. Beyond belief, some of them.

All the receptionists thought the visitor too smooth. They bleeped for Dr Burtonall and got her on the Dolf, Farnworth General Hospital's brand-new Doctoral Location Finder system.

Clare answered from the Paediatric Wing, cross at the interruption. She'd not been notified of any visiting doctor. The case she was dealing with was a request for termination of a pregnancy, the father insisting on a son this time, and his wretched wife, five months now into her third, was carrying a girl. Clare smiled a mute apology to the importuning man. His wife sat dejectedly by.

"Who is he, please?"

"Dr Harrod, Banda-Lait Sports Foundation."

The name was unfamiliar. "Please put him on."

"Good day, Dr Burtonall." Dr Harrod sounded quiet, almost amused. "I only called to arrange an appointment, not to interrupt your valued work."

"In what connection, please?"

"Advice, mainly. Did my cousin Ken mention me?"

Oh, that doctor. "Not by name."

"Might you be free later? I could come down to Charlestown, or perhaps the City Medical Society."

"I usually finish here sixish, Dr Harrod."

They agreed a time.

Clare felt almost pleased, not knowing quite why. Perhaps Ken Vane placed a deal of trust in his relative's opinion, something like that?

She gave her attention to the man opposite.

"We cannot perform a termination of pregnancy on those grounds," she said quietly. "The child your wife is carrying is healthy by every measure, including imaging scans."

The man insisted, all arrogance. "She failed me!"

"The father determines the sex of the child, not the mother."

"How much?" His palms lifted expressively. "I pay!"

Clare said quickly, wanting to nip this in the bud, "It isn't a question of money."

"I want son," the man said sullenly, darting a vitriolic glance at his silent wife. "She only give daughter."

Clare knew she was in for a long haul and settled down. As soon as the man realised that his attempted bribe had failed, he would begin talk of religious reasons. Odd, she reflected, preparing herself for an outright battle, how many gender-based arguments for abortion were couched in exactly the same terms.

That would be followed by demands to see a male doctor, who would of course understand how stupid all women doctors were. From there he'd move on to political friends in high places, then would come the rage and accusations of God-knows-what.

After his insistence on an abortion – at such a late stage, for God's sake? For no reason? – the man would become furious. He would shout, thump her desk, claim discrimination of every kind – racial, social, political. She had even been threatened by one woman's husband on the grounds that he was a smoker, that all doctors hated smokers.

It was a crazy world. She felt a pang as she thought of Bonn, at once her haven and resource. With it however came a twinge of guilt as she remembered Ken Vane. She dragged her attention back.

The man was smiling now. He'd reached the ingrate stage.

"Doctor," he said, shrugging, beaming. "You think so stupid because you are woman. Bring man doctor. He understand. I have friends in parliament..."

And so wearily on. Clare stated, asserted, tried to educate

the angry man in the law, to no avail. He left threatening to bring legal actions for discrimination of every kind and shouting stock phrases about legal aid entitlement.

She felt like a rag. She would now have to draft a report for Dr Fairchild, the consultant paediatrician who had referred them, a soul-searching hell.

Wearily she postponed the trauma. Enough for the day. She was beginning to hate religious orthodoxies, including those which deposited creatures like Bonn, that refugee from a defunct seminary, onto the street and into her life.

Better meet this Dr Harrod for a drink at the dopey Medical Society, that rest home for burnt-out doctors after hours.

*   *   *

Dr Harrod turned out to be a pleasant unassuming man of about fifty. Grey of hair, smiley, besuited and easy, he came forward to greet her in the foyer of the City Medical Society building.

A waitress took their order for tea and biscuits in the lounge. Clare settled into an armchair with a sigh of relief.

"Hard day, doctor?"

"They don't get easier."

He grimaced. She was reminded of Ken Vane, she supposed a family resemblance.

He agreed. "Like my current moan."

"Sports medicine? Interesting."

"Hardly. You have a splendid charity clinic." He chuckled. "I certainly haven't. In sports medicine, money rules."

Clare smiled, glancing around the place. Hardly anyone in at this hour, just a couple of elderly colleagues in one corner discussing the Siamese twin controversies. The hectic rampaging of the Church had concentrated moral minds wonderfully, after the accusations of medico-legal interference in the sad case of conjoined twins from the Balkans.

The famous dilemma was that both twins would die if untreated, whereas if they were separated surgically one might survive. The churches were against surgery. Doctors were mostly for an operation, thinking it better to have one living child than two dead. Already different religious sects were at each others' throats.

Dr Harrod had chosen well for a secluded chat. The place would not fill up until well after eight o'clock. Time enough. Clare felt interest. Had Dr Harrod raised Ken as a child, something like that?

"Money dictates most treatments these days," she said ruefully. "The times when the Chancellor simply picked up every tab unquestioningly are long gone. Now, wide-spectrum antibiotic therapy gets contested by some prowling pharmacy girl with a clipboard. Last week I had some clerk argue about the price of cytotoxics in cancer therapy!"

"Beyond belief."

The tea arrived. Clare relaxed. She'd enjoyed the company of two new men on different days. Were things looking up? She had lately felt in desperate need of change.

"What does your work consist of, doctor?"

"Harry, please." He smiled. "With a surname like mine, could I be called anything else?"

"Clare, then. Mine is city vagrants, street life, indigents, pavement mumpers, heaven knows what."

"I've heard about your clinic. You do good work, Clare. Why Charlestown, away from the city centre?"

"It's hardly a stone's throw. There's a small flat. And it's convenient for Farnworth General. I do locum and other work there."

"Weren't you a pathologist?"

"Once."

"So you'll be well into PEDs." He said it without embarrassment, shaking his head in exasperation. "I suffer from that little problem!"

"Performance enhancing drugs?" Clare sympathised. "I don't envy you. They're a minefield."

"Lucky that we're so heavily funded." Harry Harrod settled back in his armchair. "Unlike some of our colleagues. Before I divorced I was almost paranoid about my earnings. Now, things aren't so bad." He smiled. "Leaving hospital medicine has compensations."

For a while they talked of medical schools, where were you, I was there, the nagging undergraduate years.

The topics drifted. Harry Harrod confessed that he was subjected to many temptations from athletes.

"Mine is quite a foundation. Every athlete sees himself as an Olympic contender. The coaches are maniacal."

He was turning out to be an amiable companion, and Clare began to feel a glint of humour at her enjoyment of his company, Ken Vane of the police one day, this sophisticated doctor the next.

Reflections obviously in his mind, he went on, "Every competitor must dream of Olympic glory or vanish. Be first at your chosen sport and you're made for life. Look at the investors."

"People invest in athletes?"

He went thoughtful. "Of course! Think of some broadcasting station. They pick out a gorgeous girl swimmer, cyclist, some track eventor. Or some national metric mile hero whom they want to front a new TV sports programme. Some rival station maybe has signed a gold medallist who's syndicated in national news columns. That's how ratings wars start. It's dog-eat-dog."

"They all want to go one better?"

"That's right. They pick somebody who's certain to win at the next Olympiad. Until…"

"Until?"

Clare kept her tone light but had a sudden odd foreboding.

"Until somebody more photogenic, or more popular, threatens to win the next gold instead of their chosen one. And gets signed up to a rival TV channel."

"Bad news." She took another biscuit, seemingly casual.

"Indeed. Then for me it's the phone calls, the night visits om trainers and coaches, begging me for PEDs."

"The drugs you can't prescribe, under pain of being struck ff the Medical Register?"

"Correct. Endless." He sighed, looked away. Still so few in 1e Medical Society lounge, Clare thought. A safe place to dis- 1ss prescriptions, legal or otherwise. Cleverly chosen.

"Disappointing."

"Especially in view of the bribes they might offer."

He smiled directly at her. For the first time she noticed how rown his eyes were, almost a dark umber.

"Whatever do you say to them?"

"There sometimes seems no way out. It's very tempting." [e said into her brief silence, "The stick and carrot. No 1nctions for me, and rewards almost beyond belief."

"Almost like my work!" She laughed, still friendly.

"Not quite, Clare." More serious still. "I could literally make a ːlpful doctor independent for life, if she'd go along and help me 1t. Money's cheap. Sports sponsorships, teaching appointments, :oadcasting contracts for this track gold winner, that gold cyclist. ɔonsor everything from swim suits to bike gear, shoes, boxing obber, boats, yachts, clothes, strips, t-shirts, God knows."

If *she'd* go along? "It's hard to imagine, Harry."

"And there's the new dimension."

"What's that?"

"Political," he said evenly. "We've never had much in this ɔuntry, but it's here now. The support of an Olympic gold 1ampion would be invaluable to a political candidate. It's a atter of timing. Get it right, and the sponsor – TV company, ɔrts equipment people, political party – has it made."

"Is it that simple?"

She dreaded the conversation now, hoping she'd got ings wrong.

"Crystal clear. Direct action." He smiled with regret, sad to be doing this. "Not even two in a thousand Olympic athletes tested positive in the Seoul Olympics, yet every competitor grumbles, *They're all doing PEDs, so I'm entitled to do the same! It's natural.*"

"But surely they know the risks?" She frowned, staying professional. "HGH, human growth hormone, was obtained from fractionated pituitary glands excised from complete Sella Turcica dissections of human corpses." She shuddered. "Ugh. The thought of having that liquidised unpurified emulsified mess injected intramuscularly into your deltoid muscles, just to run a second faster than somebody else! It's ghastly! No wonder those deaths occurred from those bizarre neuropathological disorders. Remember them?"

"Risks?" He shook his head, either phoney or genuine bitterness there. "What risks, Clare? If you think risks, then you've forgotten all the surveys. American teenagers, would-be athletes, were asked if they'd be willing to sacrifice the rest of their lives in exchange for one year of Olympic and World championships! Guess how the vast majority answered?"

"But – "

"Clare, listen." Dr Harrod was speaking with intensity now, his dark eyes on her. "You naturally think of medical risks. It's what you're trained to do. They don't. The only risk to them is the risk that they'll be discovered, test positive and be sent home in shame, a failure. EPOs are available, so checks on athletes can be safely ignored. Am I right?"

Clare knew the problem with erythropoietin, that red blood cell regulating substance naturally produced in the normal body to maintain a steady supply of oxygen-carrying haemo-globin-containing cells in the blood stream. There were now synthetic and natural versions of EPO on the market, so-called SEPOs and NEPOs. They were undetectable by routine tests, and so were simply ignored at the Olympics.

"Certainly, Harry, for EPOs. But there are tests for testosterone."

"Please, Clare." He was almost scornful of her reasoning. "The days when East German competitors took testosterone and anabolic steroids willy-nilly, like sixpenny sweets in a paper bag from the corner shop, those times are over. An athlete who uses bollies or tessies, as they call them, is a simpleton, because they're not too hard to check in the laboratory."

"The testosterone/epitestosterone ratio usually falls between about point-eight to just over one, in the normal individual. That's straightforward enough, surely?"

"Hardly."

Their voices were quiet and strained now. A newcomer entered the lounge, one of the Farnworth General cardiologists Clare knew well. He sensed their gravity and veered away to a window seat, signalling the waitress for tea and a newspaper.

"The Olympic level's something a little over six," Dr Harrod said as if giving her a firm reassurance, "meaning that you can dose on it to your heart's content before you reach a ratio any athlete will fail."

"But the consequences!" Clare argued, wanting everything be honest again. "EPOs can kill. They cause circulation sludges and increased blood viscosity, strokes, thromboses, death for God's sake!"

"You mean the deaths among the Dutch cyclists? Okay, Clare." Harry leant forward, elbows on his knees, keeping the discussion confined. "That happened. Two dozen of them, after EPOs came in at the end of the 1980s. But you're missing the point. Athletes would murder for a regular supply now, even knowing the dangers."

"That can't be true!"

"Why else do you think I'm here?" he said with savage intensity, his expression still bland.

She realised that, were anyone to glance across, they would see only an animated conversation between two colleagues. It was perilous to go on, but there was no way she could withdraw. Had Ken Vane known this would happen?

She felt trapped, suddenly wanting Bonn to walk in, diffident and silent but wholly on her side.

"The tide was too strong for King Canute, Clare." Harry Harrod sounded utterly convincing. "Look at the PCV scandal. An athlete's packed cell volume of red cells is easily increased. Simply inject some of your own erythrocytes, previously stored in some laboratory, into your bloodstream. No harm, no worries about abreactions, because they're your own cells, right?"

"Isn't that illegal?"

"Banned by some old fogies on a dusty Olympic committee? That doesn't mean it's illegal, Clare. Didn't some geezer in Los Angeles set up a temporary clinic for those Yankee cyclists in a bloody motel room, for heaven's sake? And get a sackful of Olympic medals for the USA, when they'd never won a cycling gong for the best part of a century? The risks simply aren't there, Clare. *But the prizes are!*"

She stared at him, afraid to ask the next question. He sensed her hesitancy.

"GH isn't being tested for in most places. Nor is IGFO. This pair of substances are available. Human Growth Hormone is genetically engineered now. In other words, it's produced in nice clean laboratories. You can prescribe it, as long as you happen to have the right letters after your name, as we both have. So is Insulin Growth Factor One, that pumps up your muscle mass and depletes your fat. And both aren't on the let's-hunt list of international athletics."

"Why not, if they're banned?"

"There's no point in banning them. What's the good of a law that doesn't work?"

"I sympathise, Harry." The best she could do was try to edge out sideways, keep the teatime encounter casual. It didn't work. He shook his head, eyes on her.

"No, Clare. Don't go yet. You know my purpose in coming here. I want prescriptions from you, for genetically cultured human growth hormone, for EPO, steroids, norandrolones."

"Sorry, Harry. Can't be done." Shakily she found her handbag.

"You have to, Clare. Or else."

"Else?"

"Remember Ken Vane's recent pleasant sojourn – I *hope* it was pleasant! – in your flat?"

"Who I entertain is my own business," she said, but she was cornered.

"Not quite, Clare. He was one of the police medicals."

"So?"

"Therefore you are guilty of sleeping with a patient."

"Who says I slept with him?"

"Me. And he will say the same, if called upon to testify before the General Medical Council. And he will testify to worse."

"That's…"

"Blackmail?" He sighed, a dedicated professional in a sad world. "You see my difficulty. You can help me. A few scribbles on bits of paper now and again. Not much to ask for a load of money – and I do mean a load. In your position – a charity clinic, with vagrants and street indigents your main patient clientele – you can prescribe anything."

"So can you."

He chuckled mirthlessly. "My prescriptions are audited twice a week. Head of a sports foundation? The ink would hardly be dry! No, Clare. It has to be you."

"You can't mean this." She kept her face averted from the cardiologist by the window.

"Every word," he said tonelessly. "As God's my judge."

She didn't remember how she drove home, but for a long time after she'd parked her motor and flung off her clothes, she was unable to think from anguish.

The night lasted an eternity. In the dawn she thought of Bonn.

38 | Yardie – one of a criminal group affiliated by kin or origin (Jamaican slang)

Set knew things had to be done properly. When life came unglued, unsuspected messes ruined your life. He'd nothing against the old woman. She was just another mess. That was all there was to it. The kid too.

The house was an old two-up two-downer, with a dank cellar. Long before, old folk told of machines in every cellar, but how the hell did they see? Candles? Oil lamps? He'd been born on the fellside where moors began. These terraces were like houses learning to become ruins. Shit city.

He saw a curtain twitch next door as he stood, holding a clip board like he was Council, looking up at the roof, making notes. An oldish woman came to the back door.

"Is this where...?" Set tutted, flipped a page.

"Mrs Enshaw? She's not back until gone seven. Does dinners at the Home."

"Wrong one, then." Set never smiled. Council people didn't, too bloody miserable but in charge. "Ta, love."

"Are you the water and gas?" she quavered after him.

He didn't answer, walked off up the back street. She'd never remember him in a month of Sundays. The cellar would do, get in early. And with luck he could collar the lad later, lie up for the little bastard. Who'd know or care, with pensioners getting done over every night in this city by druggos scraping about for their next hack? The plod wouldn't give a tinker's toss, that's for sure. He might need helpers, though. Deirdre got buried tomorrow, if he'd remembered the days. The girls were collecting for flowers. What was it about women and flowers?

He went for a pint, time to kill in a manner of speaking. Dennis should be along, talk arrangements for shipping his product to Leeds and Sheffield. Everything was *product* to Dennis, like he was some big fucking magnate instead of hired help. Chemists were ten a penny, every polytechnic turning them out like lawnmowers. Set had got the hang of the drug business.

He'd settle up with Louse later.

*　　*　　*

Bonn was not puzzled by Clare Three-Nine-Five's continued absence, yet some new awareness was starting to trouble him. He walked into the Butty Bar, embarrassed to notice the nudging that went on among the counter girls and the glances from punters waiting for their trains. He asked for tea, paid in spite of the girls' protests, and seated himself by the moisture-frosted window to look out.

It was now some days since she had booked him. He was replete, having fulfilled one appointment at the Hotel Vivante in the Moorgate corner of the square. It had been noisy with trains, no windows ever keeping the clattering out entirely. The client was a woman who confessed to putting on airs, trying to impress people with diamonique jewellery. She had made the admission anxiously watching his eyes for disrespect. Bonn wanted to ask was disapproval what she really wanted, but his inability to actually form a question stopped him short.

He had found himself explaining that she could do no wrong, her appointment, his presence. It was correct simply because she was there with him. What she wanted had to be. Even though she seemed to listen, she still confessed that she'd not stuck to some latest diet so she was still too thick about the waist. Women, she said sadly when he smiled telling her she was ideal, only women understood.

The loving went well, was immensely satisfying. Rosalind Eight-One-Five dabbed her eyes afterwards and not quite slept.

She'd asked politely, as if for permission that might be refused, if she could "hold him". He wondered, as she felt and stroked, looking along his body with her cheek against his chest, why the euphemism now, when moments before she had grunted crudities against his face as he had spent into her. But some women insisted on riotous or even bestial coupling, yet seemed able to return instantly to social politeness without mentally breaking step. He could never quite follow the mental steps.

Bonn admired women for these things, though. He had found her earring as they left the bed. She'd beamed with pleasure. He asked could he watch her reinsert it, and she'd coloured shyly but let him stare. She had tilted her head, pushed her hair aside, and fixed the earring exactly *without using a mirror*. The feat amazed him. It must have shown in his expression because she'd laughed, swatted him with gentle playfulness and said what on earth did he think he was staring at.

She paid with a credit card, always a source of distress to him. He resolved to tell Martina that he would prefer some other means. Actual money was less worrying. They left it somewhere, usually on an occasional table or the television, and often under the rim of some ornament as ladies left a tip English fashion under a saucer. Yet they never left their payment *where they had been seated*. Why was that? They were so extraordinary. He wanted to ask, and never could.

Credit cards. The more assured clients used the suite's phone, got an outside line to the Pleases Agency, Inc, and gave the card's details before leaving. One lady, Di Three-Seven-Zero-One of the previous week, in the Royal and Grandee, Settle Street, had been surprised that he hadn't brought a form for her to fill in. A London lady, very casual, she asked him why he did this job, what he did for girls of his own age, what he "thought of it all". He mistrusted those goes, and supposed her some magazine interviewer. He liked her, though, and afterwards signalled to Rack that she might be media but to go easy. For those clients, Posser had wisely told him to prepare a false tale of upbringing, home life, studying nightly for some improbable law degree, and Bonn had reluctantly given her the sham story piecemeal. She wanted to book him the following Friday. They parted friendly enough.

She would never be allowed another booking, of course. She might try the usual ploy, coming wired with a hidden camera next time, giving a new name, using a different credit card, anything, but Rack had never let one slip through yet. The system worked, except perhaps in cases like Clare Three-Nine-Five where –

"Bonn." TicTac arrived breezily and sat opposite, waving for coffee. "You're elusive. Tried to catch you yesterday."

"I apologise, Tic. A message to Askey would – "

"No need. Got you now, right?" The other key had been a goer for two years before Bonn had been promoted to key, and openly acknowledged his envy of Bonn, so newly advanced and favoured. "Look." He bent conspiratorially. "Martina. How are things? I mean you living in her house?"

"Very well, thank you, Tic." What could one say?

"What I mean is, Bonn…" TicTac halted invitingly.

Bonn was always concerned when others faltered this way. Was it something he'd done, or more likely hadn't done? He knew he was deficient in small talk, the incidentals that made life's rubric affable and friendly. Women had the knack, and a superb attribute it was, of being able to course on without prompting, and usually in cool disregard of cohesion in converse. He envied them. One – was it that tavern dancer, who'd insisted on singing him a song? Called herself Kirsty – had begun, the instant before he had even come down from the paradise to which she had raised him, "Did you ever want to be a Member of Parliament, Bonn, sweetheart?" He had been unable to say anything, which she took as an invitation. She had instantly launched into some account, quite entertaining, of how she'd always longed to be a veterinary surgeon specialising in small pets. He had been interested yet rather shaken, and had gone home that evening to question Posser. The old man had been surprised. "Just let them chatter," he'd wheezed. "If she wants to get something off her chest, you serve by listening."

"Without reply," Bonn had guessed, worrying.

"Course."

Posser couldn't see Bonn's problem. Very like the women, Bonn thought. In the lantern hours, he often wondered why no comment from him was needed in return. Wasn't human discourse a business of observation and response, observation and response? It was always so in the seminary. A tutor stated a proposition, the student answered, and so on.

Now TicTac was doing the same.

"Frankly, Bonn, I'm asking is there anything between you and Martina?"

"Anything between," Bonn repeated, looking for clues. In the way of argument? Or perhaps...

He looked at TicTac. Could the other key mean was there anything sexual? But people didn't ask this sort of thing, did they? *Did* they? Surely not like this, in some nosh bar among commuters hurrying in for sandwiches and shoppers coming in shaking rain from their umbrellas.

"Like, are you and Martina, well, you know?"

Bonn thought. Some difficulties actually climbed about the brain, untrappable. He wondered how women coped with discussions like this. Or perhaps it was in their nature to provide details about sexual intercourse all the time. Did anyone have advice on this point? If so, who? And worse, how did one ask?

"If you could be a little more specific, Tic."

"Jesus." TicTac tasted his coffee, scalding his lips on the cup and cursing inelegantly. "I mean, Bonn," he said in a whisper, "are you and Martina, well, lovers?"

Bonn cast about for words. This was grossly improper. A man had no right to disclose a lady's sexual inclinations, activities, or proclivities. He would have sipped at his tea to buy time, but he had never had the knack of drinking scalding fluids. That too was yet another marvellous attribute of women.

"Tic," he said gently. "I think the less of you for speaking so. We are both acquainted with the lady. A man has no right to betray a lady's confidence. Excuse me, please."

"No, Bonn," TicTac said quickly. "Don't get me wrong – "

Bonn stood, almost scraping the chair back in his agitation.

"I am sorry," he told the counter girl. "I must leave before finishing my tea. It was excellent, though."

"That's all right, Bonn." The girls looked at each other, then across at TicTac.

Rack was on the pavement.

"Bonn? You've got an urgent in an hour. Royal and Grandee, 762. That Clare Three-Nine-Five. Okay?"

"Very well, Rack."

"I got something to fix first."

Bonn paused there a moment, seeing Rack rush across to the Central Gardens among the crowds. It was practically the first time that Rack had not spouted some hopelessly wild theory of society, engines, improbable politics. He looked at the bus station clock. One hour. That too was odd, because Clare Three-Nine-Five held her clinic in Charlestown about now. Or did she? And why hadn't Rack broken in on the conversation with TicTac? He had never held back before.

A car's tyres screeched. Two vehicles collided by the Bolgate traffic lights and a boy darted through the traffic. He made safety by hurling himself over the crush barrier and into the crowd of pedestrians. Folk shouted, but the lad was gone into the Asda mall. Bonn glimpsed Dag trotting after, winded. The missing boy?

He had time to walk as far as Fat George, then ask Grellie to explain away some of his unease. Too many oddities.

Clare entered the room, relieved to see Bonn but feeling worse now he was there. Her disclosure to him was now irrevocable. Had he some sort of sensor, she wondered, walking past him with hardly a greeting? Were his antennae already receiving signals? She hadn't arrived with her usual brief buss, a quip, some fond remark.

She didn't even know, she realised, shelling her coat on a chair, if he was thick, simple, cunning, brilliantly clever, or none of those. Were they, in fact, still strangers in some ghastly mogga dance, rules simply too difficult to follow when sexual compulsion was the only compelling rhythm?

Bonn seemed to be concentrating on nothing more dangerous than tea. She seated herself on the couch, from where she could watch him in the alcove, see his frowning face reflected in the mirror over the work surface as he waited with vigilance for the kettle to click showing it had finally boiled.

She knew there was a stander – Bonn had told her the term for the goer's watcher, that sentinel who prevented intrusions from drunken hangers-on or, she supposed, suspicious spouses. At first the idea of some acolyte out there in the hotel hallway had made her feel creepy until she became used to it. And of course she now knew Rack by sight, after encountering him when she'd seen Bonn at the Palais Rocco's mogga dancing. Was the stander listening even now, taking down what she was about to say?

A previous conversation flitted into her mind: they had talked about some Cybernetics Unit – was it Reading

University? – that had devised a subcutaneous microchip to register orgasms, even print them out. What would it be recording now? she wondered bitterly. Fervid anguish, a sense of hopelessness? There was guilt here too, and a sense of betrayal.

Once, her mother Esme had wept because of a new supermarket. She should have remained loyal to Ryan's, her usual corner shop. Clare's father Arthur had said he quite understood, but Clare, then fifteen, had snapped at her mother for being silly. Yet now Clare felt something similar, the guilt of the commercial betrayer. If that's all that it was, and not something deeper. But whatever affection she had for Bonn was submerged now in desperation.

Bonn slowly brought the tray across some minefield and laid it on the coffee table.

"I am in trouble, Bonn."

There, out in the open, all her carefully rehearsed phrases and tailored pauses gone just like that.

Was Ken Vane more opaque than Bonn? So little had warned her. She had also been wary of Bonn at first, even when she'd spoken to him for the very first time in the hospital grounds after he'd rescued that little girl from the angry giant bird. She had simply given Bonn a lift into the town centre, and that could have been that. With Ken she had merely succumbed, given in, his bright features and unguarded openness quite charming.

As a prelude to blackmail. How stupid she'd been.

Now, she was here asking Bonn what? For help? Yet she'd curled her legs beneath her, making it impossible for him to sit with her on the couch, a defensive distance. He drew up an armchair opposite. Had he heard her admission?

"A little boy has gone missing," he said.

"Missing? A boy?" She was lost.

See? Even now, his hopeless obliquity. Was it a mental residue from the seminary where he'd studied for so long? Or some tactic generated by those unseen signals he might have detected as she'd entered? She hated the idea that he was able to prepare responses, and that he might be able to see through her, no secrets left and open as a book while she struggled to see past his hesitancy.

"The Home Orphanage."

Clare thought, what about the trouble I just admitted? "Why are you so concerned?"

"The street is looking for him."

"The girls? The hoods?"

Heavens, she'd be calling them gangsters next, like characters from some old re-run B film in the uncontested ratings of Saturday.

"He is eight." He poured the tea, eyes intent, hair falling over his eyes. She did not feel endeared towards him, not now. Her difficulties were ignored, while he rambled on about some errant child. Weary, she asked, "When did he go missing?"

"Some days. He has been seen since, I believe."

"Won't he be miles away by now?"

Bonn held her cup, placed it gingerly in front of her, sat back with evident relief that nothing had spilled. "He chose not to be."

"Why are you telling me this?"

"I need your help."

The notion was so ludicrous in the circumstances that she almost laughed, but winced instead. People always wanted to manipulate her. And now Bonn.

"Believe me, darling," she said harshly, "I'm hardly in a position to help anyone. And I asked you first, remember?"

"I am able to help you." He tasted his tea, grimaced and laid it aside. "Perhaps I should speak first."

"Let's have it," she said, almost barking the invitation. This would shed some light on him, perhaps more than anything they had ever done or said. At last she watched his lips move.

"I would be very grateful, Clare, if you could see your way

271

to attending a funeral."

She thought she'd misheard. "A what?"

"Tuesday, at St Runwald's."

He waited for her answer, alert and apprehensive.

"You want me to come with you to a funeral? Whose?"

He coloured as he made a quick disclaimer.

"Not quite that," he said politely. "I would understand if you demurred at being *with* me. I should like to be by you at the service, of course, but if you felt more comfort seated apart I should understand."

"Silly," she said, suddenly feeling more herself. He seemed to be back again, as she'd known him all these months. "Is that the help you wanted?"

He looked surprised. "Why, yes."

"Who is it? Some relative?"

"No. The street girl called Deirdre Turnstall. We spoke of her."

The dead girl, a suicidal overdose on morphine. That explained a lot. "I would be pleased to, Bonn. We can arrive together."

He thought a while about that, then slowly nodded. "Possibly, but possibly not. I might have to accompany Martina."

"Yet you still want me there?" she ground out.

"You are utterly vital."

"Very well."

He made to speak. She waited a moment. Would it be direct and momentous, or trivial and oblique?

"This tea tastes a little stale," he said.

"It's fine."

"Please continue, Clare."

She drew breath, in for a penny. "Bonn. I am being black-mailed. You know Vane, the police? He and I … spent time together. As a consequence, I've been asked – told – to supply a Dr Harrod with prescriptions for performance enhancing drugs. The ones athletes use to run faster, become stronger. Vane claims the doctor is a relative. Those pharmaceuticals that athletes take are in great demand."

"I suppose you have refused."

"Not yet." She looked at him, ashamed. "I came to you."

"There is a penalty if you refuse, I take it."

Clare thought, he's barely twenty, God's sakes, and he accepts the sordid tale without a blink. What had he gone through? Less than a twelvemonth ago, he was practically in holy orders.

"Yes. I will be struck off the General Medical Register. Legal charges will follow. Prison is at least a possibility." Into the silence she added, "Cohabitation with Vane, a patient. Dr Harrod threatens worse."

"I shall do what I can."

"Is that it?" she asked, frantic. " I thought you might phone some influential people, try to – "

"Provide what details you can, please, before you go."

It seemed nothing. She felt her eyes begin to prick. He moved to the couch, and solemnly pushed her knees aside, frowning as if the act involved serious planning problems, and sat with her.

"The child may be killed tomorrow," he said quietly. "If not tonight. I believe evil people are searching. I shall need you with me when the threat comes."

"Killed? The same people? Can't you phone the police?"

He reached for her hand. "I want you to prevent it." He almost smiled. "I shall repay you."

"Can you help me?" she heard herself ask, aghast at her sudden gush of self-pity.

"I shall make an attempt, Clare."

She found herself laughing weakly. Why not a quick "Okay" or "I'll give it a go"?

He leaned back, viewing her. "I apologise if I said the wrong thing."

"No, darling. It's nothing. Just me being silly."

To her surprise he stood, and effortlessly raised her. "I

think we should sleep now, Clare," he said gravely. "We are both tired."

Marj Enshaw had definite opinions about stealing. She'd once had a terrible row on a bus with a woman who didn't pay her fare. Marj gave her what for. Bold as brass, though, the thief – *thief*, she was, no two ways – stalked off at the Town Hall stop, taking her time. Brazen. What sort of example was that to youngsters? It led to mugging, stealing money to buy strange powders and that funny tobacco these children – and they were still only barns – smoked in the bus shelters.

Now she too was a thief, carrying her stolen pie.

The steak-and-kidney pie was still warm in its oval dish. One for each boy in the Home, today's making. Wrong to steal, but *was* it theft when it would feed Rupert? She still hadn't set eyes on him, not properly in clear day, but she'd found traces in the cellar. She'd left a cushion and blanket down there, in plastic against the damp. They'd been used next morning. She'd found them folded like in the Home Orphanage, two along then one then two across, back in the plastic.

It was Rupert all right. She'd made him what she had: tea, hot and sugary, bread and butter, chips and some ham, two butties with jam or marmalade. Feasts! She enjoyed the secrecy, though fearful of how it was all going to end. The poor little lad, out here where he couldn't manage. She left him a clean hankie to save his sleeve, her George's old gloves and socks. They too were gone next morning. Why didn't he knock? Vainly she looked under the back door for a note. She remembered a knife and fork for the pie, wrapped the slices in Clingfilm against mice. Once, she'd gone to the Council about mice in her cellar but they'd done nothing.

The previous two nights she had listened for sounds. She'd woken cold and stiff by the dying fire and gone to bed. If a night-stealing boy didn't want to be heard, that was it. The thing was to wait. He would come into the house if he needed.

Nights were drawing in faster than ever, she thought, turning down Mozart Street. Strange how memory played tricks. Her old shoes (clogs, once) clicked on the pavement. No rain tonight, thank heavens, the traffic crossing the streets a steady shushing roar, nobody about as usual, just occasional golden sheen from one or two windows further along. A snatch of a TV soap signature tune made her smile. She must be later than usual. Well, she'd been stealing, hadn't she?

The gate was slightly ajar. She was satisfied. It was a step forward, the boy more confident knowing he'd get his hot meal from Old Marj once the street had settled down. No, she decided, it wasn't theft. She was just bringing him his dinner. A little lad had to be fed. Right and wrong didn't come into it.

She went indoors, turning the huge key in the back door. Everybody still living in the street did as they'd always done, put the heavy key under the step. The house felt different. She smiled. Had the little devil somehow come indoors while she'd been at work? Had he slept in the warm, maybe made himself some tea?

Nothing missing, no sign. She still felt him, though. There was a slight pungency. She put the light on and lit the oven. Make it hot, the scent of his dinner would bring him running the instant she left it down there. Was she brave enough to wait, maybe with a lighted candle? That might frighten him away, and the poor child would be back to dodging among the streets. She saw enough of homelessness. She was preventing Rupert from becoming one of those sleepers in shop doorways.

For herself, an egg and two rashers, one slice with a scrape of margarine, a custard tart and tea. She would have it first. By then the dish would be hot. She was using her mother's old tea

tray, though the japanning was worn through now. The rough-
ness stopped cups from sliding.

At eight o'clock she drew back the curtain to shed light into
the yard. There was just enough to see by, down the steps – the
cellar door long gone – and into the cellar.

"Hello?" she said, like entering somebody's sick room. "It's
only me."

No reply, as if she expected one. She placed the tray on the
zinc top of the old tub boiler, long unused. She ought to have
brought him a flashlight. Or maybe left a note saying to knock
if he needed anything? She'd heard so many tales of running
boys, quite like mice themselves they must be, scurrying about
frightened to be caught.

The only cover she had was the tea cosy, but at least it
would keep the dish warm. She felt all round the edge of the
boiler cover making sure it was balanced, and heard a movement behind.

"Is that you, son?" she asked, turning in the gloom.

The faint hatch of the cellar window held the vague silhouette
of a man. She smelled the same pungency, and knew he'd been
in her house.

"What is it?" she asked, feeling foolish even as she spoke.

The blow put speech and movement beyond her power and
the cold flagged floor struck her cheek. Her spectacles dug
into her left eye. She wanted to put them back on straight.
She'd be lost without them.

She tried to say, "Wait a minute, please," not realizing what
was happening but knowing it wasn't the little running lad and
beginning to feel ashamed because she felt herself wet her legs.

Her last thought was a hope the tray wouldn't overbalance
now she'd fallen, and guilt. Maybe this is what happened when
you started stealing, blows raining down like this and the
world ending.

41

Mosh – secret, disguised
(esp. vehicles)

St Runwald's had been exuberantly built, with needless cornices and gargoyles that, to Victorians, must have seemed the last word in splendour. Now, it seemed merely deformed among the brickwork and sky-reflecting glass of new office buildings. The parish had dwindled as streets decayed and people moved out. Grandeur, Bonn thought sadly, once a visual concept very like religion itself, was now only balance sheet numbers. Poor St Runwald's, with its borrowed vicar and its echoing phoney marble.

He remained outside, looking at the gravestones. Vandalised, of course, broken and tilted, graffiti on most. One grave stood unmolested, strangely sacrosanct in its curtain of wrought iron. Why did youths leave one untouched? Perhaps as bullets hailing into a crowd magically spared one person while all those about fell. Luck, then.

"Afternoon," Vane said amiably, alighting from his car.

Why were police vehicles so showy? Grinning radiators, stripes and hatchings, colours, lettering ever larger with each model. Defiance, possibly, Bonn thought, in the face of popular mistrust? The word police was first used in 1714, he vaguely recalled, to mean policy, with these new-fangled people appointed to judge if policy was being correctly asserted. So recent!

Vane was standing directly in front of him, grinning.

"I said afternoon."

"Good afternoon."

"What you hanging about here for?"

"The service."

Vane deliberately shouldered him out of the way and walked into the churchyard. Bonn had to step back to steady himself. The vicar was by the church porch, wearing his stole, cassock and cotta. He had seen the interchange. Bonn wondered if he knew who Deirdre was, what his funeral oration would say about her. So much religion was formulaic. After all, some street girl dying of drugs was wellnigh commonplace. What could religion say?

People were arriving, the girls from motors that went to park on the crumbling pavements further along and the drivers emerging to smoke in a group. The girls looked but didn't speak to Bonn. He was the only key. Two goers had already gone inside. Martina would not come, Bonn guessed. She had said nothing at breakfast when he and Posser had been at the table in the conservatory in Number Thirteen. Well, he understood. It would have been injudicious to reveal any connection between Martina's enterprises and Deirdre.

He saw Set, black-suited, arrive in a Jaguar with a tall woman wearing genuine furs. Bonn found himself staring unseeing at the overgrown churchyard. A few trees waved the wind away, shedding leaves, though wasn't that a little early in the year for that? Nobody moved among the headstones.

"Have I to stay, Bonn?"

"Please, Rack. Thank you."

Rack was in his usual casual gear, trainers, tight jeans, striped fleece with its broken zip, today with the addition of a green eyeshade on elastic that surely must be uncomfortable on his forehead.

Clare's veteran maroon Humber was parked a hundred yards away opposite a shop that had long since been vacated and boarded up.

"See, Bonn," Rack said, instantly into a lecture, "funerals shouldn't be in churches. They should be by the seaside, sand and everything. Know why?"

"No," Bonn said.

An elderly lady at a distant grave was stooping to clear away old faded blooms. Bonn noticed that she was speaking to someone behind a tilted stone angel nearby. Possibly it was her fancy to make remarks to the deceased? People did strange things.

Rack was explaining, "There's a good chance to get their energy back, see? You can't, not here. See the difference? It's ozone. You get it by the sea. The government knows this but does fuck all, see?"

"Language, please, Rack. This is consecrated ground."

"The churches want to keep things like they are, see? Or they'd have funerals down Blackpool or Fleetwood by the sea. Get it?"

"I see."

"Have I to go in?"

"Stay close, please, Rack."

"Right. Here, Bonn. What d'you reckon to that Set pillock? See that posh cunt he were with? She's not one of ours. I'm going to have a word. How much does a Jaguar cost?"

"Language, please, Rack."

"I know, I know. See that Vane prick? What the fuck's he doing here? Busy, busy. That fucker'll get his arse singed."

"Rack. Please moderate your language."

Bonn moved to stand under the lych-gate as it came on to drizzle. He saw the hearse approach. The vicar stepped forward into the church porch, a deacon with him.

"We not going in, Bonn?" Rack complained. "It's fucking taters out here, mate. Catch our deaths."

The old lady had put her flowers in a stone vase. She paused and spoke to whoever was crouching behind the leaning angel.

"I shall stand inside the porch, Rack," Bonn said as the hearse drew up and pall bearers descended from a black saloon.

"Thank Christ. Know why global warming makes things colder?"

"No." They walked past the vicar and stood in the porch.

"It's our breaths, see? There's energy when we draws breath, see? Work it out. You've only to think of China."

"Quiet now," Bonn said.

Rack silenced, narked at Bonn's whispered command. He couldn't suss Bonn today. Where was his usual please and thank you? Rack felt he'd been really helpful, giving up the chance of a shag with that new Goojer bint with the knockers who'd asked him for a starter seeing she was new on the blue string. From Scarborough, and Grellie's blue stringers all urging the new lass to start out asking time-and-a-half seeing she only looked fourteen but was seventeen. Grellie'd seen her birth certie somebody'd said. So Rack knew he'd done exactly right what Bonn wanted done today, going over every little fucking thing time after time. Once'd be enough.

He whispered, as the vicar stepped forward to greet the coffin, the bearers rocking in step, "Know why it's always wood and handles brass?"

Bonn just turned and looked. Rack went aggrieved and quiet, thinking what the fuck now? It was hard luck, any overdose always was, but it was over and done with, right? And Bonn acting like it was that gunfight coming up, OK Corral. Rack knew he'd have been a dazzler at guns, if only they were allowed, fast draws with both hands. The wind was like a knife in the porch. Rack should have listened to that girl Selina who worked Moorgate but had time off for her kiddie Tuesdays. She'd said he should get an overcoat because funerals were always freezing. Except only old people wore overcoats, over eighty. And Bonn in winter, when he was the youngest key of the entire fucking lot.

The vicar breviary's pages fluttered in the damp wind.

"I am the resurrection and the life, saith the Lord; he that believeth..."

Bonn recognised the words. The service was *not to be used for any that have laid violent hands upon themselves*, was the inflexible solemn command. Bonn had sworn that Deirdre, no suicide, had died at the hands of others. He knew it was true.

The pall bearers went in. He stood as the service began inside, the church door ajar. A bearer from the undertaker's firm peered out questioningly. Bonn shook his head. He had not glanced into the other doorway, where steep stone steps ascended to the belfry. There was no need.

Rack made to speak, but Bonn merely said, "Shhh."

The service was brief. Two hymns were sung, Bonn unable to bring himself to sing with the congregation, Rack standing beside him embarrassed in the swirling cold air. No boy appeared.

Rack's sigh of relief was audible as the congregation stirred, the pallbearers assembled and the slow shuffle began near the side door that led directly into the churchyard. No cremation for Deirdre, in case the coroner required further autopsy. Had to be burial.

"Bonn?" The stander couldn't contain himself. "It's over with, right?"

"Please stay."

"They're going outside. There's another door."

"I know. Silence now, please."

Rack peered into the church. It was emptying, everyone following outside, the old organ quivering the place. Bonn could see Clare Three-Nine-Five among the followers. She left, looking back towards the main porch.

"Rack. Would you come now, please?"

Bonn went into the drizzle, standing on the path between the church and the lych-gate, the wind flapping his coat. His head was chilled by the clinging light rain.

The scuffle began near the Marian door as the last mourners assembled in a straggling crowd about the grave. Vane was triumphantly holding a struggling boy, two other plainclothesmen with him. On cue, two black-coated priests stepped from the vestry door and joined them. The lad was shrieking, one of the

283

men trying to muffle him. They bundled the yelling boy towards the lych-gate at a rush, the more portly of the priests having a hard time keeping up. Somebody shouted a command. A police car started up and backed to the gate.

"Rack, please."

Bonn stood in their path, Rack beside him. The group slowed.

"Out of the way, you," Vane called. "Obstructing the police."

"Might I ask," Bonn asked the taller priest, "is he the boy from the Home Orphanage?"

"Shift him, Si," Vane ordered. One of the men advanced on Bonn.

"Yes," Brother Jason said curtly. "The boy went missing. He's been very disturbed. Who might you be?"

"A reporter."

"Is he fuck," Vane said. "He's one of them wankers, him and that scurf with him. Get the little sod in the motor."

"Let's see your credentials."

"Could I have a statement, please?" Bonn asked. He took out a notebook and a hand recorder.

"I am Brother Jason, the Christian Home Orphanage. This boy absconded many days ago. We have a statutory duty to return him to care."

The priest held out a restraining hand to the policemen. The stouter priest came up, breathing hard. Clare arrived, heels a difficulty in the churchyard grass.

"Deirdre!" the boy shouted, looking about.

The plainclothesman stifled his yells.

"Can I help?" Clare asked.

"I am glad to see you here, Dr Burtonall," Bonn said. "Can you advise this priest about the health of this child, please?"

"What are you doing here?" Vane stared at Clare.

"I attended the post-mortem examination, Mr Vane," Clare said. It was difficult to speak to him, direct yet detached. "Don't you remember?"

The boy's head came free. He looked at Bonn, at Rack, and

stopped trying to call out.

"Are you one of Deirdre's pals?"

"Yes."

"The old cow at the grave said Deirdre's dead," the lad panted.

Bonn looked across to the group about the grave. "Yes, she is. I'm afraid someone killed her."

"That's ballocks," Vane said. "We've the autopsy report."

"Don't let them take me!" the lad screamed. Heads turned, the crowd watching now.

"I shall not leave you," Bonn told him.

Brother Jason said angrily, "You are delaying us. Officer, get him back to the Home please."

"The boy is seriously ill," Bonn said, to Clare's astonishment. "Isn't that so, Dr Burtonall?"

"Ah, yes. He has…" Clare looked at Bonn, wanting to do the right thing, but what was right? "He has epilepsy." She almost asked Bonn if that guess would do.

"He's never had a day's illness," Brother Jason said sharply. "And we have our own medical cover at the Home."

"Into the car," Vane ordered.

"Rack, please. Get the girls. All of them."

Bonn walked with Clare as the boy was dragged to the marked police car and shoved inside. His yelling cut off, Vane mouthing obscenities as it pulled away. Brother Jason and the stout priest walked sedately towards their vehicle, a waiting taxi.

Clare asked, "Was epilepsy all right?"

"We must hurry."

"To where?"

"Please follow in your motor." He hesitated as the girls came streaming from the graveside, leaving the priest and deacon alone. "I am so grateful that you were here." He nearly smiled. "It was almost like a rescue."

"Really?" She thought she had done nothing.

"So far. Maybe it will be the real thing."

The street girls poured past them, hurrying to the cars.

"To the Home Orphanage."

Where else? Clare thought. He'd promised the lad that he would not abandon him. She ran past the row of parked cars as engines started up, fumbling for her keys.

42

True – to be believed,
whether false or not

The phone rang only minutes after TicTac came in. Martina had accepted the drink he poured, discovered that she rather disliked TicTac's aftershave lotion – a little too much, she thought; there were others milder, hinting of confidentiality. Someone should tell him.

It was Posser. "Martina? Dad." On her most protected phone number it could be nobody else.

"Yes," she said, the syllable a code: she was not alone, ask nothing that would require a qualified answer. TicTac moved to look out at the street market below, tact perhaps or, at least as likely, his best side lit in better profile.

"There's been trouble at that first church. Our friends are fine. They're going to the second church place."

"Yes."

"Drive home a different route. The traffic'll be hell. Okay?" Her silence called for more. "Our friend is fine."

"Yes."

She heard Posser's click and replaced her phone in her handbag. A handbag, she had learned from a brief fling with a stern feminist three years before, was a symbol of women's servitude, being a descendant of the chatelaine of the bonded housekeeper. *So many handbags have reminder chains* was one of Belinda's slogans. Or was that Clarrie?

"Have you bought the Worcester Club, then?" TicTac asked easily, returning to sit with her. "Just ripe for development."

"I am unsure."

Martina knew very well whether she owned the Worcester

Club and Tea Rooms or not. A persistent manageress had used arcane methods and clever accounting to wrest control from the previous owners. She had surrendered her possessions and left hurriedly. She would not be back.

"Isn't it time we went on holiday?"

TicTac was the most pleasant of the keys, Martina thought. Unfazed by her position of authority, a clever dresser, all sorts of interesting features. Was that what troubled her, features? Like aspects of a cliff, or an architectural triumph? Too often this was the man's allure to a woman. Teenage girls gawped at hulks, seeing the size, brilliant teeth, the tan, the shining smoothness.

"Where to?"

He grinned charmingly. "Cruise? The Med? Florida between hurricanes? Las Vegas?" He almost jumped at a sudden idea. "Somewhere we don't speak their language! How about it?"

"When?"

"Tomorrow morning! Give you time to leave messages. How about it?"

It was tempting. But there was Dad, now so sickly he needed round-the-clock care and the doctor permanently on call. And could Bonn be left? She felt a spurt of anger at the image of Bonn. What the hell was going on? She turned her back for a second and all sorts of mayhem broke out. Dr Burtonall, the corrupt bitch, must have caused all this. Her instinct to rid herself of the horrid cow had been right. She should have gone through with it, faced Bonn down.

"It would be nice."

His real name was Jeremy, she remembered. Bonn's, she'd no idea. Why not? Even to the police Bonn was known only as James Whitmore, some old screen actor's name. She paid everybody through the nose, yet was kept in the dark. Everything was wrong.

TicTac came closer, took her drink and placed it on the table.

"I'd do my damnedest, Martina, to make it a holiday to remember. There's so little chance in the city. You under such pressure, and me with ... the work." He gave his charming grin. "Say you'll come, Martina. We're all right together, aren't we?"

"Probably."

"Well, then! What's stopping us?" TicTac rose, his lithe form spinning as he clicked his heels in a pretended dance. "Spanish! Mexican! Or Thailand." He laughed, trying to curve his hands like a temple dancer. "Ouch. Can't do it."

He returned and held her face.

"Please, Martina. Say the word and we'll be there tomorrow. Wherever. I'll pay!"

His charming grin was getting on her nerves. Where were the messages? Where was Rack? He should be ringing in no later than five minutes after a call from Posser. Rack had strict limits about what could be safely executed. There had been instances when he'd taken the bit between his teeth, with terrible consequences. It was too much.

"Better leave now."

"What?" The charm vanished. TicTac sat upright, his hands moving off her. "What?"

"I have something to do."

"You mean go?"

"Now."

She sat keying her phone as he got his jacket. His inviting pause at the door would have been charming, in other circumstances. She did not look up as the door closed. Timpo was his stander. She would transfer TicTac and Timpo when things cooled.

43 | Mined – (of illicit deals)
          properly done

"This is ridiculous," Cheryl told Grellie. "I'm pissed off."

They were waiting outside the main entrance of the Christian Home Orphanage. Grellie had seen her discontent grow.

"Stop smoking," Grellie said back.

"Seven of us." The Cockney girl hadn't stopped grumbling since they arrived. Grellie was close to snapping.

"Shut it."

"Who said we've to fucking stand here, broad fucking daylight?"

Cheryl was sulking because she'd detected the aroma of coffee from a florist's van parked opposite and wanted to chat up the driver. Grellie had forbidden any such thing.

"Bonn."

Cheryl stared. "Bonn? Making us do this?" She saw sudden high points on Grellie's cheeks and should have bit her words off but curiosity won. "What, half the entire fucking green string loitering here like a flag day?"

She stubbed out her fag and opened her handbag.

"No more fags. Schtum now."

Cheryl gazed at the Victorian building. "A kids' home, innit?"

"We've a job on."

Grellie looked along the line of her girls as the mobile phone shrilled. She listened, said okay and beckoned. Two reporters with stupid press badges on their lapels crossed the road.

"About time, Grellie. What's on?"

"Wind your cameras up. Your video goon in the van awake, is he?"

"Keep your hair on."

Roy was the younger of the two, always wanting explanations. Grellie had already had a run in with him, forever looking at his watch and moaning he ought to be at the football for a new overseas signing. The older reporter Poke was more observant, gauging the street as the girls loitered.

"Two girls blocking the postern door, Grellie?" Observant. His camera was as old as he. "They staying there?"

"And the rest, Poke."

Poke checked his lens against rain and moved to one side. "Come on, Roy. Ready, steady."

"Listen." The girls clustered around Grellie attentively. "We're here to show sincere fucking sorry, right? So you're all sweet angels of fucking mercy, right?"

"Three girls together," Mandy warned. She was an astute St Kitts girl who prided herself on knowing the law. "The plod can say we're a brothel, any three of us together even in the road. If we spread about they can't."

"We all know that, Mand. We're legit, showing sympathy. Leave talking to me. They're on their way now, from her funeral."

"I wanted to go," Cheryl groused. "I like a funeral."

"Cheryl, piss off." Grellie had had enough.

"But – "

Grellie lashed the girl's face and swore. "Get gone, you gabby bitch. You're docked."

"Grellie!" Cheryl wailed, sobbing with a hand at her face, backing away. Grellie warned Roy and Poke with a raised finger to ignore the incident.

"So everybody polite, yeh? Neat and tidy, yeh? Fags out. Smart ladies. No trolling anybody, right? Eyes on the floor. Cry if you like but don't overdo it."

"Christ," Iris said. "Does Martina know we're doing fuck all?"

"Watch your language," Grellie ordered coldly. The little Channel Isles girl was quite good but she ran off at the mouth and soon would be heading for it. "They'll be here any minute. Get the flowers."

Three girls clipped across the road to the florist's van. They trotted back, comparing blooms.

"I hate maidenhair fern," Iris said. "They can't think of anything else. And always frigging chrysanths."

Grellie sighed. "He's not a real flower bloke, stupid. He's the video."

"Still, you'd think he'd have taken the trouble – "

A marked police car came at speed round the corner, tyres screeching as it pulled up. Two uniformed plod got out, holding a struggling boy. He was white-faced and frightened. The two reporters closed in, Roy and Poke talking non-stop, the girls gathering on the pavement between the car and the Home entrance.

"Out of the way," Vane called.

Poke shoved Roy forward. The scared younger reporter held his microphone out before him.

"Mr Vane. Can you give us an interview about the events of today at St Runwald's church?"

"Not now. Shift, you lot."

Poke spoke up. "Mr Vane. The *Standard* has had a report that the deceased girl was – "

"I said not now. Move."

"Please, Mr Vane," Grellie begged. She heard rather than saw other motors arriving and the pavement starting to throng up. "Can we accompany you inside? We have floral tributes, marks of respect."

"Shift them," Vane ordered the uniformed police. Another swerved up on a motorbike. "What the hell you lot doing here anyway?"

"The Home Orphanage was Miss Deirdre Turnstall's favourite charity. We collected money. We've a right."

Grellie stayed put. The girls formed a phalanx before the door as the police tried to shove through with the boy. More girls arrived to join them.

"She would have wanted us to pay tribute."

Three of the girls started arguing, calling. Rula, always a show-off, did her imaginary injuries, emitting a shriek about her leg. "Mind me shoe, stupid!"

Brother Jason pushed but yet more girls arrived, doors slamming, and came into the press, chattering, crowding up, several exclaiming at the bouquets and telling the others about the church service in a babble. Brother Paulo hesitated, made for the postern door but found himself impeded there too.

"I want to talk to the head priest." Grellie shook Brother Jason's hand off her arm and kept on at Vane. "We want a service here, see? We had collections every week for Deirdre's charities."

Bonn walked up, Rack with him, from Clare's double-parked saloon. Bonn took the boy's hand.

"This child is unwell," he said. "Dr Burtonall, please."

Clare nodded. "He should be admitted to hospital immediately." The girls edged aside, making way, some gazing in awe at the boy and at Bonn. "Yes. He is definitely pre-epileptiform." She looked about. "He needs transport to Farnworth General. Can you police provide us with an escort, please?"

"What now?" a uniformed officer asked Vane doubtfully.

"Get him inside first," Vane ordered, but he was losing conviction. People crossing the end of the street had paused, some turning to drift down and see what was causing the concourse. Cameras were half the attraction.

"We have a doctor of our own on the premises," Brother Jason put in. "For the boy's security – "

"Get us through, lads," Vane ordered.

The police made a concerted effort but the girls started screaming, two or three falling over and screeching. Rula, tawny haired and tall, let out a wail, falling dramatically against the nearest uniformed constable and going over, legs in the air. For once Grellie didn't mind the exhibition.

Two new cameramen appeared from behind the florist's van. An assistant held the sound boom. All wore Granadee TV insignia. Poke was in the thick of it, shouting questions and dragging the inept Roy along, shoving the girls creating more mayhem.

Hassall arrived and forced through to the entrance, saying "Excuse me, miss. Excuse me, miss, just coming by, please..."

Some girls noticed him and quietened their performance, edging aside to let him pass. Others were so into their acts that they were reluctant to stop and fell about all the more, for once sure they were doing right, pleasing Grellie in the madness.

"This the missing boy, Reverend?" Hassall shouted.

"Yes. I am trying to get him inside."

"Leave it to me, sir." Hassall nodded to the men. "Stand easy, lads. You Rupert, son?"

The lad struggled in new terror. Bonn spoke quietly to him and he stilled. Hassall called Vane.

"Calm this lot down and at least get the doorway clear. There's enough of you."

The ferment slowly settled. Bonn held the boy's hand.

He said, "If they take you inside, I shall come too. You will not be left."

"Promise?"

"I promise. I am with you."

"Right." Hassall beckoned Clare. "Will you come inside with us, Dr Burtonall? And the reverends. The boy. And you, I suppose, seeing you're making lunatic promises you'll never keep."

Bonn almost smiled, his eyes on the boy. "We know different, don't we?"

"Yes." The boy said shakily, "I saw them kill Marj."

"Please be sure," Bonn said, quietly conversational as if they were alone. "She helped you, then."

"It was him."

Bonn didn't even look in the direction the lad indicated.

"How terrible. How very sad."

"He hit her with an iron thingy in the cellar. She fell down. He kept on hitting her with it."

Clare heard the world go silent, the girls, police and priests listening.

"Poor lady. She was your friend, then."

"She left me my dinner on the boiler."

"You hid there."

"I were scared. I saw him in her house. I went down the cellar steps when he went for a pee in the yard, and hid in the cellar."

"The old lady went to give you your dinner, I suppose."

"Yeh. He come after her and hit her. It was iron. He kept hitting her."

"You stayed there until he'd gone."

"Yeh. I counted to a thousand after I heard the gate go."

The lad was weeping, the girls a frozen tableau around him on the pavement. Vane made to speak but Hassall snarled him to silence.

"You tried to wake the old lady," Bonn said.

"I shook her. I kept saying, 'Wake up, Marj, wake up.' But she couldn't. I didn't have my dinner. I was frightened. I counted another thousand and heard some old woman going down the back street and went out and ran."

"I was nowhere near," Set said. "The little bugger's lying. I've an alibi."

"That'll do, you. Not another word." Hassall said to Bonn, "Ask some more."

"She wouldn't wake up," Bonn said sadly, his eyes streaming and his vision blurred.

"He killed her. Honest."

"You were scared he'd hit you too if he knew you were there."

"I saw him talking to him over there. In the square."

Rack lifted his chin to prompt Grellie, who said, "Set? You hurt an old woman?"

"I were nowhere near."

"Near where?" Hassall interrupted. "Swinton, take Mr Set in. Do the words."

"You were looking for Deirdre's friends," Bonn was saying.

"No. I was looking for Deirdre." The boy shuddered, racked with sobs. "I thought she was getting married at church, something like that. They said it was her service. I didn't know…"

"No, course not. You said on the phone that you were ringing for Mrs Spencer."

"I ducked behind a grave, but an old woman saw me and said I should go home. I kept looking for Deirdre's friend. I heard people talk. Everybody said Deirdre's friend had got to be told first because he's her friend, see?"

"You don't know him, though."

"No. But he'd help me."

"Her friend," Bonn said seriously.

"Yeh. He's called Bonn."

"Found him," Bonn said. "He's me."

"That it?" Rack said, eyes on Set.

"You the geezer from the Triple Racer?" Vane's belligerence was unconvincing but he stayed there, his voice truculent, still trying.

"No." Rack kept his gaze on Set.

"One of your employees, Reverend." Hassall was benign, wagged his head to bring uniformed officers forward. "Was found battered to death in her cellar this morning by a neighbour."

"I saw him do it, honest," the lad told Bonn.

"I know you did."

"Could we speak in your office, sir? We'll bring the boy in for a chat, eh?" Hassall asked.

"I shall come," Bonn said.

"Keep that bloke, Swinton." Hassall beckoned Vane. "And Swinton? Make sure you get the first go at that video they're doing across the road. And a copy of Poke's tape. It's all blinking electronics these days." He smiled at Clare. "Wouldn't you say, Dr Burtonall?"

"Partly." She stood with Bonn and the boy.

"One thing, doctor. This kid isn't going to foam at the mouth or anything, is he? Only you said he was going to throw a fit."

Grellie and three of her girls came with them into the doorway, eyes everywhere.

Bonn paused. "Rack. Don't wait."

"Right. I'm going to the fair, okay?"

The senior policeman paused at the door to allow Vane to go ahead. Hassall held up three fingers. That number of police went inside after them all and shut the door.

44 | Cushy, Cushtie – profitable, easy (Romany)

The fairground wasn't even crowded when Rack got there. It was getting on for dark. Four of the five synthetic trees by the trailers had been nicked. Rack laughed, kids round here.

"If Olivio'd paid a bar to some brat, they'd have been left alone. Know why?"

"No."

"Basic, they're honest like murderers are basically holy, see?"

Louse, hands in pockets, stood while Rack eyed the shop-soiled dancers bellying half-heartedly on the garish catwalk.

"Would you give any of them the time of day, Louse?"

"No."

Louse was terrified. He'd never been told to come along with Rack like this before. The fair still had eight days to run, and Olivio was making a mint from the Ecstasy and miraa packs. He tried to work out a way of giving Rack his rightful share, which was about thirties, or whatever percents Rack said. But if Rack didn't know fuck all, how could Louse admit he'd been dealing?

"You're wrong, Louse." Rack gazed up at the girls, face shining with delight at the smooth bellies moving in the flashing pulses from the strung illuminations. "Know why?"

"No."

"Because you don't listen."

"I done what you said, Rack." Time to confess.

Rack hummed along. "What's that song, Louse? Yank marching tune, right?"

"Think so, yeh."

"Wrong! It's that fucking BeeGees thing fifty year gone, see? Know how I knows?"

"No."

Rack walked off, Louse hurrying after.

"It's in the air, see? Played too often, it gets in wet electrics. No sodding good, though. Wait here."

And Rack vanished near the bumper cars. Louse strained to follow his progress among the thin crowds, should have been easy but wasn't because Rack never walked straight, always ducking and diving, talking, turning to have a laugh then vanishing to reappear somewhere else. A fucking menace.

Louse wanted a pee, desperate. He wondered about peeing against the oiled canvases behind the roll-a-penny booths but some housewife was sure to raise the plod, howl that some pervert was flashing his dick at the fair with public everywhere. He waited an hour.

The fire was not even noticed at first, just one more dazzling flash among so many, a fairground after all. Except it was from the line of trailers. That too was nothing special except it settled down to a growling fire, flames erect and yellowing, reddening, then giving out a whoosh that caused folk to look round and women start screaming.

A father shouted at the sight, grabbed his two little children, yanked his wife away from a hoopla stall, she trying to win a goldfish in a plastic bag, and hurried them towards the street calling out for folk to get the fire brigade. Other folk started yelling for children, stop that ride quick there's a fire, the usual stupidities. Louse began to wonder why he'd been told to stay where he was.

Then he saw Dag, thin as a lath, smoking, standing watching him. When Louse turned to run, Dag just lifted a finger and Louse froze. Stop there. You've been told, no running away for you, Louse, no more running.

Two women were talking quite casually among the panicking people, almost like they'd been planted. Strawers, Rack's lot

300

called them, whose job was to perjure themselves on command. Paid a retainer, steady income for nothing week in week out, until the call came.

Louse saw Dag nod to them, then in his direction. The two women – was one that woman from Breightmet, Rack used her sometimes in an afternoon, had two kids at St Joseph's, husband a pro golfer – gazed his way long enough to recognise him when the time came to give the evidence they'd learned by heart. One even had the nerve to give him a friendly wave, just before she was almost knocked over by teenagers rushing to see what trailer home was afire. She gave them a real mouthful of abuse. They laughed. Louse knew it was Olivio's, of course an accident, some Heath Robinson bottled gas connections, the usual. Nothing spectacular where Rack was involved.

Louse stayed put, almost weeping from dejection, as the fire people came wailing into the fairground but not in time to prevent the fire spreading to two other trailers, the third one going up with a whoomf as the heat took hold.

Eventually police came to clear everybody out. One plod approached the solitary figure and asked what was he doing standing there like a prick. Two women who happened to be visiting the fairground were in view, pointing Louse out from by the infants' carousel, saying what they'd seen Louse do near the trailer before it went up in flames.

End of the road.

The two young ladies were beautifully turned out, stylish without being presumptuous. Dr Harrod was pleased it was a social call, nothing athletic or medical. The Banda-Lait Sports Centre receptionist, who'd thought herself smart until their arrival, became sulky. Dr Harrod wondered contentedly about women's rivalries. More refined than those of men, and twice as interesting.

He was charmed to be invited to accompany them.

"Dr Burtonall is waiting to discuss her agreement with you, Dr Harrod," the dark-haired girl said.

"She is in full agreement with your proposal," added the blonde.

Harrod couldn't resist a glance at the wall panels. The CCTV, common these days in all doctors' surgeries, had now recorded Clare Burtonall's criminal complicity.

"Dr Burtonall has arranged supper at a hotel, sir," from the raven-haired model with the mellifluous voice. She looked dynamite in blue.

The sports doctor wondered how far Dr Burtonall was prepared to go in appeasing him. Quite a distance, evidently. Ken Vane had certainly given a superb recommendation for the worthy doctor. He would play it off the cuff, press her only when she was in deeper, maybe after a few transactions.

"Limousine transport is waiting, sir," said the quieter but more enticing blonde. She looked brilliant in scarlet.

The surgery office was sound-proofed, so necessary for certain selective treatments Dr Harrod meted out to the athletes, narcissistic poseurs all. But the two models' arrival had been clocked by the closed-circuit TV. All safe. He asked for a moment to gather a folder, and he was ready.

They left together, his two visitors asking about this runner, that muscly pentathlete, almost whimpering with delight to learn that he knew them so well.

Curtains slid to as the stretch limo cruised away, the two charmers offering him drinks that he had the sense to decline. The journey took a mere ten minutes, by the conclusion of which he had learned their names and heard a little of their adventures as hired hostesses to the affluent.

It was only when the motor dropped them at the main entrance to a seemingly derelict mill that he realised something was either badly wrong or very strange. The car drifted off, despite his despairing call for it to wait. The two young ladies were reassuring, joking about his temerity, laughingly pulling him along, one going ahead to bell the lift. One bare bulb lit the space. They ushered him inside. The gate crashed to, the two girls still chattering as the industrial cage creaked upwards.

"I think I'll just call my office," he said after a few moments, smiling with more confidence than he felt. "I forgot to let my secretary know my precise location. It's my rule."

The phone was not in his folder. He was still casting about for it when the lift jerked noisily to a halt and the crisscross gates rolled apart. He was conducted out onto a vast floor area the size of an arena. In the centre was a brightly-lit tented arrangement evidently constructed of dense plastic. The windows in the mill walls were blacked out. No light would be visible from outside.

Harrod could hear faint music from some radio, the announcer talking over some jocular comment with a laughing woman. The news would be along in five minutes, football results would follow. He could just discern a figure moving about inside the bright cocoon and pale blurred rectangles that might be oscilloscopes.

"What is this?" he asked, wondering now how these two

girls had managed to get everything completely wrong. "Is it some sort of laboratory?" Had Burtonall some illicit lab already on the go?

Surely there couldn't have been some mistake? He asked his two companions this, got back the same laughing reassurances, was told not to be silly.

"Who the hell's that?" a man called.

"Do go ahead," the blonde invited. "We've been told to wait here for you, help you carry the materials."

"Materials?"

The same voice shouted, "Set? You weren't due for another hour. Hang on a sec."

The radio quietened. Dr Harrod was encouraged forward towards the tented arrangement. He approached tentatively.

"I've to decontam," the figure called. "The extractors have been swines, stop-starting since four o'clock, a right game. I'll need new next week."

"Ah, are you her partner?" Dr Harrod called.

The shadowy silhouette froze. "Who's that?"

"I'm a colleague."

Dr Harrod looked about but the two models had gone. He walked quickly to one side, peered back at the industrial elevator, saw nobody, crossed to the opposite side. No models.

"Whose, Set's?" The man appeared. "Who are you?" he said, staring. "Did Set send you?"

"I was invited here by Dr Burtonall," Dr Harrod said, trying for control. "Is she here?"

"Never heard of anybody by that name. You've no right to be here."

"Two ladies brought me at Dr Burtonall's request." It was clearly time to leave. "It seems I was misled, through no fault of my own."

He thought of other platitudes, even murmured a few. You never knew what cameras were filming for evidence, drug entrapment being what it was these days. And there came a smell of aromatic compounds. The young bespectacled man was obviously working some drug scam. Solvents were the very devil to get rid of, hence the plight in which sports medicine found itself. Harrod had glimpsed a cryostat, a sophisticated centrifuge, and autotitration racks as the man had emerged from his improvised laboratory. It was an illegal synthetic drug factory, and he'd blundered right in.

Time for out.

"Look. It's a clear mistake. Sorry to have interrupted."

At that moment a loudhailer stunned him.

"Police! This is the police! Stand still! Do not attempt to move. Police!"

Dr Harrod always had been quick thinking, a real talent. He smiled affably, raising his hands and letting his leather folder fall. The idiot biochemist started to run from side to side like a headless chicken, even trying for the lift cage, until police officers came stepping from the gloom and stood about them in a crescent.

"I was just remarking that I seem to have blundered into some sort of industrial complex," Harrod said over his shoulder, smiling with that casual benignity nurses had always loved. "I was misled by two ladies who brought me here at the request of a colleague, of whom I have details in my folder. You can phone my secretary. I am telling the truth."

He heard the standard caution and arrest warning with sheer disbelief.

"I can't possibly be under arrest," he said, still outwardly calm. "I've never seen this man before. My presence here is quite accidental."

"You Dr Harrod of the sports foundation?" one officer said, retrieving Harrod's folder from the floor. "That your motor outside, is it?" And the officer smiled. "We've already checked, sir." He signalled to the others. "Tape it off, lads. We've a night's work here."

The biochemist started to cry, tears rolling down his cheeks and trying to choke out explanations. A constable said no, he couldn't go back inside the plastic tent for his coat, and if he wanted to telephone anyone they could arrange that.

Harrod thought, Ken Vane. He's the one to put things straight. The only one left, until the CCTV in his surgery showed how he'd been tricked into accompanying the two beautiful models. It was a clear case of wrongful identification, and would be easily resolved.

"The money, son," Hassall said not unkindly to Vane. "See what I mean? Three accounts. And you openly buying a motor with notes, bunce in hand. Nobody does that."

Vane sat bemused. "I asked you to represent me at the enquiry, Mr Hassall, not fit me up."

They were in a corner of the police canteen, the hubbub all around keeping its distance and nobody joining them.

Hassall sighed. "I'm telling you where you stand. This cousin, Dr Harrod. He states you had a deal."

"That's a lie."

"The miraa packs in your garage aren't illegal, but the six thousand appies are. Virtually pure Ecstasy, worth a mint on the street. That lunatic burke Dennis made them. Admits it. It totals a lot of gelt."

"Can Forensics prove they came from the mill?"

"They already have."

"Honest. I had nothing to do with it, Mr Hassall." Vane drew breath and went for it. "Look. It's true, part of it. Dr Harrod and me met sometimes at the sports place. We talked. I mentioned Clare, Dr Burtonall. Said I was seeing her. He said she'd just be the one to supply prescriptions. His prescriptions are audited."

"This true?"

"Honest to God, Mr Hassall. I told her to see him, pressed her a bit. Technically I'd been her patient – the police FFIs that we attended. You too, remember?"

"Go on." Working out the sequence, Hassall wondered how

honest Vane was being. It could fit.

"She met Dr Harrod. He blackmailed her to cough up some scrips for performance enhancer chemos. I'd be paid when she came good."

"Did it get that far?"

"No." Vane said miserably. "That's…"

"When it all went wrong, eh?"

"I don't know what happened after that."

"That Set. Did you ever meet him?"

"Never saw the bugger before the funeral. That's the truth."

Hassall was irritated by officers at a nearby table talking, heads low, with frequent glances at him. "What you looking at, Forrest?" he called out loudly. "Forgot your manners? Want to ask if this officer nicked your bike?" Other uniformed police hid grins, the desk constable's bicycle being the frequent target of estate kids. Stung, Forrest looked away.

"See," Hassall sighed, "Marj fed the boy. She nicked food for him. Several nights, in the cellar where she got done."

"Nothing to do with me, Mr Hassall."

"Never said it was. Listen, though. The lad's story holds. He's lurking, the grub's there, the killer tops the old lady. But."

"But what?"

"Set set up the e lab with his maverick biochemist. Then supplies packs of the bloody things to Brother Paulo at the Home Orphanage. The drugs are distributed in the guise of everything from sacred hosts to altar wine, holy goods being virtually sacrosanct, see? A bonny scam, right?"

"Nothing to do with me, sir."

"The drug money's still being traced by AO. Brother Jason was having to pay out increasing guilt gelt, hush money, to kids who'd grown out of the Home and were making threatening noises. Like in Eire, remember? The Church there's forking out hundreds of millions in abuse payments." Hassall eyed Vane. "They admit no liability, but are still shovelling out tens of millions at a time to thousands of abuse-damaged children."

"They can't pin anything like that on me, sir."

"Can't they?"

"No." Vane had to fight to keep his voice low, conscious of the eavesdropping officers' increasing belligerence across the canteen.

"See my problem? This Set scurf knows Dr Harrod, who is found at the biochemist's improvised laborarory. And Dr Harrod's your partner in crime. You've admitted that, right?"

"I didn't know he'd anything to do with Set, or any illegal drugs factory."

"The money from which goes directly to fund Brother Jason's abuses. A horrible chain, lad."

"It's still none of my doing."

"And Set was witnessed killing Marj, who was protecting the boy. One thing. Why didn't the old lady simply tell Brother Jason at the Home, or bring the kid in? D'you think she guessed about the abuse, and was simply trying to keep the boy hiding out in safety?"

"I know nothing about it."

"If you do, say so now before I meet your lawyer." Hassall smiled wistfully. "Makes you think, doesn't it? Old ladies like Marj. Absolute angels, plodding on for decades simply doing good, never complaining. It would restore your belief in mankind, if the rest of us weren't such bastards."

"Look, sir." Vane was on the point of break-down. "My only crime was persuading Clare Burtonall to meet Dr Harrod when he asked me to. About prescriptions. It's a professional matter between two doctors. That's all I did. It's the absolute truth."

"You mean," Hassall said sadly, "that your life was absolutely fine until you met a woman?" He scraped back his chair. "Doesn't sound much of a defence. Let's get back and see what I can make of it with your lawyer. Any good, is he?"

Vane rose and followed, avoiding the looks he got from all over the canteen. He had to step carefully over a tangle of thrust-out legs.

47 | **Mogga Dancing** – that type of ballroom competition dancing where each couple changes their dance rhythm to a different style every few bars – usually four or six – throughout a single melody

The morning brought a headache so profound that Clare feared she might faint the instant she got up. It passed off with tea and a prolonged soak. She dressed slowly, promising herself a two-hour booking with Bonn at six or so. She might even test room service by ordering supper for him. That would be good, give her time to bring their thoughts together. She had plans for that encounter. How would Bonn answer? After recent events, she knew her mind. Everything – every*one* – else was over. She was determined.

Bonn deserved more than a reward, rescuing her from Vane and Dr Harrod. What could she possibly give him besides herself? She had no idea of his circumstances except that he was mind-bendingly wealthy from the Pleases Agency's activities. She knew he lodged at 13, Bradshawgate North, with that ice maiden Martina and her ailing father, and that was about it. She knew nothing of his family, his upbringing. Sometimes he was remote and ascetic, only becoming real when they were together. Tonight, though, she would reach him and win.

Getting ready to leave for the surgery, she keyed in her programmed responder. Surprisingly she had no appointments for the morning. Unprecedented, but a relief. It crossed her mind that maybe some order had gone out from Martina to spare her work today. Unlikely, yet all to the good, for what she planned. She rang the Pleases Agency and got the distant quavery voice. Clare went straight into it.

"This is Clare Three-Nine-Five. Please may I book Bonn

for two hours today, six o'clock? I prefer the New Amadar in Deansgate."

"Thank you for calling, Clare Three-Nine-Five. I regret that Bonn is not available. Thank you for using Pleases Agency, Inc."

The line went dead. Clare stared at the receiver, slowly replaced it. That too was strange. She sat, coat on, handbag on her lap, staring unseeing at her floral arrangement on the sideboard.

Something was wrong.

When Bonn was unavailable, they usually offered her an alternative date. If she declined, they then suggested a time later in the week. And if she couldn't make that, the next offer was of some other goer. As a regular client of the Agency – and she was – it seemed to be their fixed routine. Fixed no longer. Why?

Slowly she found her keys, carefully locked up her flat and left for the surgery, thinking hard. Had some unpleasantness recurred? Some legal nicety needing resolution? She had assumed it was all over.

Her interviews with Hassall and the other police officers were finished. The lawyers for Dr Harrod and Vane had jousted and been repulsed. Those issues had fizzled. What else? Well, the terrible abuses at the Home Orphanage and the arrest of Brother Jason and Brother Paulo had reached the headlines, had come and faded, and now were mere footnotes in the middle pages and sidewipes on TV's *Look North*. The murder of the poor old lady who had protected the missing boy, the death of the fairground proprietor and subsequent arrest of the arsonist caught red-handed by the carousel, all had receded. She had been named by Dr Harrod and Vane but their evidence was widely disbelieved. Both were awaiting trial. Hassall said frankly to forget it ever happened – double meaning there, but perhaps she'd misinterpreted his wry expression.

Now this. The very day she thought she would get back to normality, sudden disquiet. No Bonn. A curt response from the booking ladies at Pleases. No patients booked in her surgery. What had she missed?

Reaching her surgery door, the key jammed. Foolishly she tried her other key, knowing it belonged to her hospital office. After more struggle she faced the truth: the lock had been changed.

"Doctor."

Clare turned. A dark saloon was parked by the kerb, engine running. Martina's face appeared as the rear window wound down. Clare felt her throat catch as she walked towards Martina.

"Good day, Dr Burtonall. On behalf of the charity I wish to thank you for your excellent doctoral services. Your contract is terminated forthwith. Your flat is repossessed, and your surgery closed."

"My – ?"

"Your goods are going into store, with immediate effect. Your patient records will be taken over by a new doctor appointed for the purpose."

"This is – "

"Outrageous, Dr Burtonall?" Clare could see the glint of satisfaction in the girl's cold eyes. "No more than your association with the police and other criminals. If you insist on trying to remain, you will be struck off the Medical Register for reasons you already know and which, through my good offices, you managed to evade. If you accept this dismissal without question, you will be paid a generous sum. The choice is, as they say, yours. Make it now."

Clare glanced about. The cool morning street was thinly peopled. Two buses ambling along, children heading for school. And her world was being taken away.

She blazed, "That is no choice and you know it!"

"Remove your personal belongings from the flat by noon or they will be incinerated. A removal firm is on its way. Storage charges will be paid until the end of the month. Your severance salary and redundancy money will be transferred to your bank account in one hour."

Clare tried to speak but rage stifled her. Eventually she managed to get out, "The flat is mine. Freehold."

"I have ordered its confiscation. Quite legal, you'll find, though you are free to contest that."

Clare felt broken. "Why are you doing this?"

"Any guesses you might make, Dr Burtonall, are probably as accurate as mine. Thank you for your excellent work for the charity. Goodbye."

The motor glided away leaving Clare standing on the pavement. She sat in her motor waiting for the receptionist and nurse, but nobody came. The removal vans, inordinately huge for the slight task ahead, arrived. In silence she went and supervised the clearance, then drove out of Charlestown into the city.

She parked and walked to the Café Phryne across from the street market by Rivergate. She was reluctant to enter. A passing glance showed that it was fairly busy, perhaps a score of ladies at their elevenses with the clever Carol on reception. For a while she wandered among the market stalls to keep watch. There was no sign of Bonn.

After an hour's slothful shopping she went to the Weavers Hall, avoiding the central square, and sat facing a cup of stale coffee in the cafeteria until it was time, her thoughts a tumult.

By the time she left, she knew exactly what she would do.

*　　*　　*

The Palais Rocco was at its desultory practice. Today's dance leader was Nino, exotic in sequins and Florentine rainbow stripes. When Clare entered he was being scathing to the scatter of hopefuls on the dance floor. The band was due in an hour. Waitresses drifted or chatted idly. The lights were low, spectator tables and chairs still stacked against the walls. She was not even charged admission. Clare seated herself against a pillar facing the stage.

Her numbness and shock were fading. The instant Martina's saloon had driven off, Clare's first urge was to dash to a lawyer and sue the frozen bitch for every rotten corrupt penny she possessed. Now, the turmoil was gone and she began to calculate the odds against her.

Martina's resources were almost infinite. As her charity probably paid for the lawyers who'd acted for Clare in the first place, Clare realised she was in no position to demand that they act against Martina. The horrid bitch knew Clare was helpless. Clare estimated her assets. Alimony from Clifford, and some savings. She still had her job at the Farnworth General, or had she? Cold appraisal left her in no doubt. If Martina wanted her out, that was it.

The question was Bonn.

The fling – had it been real? – with the moronic Ken Vane had been a hideous mistake. All right, she'd felt empowered by the encounter, full of herself and living the trendy life. Until he'd started the blackmail process, then it had turned to sawdust. She knew she'd been lucky to escape, thanks to Bonn's arrangements. Now she was being made to pay. Martina's vicious gratification at getting rid of Clare would stay in Clare's mind for ever.

Another couple drifted onto the dance floor as the piano played. Still no sign of Bonn. He usually positioned himself on the balcony, from where he could see the band and the dancers. Rack often came, inevitably creating a disturbance, joking inanely. She worried that Rack might tell her to leave. If he did, she would have no choice. So many choices now out of her hands.

"Good day, Clare," Bonn's voice.

He was standing beside her. She started, almost rose but gestured him to a chair. Two waitresses started setting out the chairs and tables for spectators.

"Hello." She gave a mock grimace. "I would have said a good-day back, but it's hardly that."

He deliberated, gazing at the dancers and Nino posturing exotically among them. She wondered how he might seem to her now, were this their very first meeting. Would his hair, mildly unruly, cry out for attention? Would his attire, surely off the peg from some city home stores, irritate her so much that she would think him careless? Perhaps his pauses, the evident pondering of even the most casual greetings, would drive her mad and she would stalk out in exasperation? Except there was a problem. All those annoyances had surfaced in her end-lessly, time after time, and she loved him all the more.

They had talked of love. Its chemistry, its positions, the mechanics and physiology, the neurobiochemistry of the processes, the endocrine balances and reciprocal pathways, and he had simply showed nothing but rejoicing in the making of it. She had been baffled by his response, and now here she was, brought round to his way of seeing beauty in his world of sordid streets, a thronged chaos that nobody rational could make any sense of.

He remained standing.

"I am happy to find you, Clare. I wish to ask what you intend."

Always the statement, never the question. She once asked if he worked syllables out on the way to an appointment. He gravely considered the question, then said no, when all the time it had been her light-hearted joke. It had earned her a rare smile.

"I've decided. If you agree, Bonn, I'll become an independent medical investigator. Would that madden your employer?"

"No." He looked so sad. "She would see it as evidence of your failure. Your office however should not be in Martina's area."

"The city centre? Darling, I shall have no surgery. I'll rent. I'll be independent, only take the cases I want, follow them through exactly as I wish."

He nodded. The piano struck up, Nino shrieking abuse, undulating away and posing among the stolid pairs of shuffling dancers.

"I believe that Nino only teaches this session in order to show off," Bonn observed, frowning. "An uncharitable thought."

Clare almost laughed, except it would have brought tears. Bonn was master of the obvious, yet so profound it was painful to see him trying to grasp words that would do.

"Darling. I think you and I should live together. You are allowed a private woman. Am I right?"

"We are."

"Then let it be me. Will you?"

She wondered what Sister Conceptua would say now, Clare offering herself as a kept – keeping, keeper? – woman. Well, that stern tutor should stay in her rotten old convent and mind her own business. And Clare had done worse lately, and condoned even worse than that.

"I shall, for two months in the first instance," Bonn replied, watching the dancers.

Clare stared, her heart racing. "Yes? You mean yes?"

"Indeed." His eyes dwelt on her face. "It will be problematic."

The music started up, Nino swaying, clapping, shouting, flapping demonstratively at the dancers. Clare remembered how she had seen mogga dancing for the very first time, and how she couldn't see the logic of the erratic successions of random dances done to one constant melody. It had seemed impossibly weird. At first. Now, it seemed sensible, manmade order coexisting in the madness of maelstrom.

"Everything is," she said. "They wouldn't let me book you today."

"I heard."

"I shall find a place by this evening."

"Very well." He hesitated and finally made it. "Where shall we meet?"

Clare answered his question, smiling.

"You tell me," she said. "We'll go there together."